TO TAME THE WILD RAKE

THE SAINT AND THE SINNER

JUDE KNIGHT

ISBN: 978-0-9911543-1-6

❊ Created with Vellum

TO TAME THE WILD RAKE

The whole world knows Aldridge is a wicked sinner. They used to be right.

The ton has labelled Charlotte a saint for her virtue and good works. They don't know the ruinous secret she hides.

Then an implacable enemy reveals all. The past that haunts them wounds their nearest relatives and turns any hope of a future to ashes.

Must they choose between family and one another?

This book is dedicated to all the readers who have been asking for Aldridge's story since he first appeared in A Baron for Becky. Thank you for your encouragement. I hope you think I've done him justice.

AUTHOR'S NOTE

To Tame the Wild Rake is the last novel in the series *The Return of the Mountain King*. Can it be read as a stand-alone? Yes, it can. The main plot line is the romance between the Marquis of Aldridge and Lady Charlotte Winderfield. In this novel, you'll find out about their history, together and separately, what stands between them, and how it is resolved. And I'll give you a glimpse of their happy ever after in the epilogue.

If you want to know the full story of the villain's dealings with the two main families in the book, or the stories of the married son and daughter of the Duke of Winshire, and of Charlotte's sister, you may wish to read the other books in the series. They're listed in order at the back and on my web, and on retailer sites, you'll notice that the novels are numbered on the cover.

Beyond that, I write historical romances set in a complex Regency world of my own imagining, where all the most powerful families know one another, and a main character from one book may be a secondary or background character in another. For example, Aldridge has appeared in more than thirteen of my novels, novellas, and short stories, and not only in this series. When I edit, I have to discipline myself to cut out all the detail about these extra people that doesn't have anything to do with the plot lines of the particular book I'm writing. I don't want to confuse new readers. But I know readers of my other books enjoy these glimpses of old friends.

This book has one unresolved plot line from the series. What becomes of the relationship between Aldridge's mother, the Duchess of Haverford, and Charlotte's uncle, the Duke of Winshire? That story will be published as *Paradise At Last* in a three-part set later this year. I'm aiming at 15 December. The set, The Paradise Triptych, will include the duke's novella, *Paradise Regained*, the duchess's memoirs, *Paradise Lost*, and *Paradise At Last*.

PROLOGUE

FEBRUARY 1812

The Marquis of Aldridge was closeted with His Grace. The Duke of Winshire, Charlotte's grandfather, had permitted no visitors for months, ever since an apoplexy robbed his movements of precision and slurred his speech. But this morning he had agreed to see Aldridge.

"He can't force you into the marriage," her twin sister Sarah whispered through the spy hole from the servants' passage in the wall, when she came to tell Charlotte about the visitor. Whether Sarah meant Aldridge or Grandfather, Charlotte wasn't sure, but Sarah was wrong. Grandfather had already assured her she would be Aldridge's bride if she had to be carried into the mansion's chapel bound and gagged.

"My chaplain will marry you right and tight, without you saying a word, and once Aldridge has his hands on you, you'll obey him like a wife should or suffer the consequences. The boy takes after his father. He'll know how to handle a reluctant wife."

Aldridge wasn't like that. Was he? Five years ago, when he and Charlotte were friends, she would have been certain of him. But his friendship was a kindness to a child. By the time she was old enough to be in Society, her confidence in men had been shattered, and the whispers about Aldridge's women had been a minor factor in her adamant refusal of his first two proposals.

This time, though, his father and her grandfather had brokered the arrangement, and the Duke of Winshire was determined to bring the unwilling bride to heel. Charlotte was fighting the match with all her powers, but those were few. "I'll tell Aldridge why I'm unfit to be a bride," she threatened her grandfather.

"Do that, and I'll put you, your sister, and your mother out into the street in your chemises," the old man promised. "Useless coven of females."

The danger wasn't as dire as it sounded. Aunt Georgie would make sure they were clothed and fed, and had a roof over their heads.

But Charlotte's threat was even more toothless. Her work depended on her reputation in Society, but even if she was prepared to lose that, she couldn't condemn her mother or her beloved sister to forever living on the fringes of the Polite World, hidden from view, their very existence an affront.

Would it be so terrible to be married to Aldridge? Yes, and precisely because he was, in his own way, a decent man. She could very easily fall back in love with him as she had when she was fifteen, and that way lay unending heartache. Even if her own scandal remained a secret, he was a rakehell. She could not expect him to remain faithful to any woman, especially one who hated being touched. To love a man who sought his pleasure elsewhere—however discreetly—would be a kind of hell. And then there was the other…

The key rattled in her door and it swung open at the hands of the tall footman who stood guard over her and followed her everywhere she was permitted. Neither he nor his colleague would meet Charlotte's eyes. "His Lordship the Marquis of Aldridge awaits you in the green parlour, my lady," said the one in the lead.

Charlotte briefly considered refusing, but they probably had orders to carry her if she wouldn't go. She tried for a sort of freedom anyway. "Please tell the marquis I will be down shortly."

The footmen exchanged glances. "We must escort you, my lady," said the spokesman.

Might as well get it over, then. If Aldridge was determined to go ahead with the marriage, she would tell him all and let come what may. If she made him swear first not to tell His Grace his reasons for crying off, would he keep his word? He was known for always keeping promises, but most men didn't believe their honour compromised by breaking promises made to women.

With her mind on the coming interview, she was out of the family wing and on her way down the private stairs before she realised that the halls had been a stirred ant nest of activity, and here, hurrying up to brush past her with a chorus of murmured apologies, came the duke's covey of physicians.

She turned to watch them ascend and disappear through the door into the family wing. "Is something wrong with my grandfather?"

The quieter of the two footmen replied, "They say he took another fit, my lady. When he was seein' Lord Aldridge."

Another apoplexy. Each robbed him of a little more function. She found it hard to summon any pity for the old tyrant, especially since he had undoubtedly set things up to rule them all from beyond the grave. Even if he had not, the unknown uncle who would succeed him was sure to be cut from the same cloth, as had been her father and brother.

If she weren't so damaged, a dynastic marriage to Aldridge would have been preferable to remaining under the rule of the men of her family. As long as she could avoid the stupidity of falling in love. Kindness and respect lasted longer, and Aldridge was kind to his mother and sisters. Though who knew what a man was really like behind closed doors?

In any case, the point was moot. She would tell him all—or most —and it would be over.

He stood as she entered the parlour. From the artistic disorder of his fair hair to the mirror-gleam of his boots, he was dressed with his usual elegance. His coat fitted his broad shoulders like a glove. The single emerald on the gold pin that anchored his snowy cravat echoed the embroidery on his waistcoat and the glints of green in his hazel eyes. His tight pantaloons lovingly shaped slender hips and muscular thighs. Which she was not going to look at.

He'd chosen a seat on the far side of the room from the door, and he now ordered the footmen to wait outside. "I require a few moments of privacy with my betrothed." After a moment's hesitation, they obeyed, leaving the door wide open.

As she took a chair, he murmured, "Are there servant passages near us? Can we be heard if we keep our voices low?"

So that is why he'd chosen a seating group by the outside wall. "Not if we are quiet," she confirmed.

He was examining her in the way that always made her restless —a steady look, as if he could see her innermost thoughts. "You asked to see me," she reminded him, to put an end to it.

That broke his gaze. His lids dropped, and he laughed, a short unamused bark. "And you would like to see me in Jericho. Straight to the point, then, Lady Charlotte. Your mother told my mother that you are being threatened with dire consequences if you do not marry me."

He leaned forward, meeting her eyes again, his voice vibrating with sincerity. "I have never forced a woman, and I don't plan to do so. I will not take an unwilling wife."

Charlotte tried to hide the upwelling relief, but some of it must have shown, for he sighed as he sat back, his shoulders shifting in what would have been a slump in a less elegant man. "It is true, then. Given a choice, you will not have me."

Charlotte had not expected his disappointment, the sorrow deep in his eyes, swiftly masked. Before she could measure her words, she leapt to reassure him. "It is not you. I do not plan ever to marry."

He grimaced. "That is what my mother tells me. Is there nothing I can say that would change your mind? You would be an outstanding duchess."

No. She really wouldn't. Like everyone else, he saw only the duke's granddaughter, not the woman within. Perhaps, if he had been a man of lesser estate, if he had spoken about affection and companionship, she might have risked it. Not love. Charlotte did not trust love.

Again, he read something of her mind, for he sighed again, and gave her a wry smile and the very words she wanted. "We were friends once, my Cherry, were we not? Long ago?"

Her resolve softened at the nickname he had given her that golden summer, before it all went wrong. "I was very young and you were very drunk," she retorted.

He huffed a brief laugh. "Both very true. Still, we could be friends again, I think. I have always hoped for a wife who could also be my friend." He frowned. "Is it my damnable reputation? I am not quite the reprobate they paint me, you know."

Charlotte shook her head, then rethought her response. His reputation might outrun his actions, but he was reprobate enough, and the lifestyle he brushed off so casually had destroyed her brother. And her, as well, though not through her own fault.

"Not that, though if I were disposed to marry, I would not choose a rake. Marriage is not for me, however." She should at least hint at the reason. "I cannot be your duchess, Aldridge." She hesitated. How should she tell him? Blurt it out? Make a story of it?

The words wouldn't come, and he must have assumed that she'd finished. His social mask dropped back into place, proud though affable. "I have told your grandfather we will not suit. He asked if you had told me what he called 'your maidenly reservations', and I assured him I had not spoken with you. I let him think that the marriage arrangement was my father's idea, and not mine."

Marrying her had been Aldridge's idea? Charlotte put that away to think about later. "Thank you. He has had me locked in until I agreed to receive your proposal."

Aldridge nodded, unsurprised. The mother network must have included that information. "I am afraid my repudiation of the arrangement made him ill again. I'm sorry to say he took a fit."

Charlotte shrugged. She couldn't be sorry, even if that made her a horrible person. Again, Aldridge seemed to know what she was thinking.

"He, like my own sire, is too used to everyone leaping to his commands. We can't let their refusal to brook denial shape our lives any more than they must." He stood. "Still, I must hope I haven't killed him. Will you let me know?"

"I will. And thank you." She held out her hand in farewell, and he took it, turning it over and placing a kiss in the palm.

Once again, his mask dropped away, and something unfathomable stirred in his eyes. "If you change your mind, or if you ever have need of anything I can do for you, let me know, Cherry. I will always come at your command."

With that, he dropped her hand and strode for the door, leaving Charlotte less happy than she expected. If he had been a yeoman farmer, or a lawyer, or some other humble man to whom she might aspire—someone who did not require from her the primary duty of a peer's wife—they might have been happy together. But then, he would not have been Aldridge.

1

October 1814

Wintermount Street had gone down in the world since its heyday in the middle of the last century, when the houses that lined it were occupied by comfortably placed widows, younger sons with a creditable profession, and merchants with pretensions to the gentry.

Travelling the old street's length from west to east, Charlotte's carriage also traversed its slide into penury and disgrace. At the western end, a few of the houses still clung to the remnants of their former grandeur, a little scuffed and down at heel. Halfway down the street, boarding houses abounded, offering rooms for respectable ladies of diminished means, or gentlemen down on their luck, but never the two together. The eastern end merged almost indiscernibly into the slums of the streets beyond.

By design, the school—Charlotte's destination—was almost at that end. It was within an easy scurry through shadows for the children who sought a future away from the grog shops, the gangs, and the brothels. It was outside of the territory of the slum masters who might object to even their least significant subjects escaping their command.

The carriage pulled up in front of the school. Charlotte remained seated as she had promised the Duke of Winshire, her uncle, back when a Winshire carriage was attacked in a London street not dissimilar to this one. The attack had been the year before last, but still, he insisted on supplying her with armed footmen and two of his personal retainers as outriders on the days that she taught here.

She made no attempt to evade the escort, since she had grown to love her uncle, who was a very different man to his father and brother. She knew he loved her and worried for her safety this far from the wealthier streets where ladies were safe with no more escort than a maid.

One of her outriders knocked on the door, and only when it opened did a footman throw wide the door of the carriage, and offer a hand to help Charlotte descend. The outrider at the door would come with her into the school. The rest of her escort would return to the Winshire townhouse with both horses and the carriage, and would collect her again in two hours.

"Lady Charlotte." The matron waited at the door, unsmiling, and Charlotte hid a sigh. Mrs Porter was devoted to her work, but her preconceptions made managing her a challenge. Charlotte hoped that the thirty minutes she had allotted to taking tea with the woman would be enough to give the shrew's thoughts a better direction. From Mrs Porter's expression, it would probably take longer.

Inside, the house was austere, clean and quiet. Not silent, precisely. Young voices chanted times tables, the sound muffled. The little ones, presumably. Her own mathematics class had advanced well beyond such chants.

Charlotte allowed Mrs Porter to usher her into the matron's sitting room and pour her a cup of the inferior tea that the house offered its aristocratic patronesses and volunteers. Presumably, it was the same as the tea they drank themselves, which was very egalitarian of them. Charlotte instructed herself to admire their principles and sipped the tea without complaint.

It took ten minutes of general platitudes about the weather, the price of flour, and the progress of the war before Mrs Porter returned to the same arguments Charlotte had been hearing since she first offered herself as a volunteer teacher.

"These children have no use for anything but the simplest of arithmetic, Lady Charlotte. They are workers' children, at best. Not even that, most of them. Few of them are fit to be servants even in the home of a merchant or tradesman, and none of them can expect a more exalted role. What use is algebra to them? Or trigonometry? It is a ridiculous waste of your time."

Years of practice allowed Charlotte to keep her voice even. "It is my time to use as I see fit, Mrs Porter."

"The children, however, are my responsibility. You encourage them to defy me, Lady Charlotte. It is hard enough running a school in this neighbourhood without one of my teachers undermining me at every turn."

Charlotte lifted her eyebrows. "Clearly, some particular incident prompts this expression of your concern." The word diatribe would only exacerbate the situation. "Tell me what has happened, Mrs Porter."

Before the matron spoke, Charlotte knew the name of the pupil who had set off the storm. It would be Tony Tweedy, of course. A child of the slums—sly, wild, and defiant—he had been ruffling Mrs Porter's feathers from the day Charlotte tempted him into her lessons with a demonstration of Euclid's third apostolate.

His face—his uncanny resemblance to a portrait in the home of her godmother the Duchess of Haverford—had won her attention. His restless intelligence held it.

He had already been able to read and write after a fashion, but had taken to other lessons with hungry enthusiasm, as long as his teachers did not try to curb his rebelliousness or his imagination. His passion, though, was mathematics.

Outside of lessons, or in lessons he didn't enjoy, he found creative—even inspired—ways to circumvent every rule of the school, and he loathed Mrs Porter almost as much as she loathed him.

Mrs Porter was too well behaved to spit, but the way she said Tony's name came close. "The Tweedy boy. He is disruptive and disobedient. It is your lessons, Lady Charlotte. You mean well, I suppose." The expression on her face suggested she supposed no such thing. "But treating a slum boy as if he is intelligent? It gives him ideas above his station. He is—"

Charlotte interrupted the tirade, which she had heard before. "What happened this time?"

Tony's trespasses were of three kinds: pranks that displayed a creative sense of humour and a sharp awareness of how best to annoy; an insouciant defiance of those he despised that skirted the edges of outright rebellion; and a wilful misinterpretation of any rules he regarded as unnecessary or stupid.

Today's escapade had been all three, eclipsing even the introduction of a piglet into morning prayers and Charlotte's personal favourite, the day Tony had managed to marshal the entire school, plus a succession of idlers from the street, to search the building for suspected smugglers.

"Let me see if I understand you," Charlotte ventured, after Mrs Porter had interrupted her involved explanation for the fifth or sixth time to repeat her vituperative assessment of Tony's birth, intelligence, and moral character. "Someone stole your chamber pot from behind the screen where it is kept, filled it with slugs, and balanced it on the door to your private study." Mrs Porter coloured, whether at the direct reference to the receptacle—she herself had only hinted at its personal and private nature—or at the insult to her person.

"Not someone," she insisted. "It was that little slum rat. Tweedy."

"Someone saw Master Tweedy during his commission of this activity?" Charlotte asked. Not that she had any real doubts about the rascal's guilt, but Mrs Porter would have blamed the boy anyway, even if he were completely innocent.

"It was him, Lady Charlotte, and you know it. If he hadn't run off, I would have bea—got it out of him."

"The boy has gone? But today is my lesson!" A silly statement.

As if he would wait around for a mathematics lesson when Mrs Porter was breathing fire and talking about calling the constable.

Mrs Porter breathed deep, thrusting her bust up like a poulter pigeon. "I shall be writing to the Board of Trustees, Lady Charlotte, to ask them to close down your mathematics classes. You give these children ideas above their station."

Charlotte took her own deep breath before she spoke, the better to keep her voice calm and even. "And what, Mrs Porter, is the station of a boy who is brilliant at mathematics, to the extent that he has, in two lessons a week for six months, come from simple arithmetic to grasping concepts and solving equations that university students find challenging?"

"I know that the little brat has pulled the wool over your eyes, Lady Charlotte. You see what you want to see. I'll not deny that he's sly; his sort are. But you won't find real intelligence in the son of a whore."

"I disagree, Mrs Porter."

"If you will excuse me saying so, Lady Charlotte, you are a woman. I am sure the Trustees will understand the damage caused to these children by allowing a young noblewoman to practice her hobby. As if a woman could understand higher mathematics any more than a slum brat."

So. The gloves were off, were they? Charlotte smiled, though it really wasn't funny. "Go right ahead, Mrs Porter. However, I can assure you that it is not my place at this school that will be questioned. Remember that the patroness of this school, my godmother the Duchess of Haverford, is an ardent supporter of the right to education—for the poor, as well as for women. And she has chosen Trustees who agree with her."

Mrs Porter glared. "You nobles. You think you know so much better than anyone else. You don't know what those wicked children are capable of, and Tweedy is the worst of them all."

"You might be happier in another job, Mrs Porter," Charlotte suggested. "If you cannot subscribe to the same principles as the Trustees, you will be unable to carry out your duties here. I will teach mathematics to those capable of learning, and other teachers will also present opportunities to those with different talents. I suggest you think very carefully about whether you have a future here."

And Charlotte, who had no heart for the lesson that should have commenced half an hour ago, would go and teach the students who remained while fretting about the one who got away.

2

Aldridge poured the Marquess of Sodfield another brandy, and held it for him while the Marquess took his turn at the billiard table. Sodfield was the last hold-out, and even he was beginning to bend to three weeks of persuasion, logic, explanation, and all the considerable charm Aldridge had at his fingertips.

After nearly a year as Duke of Haverford in all but name, Aldridge seldom had to convince someone to accept his authority. Sadly, when it came to bills before the House of Lords, even bills to allow a canal across land that included a Haverford estate, he was on the same footing as any other landowner's steward. Which was shaky footing indeed, when the men responsible for blocking the bill were long-time adversaries of Haverford eager to put the boot into the duke, now he could not defend himself.

Sodfield missed his shot and retrieved his brandy. "At least you are not trying to sell me shares in some railway," he commented, as Aldridge studied the table.

Personally, Aldridge was betting on railways becoming commercial propositions sooner rather than later, but the canal was going to go ahead; the mills and collieries it would serve couldn't wait a decade or more for alternative transport. Taking the more circuitous route that opposition to the canal demanded would add months and thousands of pounds to the construction. For those bankrolling the project, the extra time could make the difference between recovering costs or going bankrupt.

"In time, Sodfield," he predicted. "For now, a canal on the route we've agreed will give us the best return." Sodfield had heard all of his arguments. No point in repeating them. He managed a cannon off the other two balls and stood back to give Sodfield his turn.

He'd finally convinced enough of the doubters to his side that he was almost certain the bill would go through. Sodfield would make it certain.

It had been frustrating. He'd been obliged to find social occasions to corner the lords who held the future of the canal in their spiteful hands. He'd been in and out of balls, musicales and routs, often several in a night. Every evening another dinner party. Every afternoon a round of the clubs. There, at least, he could breathe easily, for they were male-only preserves.

"Will you be at the Weston ball this evening?" Sodfield asked. He chuckled. "M'wife wanted me to make you known to my daughter. She's a taking little thing, but you needn't worry. I know she's not up to your weight. Only seventeen, you know, and if she has a thought beyond ribbons and fans, I've never seen it. M'wife has windmills in her head, and so I told her, but I promised I'd ask."

Thank goodness for a man with common sense. "I would be pleased to meet Lady Sodfield and your daughter," Aldridge replied. Sodfield had just potted the red ball and was ahead on points, but the move had left the man's cue ball vulnerable to counterattack.

Mothers and marriageable daughters everywhere he looked, hounds to his fox. In the vicious hunt most debutantes and their mamas made of the marriage mart, a title, wealth, acceptable looks and amiable disposition marked a gentleman as a prime quarry.

He would retire to the country to become a hermit, if he could. The business of the duchy required him to be social and in London, but the risk of being saddled with a wife he hadn't chosen required constant vigilance.

Sodfield shrugged as Aldridge took his revenge, though the two points scored still didn't remove Sodfield's lead. "Everyone knows you're not putting your head in the noose. And I daresay you'd not make my Felicia a comfortable husband if you were fool enough to offer for her."

Aldridge's abysmal reputation remained something of a defence, then, at least with careful fathers. Add to that his constant vigilance, and the willingness to be ruthless when required. Even so, the inevitable gossip about his father's swift decline and approaching demise had sent the hunt into a frenzy, and the usual measures were no longer enough.

And if his reputation was no longer protecting him from the marriage-minded, it was a positive incentive to widows, bored wives, and reckless spinsters looking for a companion in pleasure. He had long since lost any taste for casual sex, so had been ignoring lures and turning down blatant invitations for more than two years, but polite refusal seemed to spur some women on to even more flagrant attempts.

Baroness Thirby, for example. He had entertained the lady some years back, shortly after she was left widowed and wealthy. The marriage bed—or, more properly, Baron Thirby in the marriage bed—had bored her, but she discovered a new enthusiasm for the act with Aldridge and had spent the last four years experiencing—or so whisper had it—a wide variety of partners and encounters.

Now she seemed determined to revisit their brief affair, and did not believe that his 'no' was sincere.

Sodfield heaved a sigh of satisfaction as he managed a difficult carom that sent both Aldridge's cue ball and the object ball into the pockets, and racked up enough points to finish the game.

"Excellent, excellent!" he exulted. "A good game, Aldridge. I thought you had me early on. I had better call it quits, least Lady Sodfield become anxious about her evening. Another game next week, perhaps?"

Aldridge bowed his agreement. "Of course." *Damn. How long was Sodfield going to string him along.*

Sodfield was examining him closely. "Even if I say no to your canal?" he asked.

Aldridge summoned a smile and a nod. "You are a worthy opponent, Sodfield. It is a pleasure to play you."

Sodfield chuckled. "Excellent manners. And all the while you are wishing you could roast my gizzard. Very well, Aldridge, I'll sign your papers to let the canal cross my land, and I'll back your bill in the House. But I still want another game, mind." He held out his hand and Aldridge clasped it to seal the agreement.

"Tuesday next? Three o'clock in the afternoon?" Aldridge suggested.

"Done, and come and look me up tonight at Weston's. I'll present you to my wife and get it over. You're a good man, Aldridge. You'll have to marry one day. A duke needs an heir. Don't make it to a foolish yearling like my girl. Marriage is forever, and a man needs more in a partner than a pretty face at the breakfast table."

Which was good advice, but made one wonder about Lady Sodfield. Foolishness would not be a problem with the choice of Aldridge's heart, Lady Charlotte Winderfield.

She was the extra goad that lifted the gauntlet he ran at every social occasion from discomfort to torture. In the past, both she and her twin avoided the broader social swirl, attending mainly those entertainments put on by family members. Aldridge did the same, and so they encountered one another perhaps twice a month, even at the height of the Spring season. The Haverford and Winshire families were estranged because the Duke of Haverford had declared it so, setting himself against the new Duke of Winshire when the man first appeared in London two and a half years ago. Indeed, he had gone so far as to attempt to have the man's children declared illegitimate, and had even paid for at least two assassination attempts.

However, this month, Aldridge had been on a mission and so, apparently, were the twins, for every time he turned around, there was Charlotte. Encountering her night after night, sometimes several times a night, was further abrading his already raw spirits.

Most people thought her twin sister, Lady Sarah, was the lovelier of the two. The Winderfield Diamond, they called Sarah. Aldridge had never agreed. He freely acknowledged that Charlotte's colouring was less fashionable than her sister's: brown hair to Sarah's fair and brown eyes to her sister's blue.

Charlotte's curves were subtler, too. She was the twin, though, who drew his eye, whose shape, mostly guessed at as the fabric of her gown shifted around her, fueled his dreams.

After his last failed proposal, he had put his raking days behind him, hoping Charlotte would soften towards the idea of marrying him. But she continued to be uncomfortable in his company, giving him little more than common politeness.

Sooner or later, he was going to have to accept that she really had sworn off marriage or that it was him, in particular, she objected to. And why wouldn't it be? With his tarnished past, what had he to offer to someone who had earned the *sobriquet* Saint Charlotte as much for her immaculate behaviour and unblemished reputation as for her good works?

A sinner might aspire to admire a saint, but never to touch one.

Nonetheless, he poured himself another brandy, and sat looking at the fire, remembering a certain summer when he ran away to drown his sorrows in alcohol and willing women, and found an unexpected friend.

His lips curved as he sipped. Who would have thought that the most precious memory of that long-ago orgy would be an innocent schoolgirl, all skin and bone after an illness, brown hair in plaits as if to remind him to mind his manners? He could not, seven years later, recall a single woman from the house-party. They blurred into a vague impression of perfume, paint, giggles and curls. But he remembered Charlotte Winderfield.

1807, Somerset

"Mathematics is truth," the girl told Aldridge, her thin face glowing with passion. "It is beauty. The world is patterns of logic and shapes, and the task of mathematicians is to understand those patterns, Lord Aldridge."

Aldridge was drunk, but not so much that he didn't know he was in dangerous territory. He should not be trespassing on the wrong side of the pond that marked the boundary of the estate he was visiting. He should not be alone in this quiet folly with a girl who was both younger and better born than he had at first assumed. He should not be listening, enraptured, to her explanation about why she was beguiling her convalescence from an embarrassing childhood illness by solving puzzles.

Richport's house was hidden from their sight by a small tree-covered hill that rose on the other side of the pond. It was filled, as Richport's houses tended to be, with lustful women, good liquor, wagers of all kinds, and countless inducements to forget the sins, follies and betrayals that haunted him.

Yet he had been here for nearly an hour, in peaceful conversation—intellectual conversation—with a chit not yet out of the schoolroom, and he was already planning to return tomorrow.

"You know my name, my lady. May I know yours?"

She blushed, then, and cast her eyes around as if a suggestion might be written up in the rafters of the folly. "I am called Charrie."

He looked up to the tree that shaded the little building and then down at the basket that held cherry pits, all that was left of the fruit they had been sharing, and raised one eyebrow.

"Not Cherry," she told him. "Charrie."

"Cherry suits you better," he told her, though he was by no means drunk enough to explain why. An errant memory surfaced. Didn't Elfingham refer to his twin sisters as Charrie and Sarrie? And didn't Elfingham's grandfather have an estate somewhere in this area?

She was Lady Charlotte Winderfield, then, and the granddaughter of the Duke of Winshire. Highly eligible. Still too young, but she would be marriageable in a year or two.

And if he was thinking such foolish thoughts, it was high time he found another drink. He had not been sober for more than a month, and he had no intention of starting now. He stood.

"I must take my leave, Cherry, but I will visit tomorrow, if you will admit me. I shall present my card at the door." He gestured to the open side of the structure.

She giggled at his fooling, but said, "If we are to be friends, and if you are to call me Cherry"—the blush deepened—"then I shall call you Anthony. That is your name, is it not?"

Hardly. It was one of a string of names that had been bestowed on him at baptism, but no one had ever addressed him by anything but his title. He was Aldridge even to his closest relatives, and would remain so until his father died and he became Haverford. If she called him Anthony, he would look around to see who was being addressed.

Still, fair was fair. If he insisted on calling her by a name he had selected, she had every right to choose what to call him.

"Then we shall be Anthony and Cherry. Friend."

3

ovember, 1814, London

The Winshire townhouse was unusually quiet, with most of the family gone from London. Even Sarah had left, though just for two weeks to attend a house party. At twenty-two, Sarah had decided it was time to take a husband, and was hoping that two weeks under the same roof as three of her suitors, in the more relaxed environment of a country house, might help her to further her plan.

The small army of servants and retainers were scattered across England with the particular family members they served. Only Charlotte and her own personal attendants remained, and that only because she had obligations to fulfil.

The disappointing mathematics lesson at the ragged school had been nearly the last of them. Tomorrow, she had a meeting to attend, and then she would join Sarah in the country.

For tonight, she was eating dinner alone in the small dining room, at a table that, even with all the leaves removed, could seat ten. The room was laughably named when Charlotte thought of some of the dwellings she entered in the service of her students, but still just a fraction of the size of the banquet room, where one hundred and fifty could sit comfortably at the long tables, and two hundred could be squeezed in at need.

This evening, Charlotte had sent away the maid who was playing chaperone, the footman who had served the dinner, and Yahzak, the guard on duty, and was indulging in the forbidden pleasure of reading at the table, but she leapt to her feet when the door crashed open.

"My lady." Yahzak's calm tone showed no strain, though his arms confined a twisting, wriggling, fighting figure. "This urchin begs a moment of your time. A clean tongue, boy!"

The steady stream of imprecations, or rather the voice in which they were uttered, identified the intruder before Yahzak released him to fall to the floor a few feet from Charlotte. Yahzak followed in two swift paces. "Your pupil, I think?"

"Tony! What are you doing here?"

Tony gathered himself from his sprawl and glared up at Yahzak. "Ain't no call to be so rough, guv."

"The boy had no call to kick me and attempt to flee," Yahzak observed. "I recognised him from the school, my lady, and thought you might like to ask him why he was attempting to sneak into the house before I slit his throat and bury him in the garden."

Tony turned an alarmed face to Charlotte.

"He is joking, Tony. Sit down and tell me what the problem is. I take it you came to see me about something? Yahzak, you sit, too." No point in telling the warrior to leave them; he wouldn't until he was certain that the boy was no threat. Yahzak was one of the retainers the new duke had brought from his kingdom in the mountains north of Persia, his personal guard.

Tony took the indicated chair, keeping a wary eye on Yahzak.

"I assume this is about school?" Charlotte prompted.

Tony twisted to face her. In his unease, he forgot to speak the form of English he'd picked up from her and the other teachers, absorbing both accent and vocabulary like a sponge. Charlotte had less ease with his dialect than he with hers, but managed to pick up a scornful negative, followed by an explanation she could make neither head nor tail of.

He must have seen her bewilderment, for he took a deep breath and began again. "It's the Beast, me—my lady. He sent his men for me, but one of his pets used to be a mate of mine, back before the Beast collared him, and he…" He stopped mid-sentence and turned on Yahzak.

"Here, you can't say nothin'. If'n he tumbles… If the Beast finds out how I knew to run, my mate's neck won't be worth a farthing. Powerful nasty when he's crossed, is the Beast. He's, like, the duke of the tenements."

"I promise my silence, çaga, on all matters that do not touch on the safety of my kagan and his family." The boy's face said the words did not satisfy, and Yahzak added to them. "My lady's uncle, who is a real duke."

"The Beast is real enough to us as live in the tenements," Tony argued, which was true enough. The villain who ruled the particular noxious slum Tony called home had crossed paths with the Winshires before, if the intelligence recently brought to Charlotte's uncle was true.

He had once been known as the Duke of Devil's Kitchen, and had, in that persona, twice chosen the wrong side to back, first providing assassins for hire to Charlotte's uncle's enemies, and then involving himself in a plot against her cousin Ruth and Ruth's now husband, the Earl of Ashbury.

The Winshires had crushed his organisation after the second incident, but the villain himself had escaped custody with some of his accomplices. Winshire had recently learned that, instead of fleeing to the West Indies, as they had believed, he had hidden somewhere and was now taking a large chunk of the slums back under his control.

Opinion was divided on whether to go in after him. "We know his weaknesses," Charlotte's cousin Sutton had argued. "Destroy him altogether and another will rise that we have to learn all over again."

One of those weaknesses was pretty children. He kept several with him at all times, dressed in silk and treated like household pets, right down to the gold and silver collars they wore around their necks. No wonder Tony had run.

"You can stay here tonight and tomorrow," Charlotte decided. "I'm travelling into the country to a house party the day after that. You can come with me. As a groom, perhaps? The Beast won't be able to reach you there."

Aldridge could not sense the presence of Lady Charlotte behind him. The idea was ridiculous. And he could not possibly smell the delicate mix of herbs and flowers that drove him wild every time he was in Lady Charlotte's vicinity.

For a start, she would rather die than enter the chambers of any man, let alone the notorious Marquis of Aldridge.

For another, he was not in a position to sense anything outside of the strong musky perfume of the two naked women on the bed before him. They must have drenched themselves with it before casting themselves onto the sheets. Certainly, they could not have crept past his footmen to intrude on his peace while stinking like a bordello. Lady Thirby had gone too far, this time. And she'd brought her friend.

He'd been having a bath in his dressing room when he was called to deal with the intruders. He found the pair of them already naked in the big bed in the chamber he had long since abandoned to the ghosts of past *bacchanales*. Apparently, they expected a *danse de trois*—rumour had it that neither went anywhere without the other, but he had not thought the comment quite so literal.

They were doomed to be disappointed. Beyond a mild stirring of his least respectable body parts, he was not particularly tempted by the two ladies, which was depressing in its own way. However, using them to submerge his discontent in physical pleasure would show no respect to them or to himself. Now he had to get rid of them.

Perhaps he should claim a head cold or an emergency on one of

the estates. The one in the far north of Scotland might be sufficiently distant.

Suddenly, Lady Thirby stiffened, abandoning her odalisque pose
to point at something behind her. "What is she doing here?"

Standing in his doorway, her lips pressed into a tight line and
her face white except for two spots of high colour on her cheek-
bones, was the woman of his fondest dreams. And she didn't look
happy to be there.

A cold breeze down below warned him that his hastily-donned
banyan had caught on the bed as he turned. He hurriedly wrapped
it back around him, veiling that part of him that the lady could not
have expected to see.

Behind him, Mrs Meecham whined, "She's never here for a
romp, Margaret. She's one of the Winderfield twins."

Aldridge sighed. He could not imagine what sort of a crisis had
brought Saint Charlotte here, but clearly, he was going to have to
deal with it. "My lady," he said, "if you would be kind enough to
wait in the next room, I'll join you in a moment."

She pulled her fascinated gaze from his lower torso, and glared
at him. "You'll need clothing. You have to come with me and we
have no time to waste."

"He can't go out," Mrs Meecham objected. "Aldridge, you can't
go. We came to play."

Lady Charlotte said nothing; just retreated into the next room.
Aldridge sighed. "Ladies, I have already explained that I am not
available for such games. Not this evening. Not at all. And now, I
must leave you. The messenger—who, by the way, neither of you
saw,"—he gave them the ducal look learned from his father and
honed over years of acting in his father's place—"brings me word of
an appointment I cannot miss. My heartiest regrets."

He raised his voice. "Richards!" The butler must have been
hovering at the door, for he was bowing to Aldridge before his name
was out of Aldridge's mouth. "Escort these two ladies to a room
where they can dress, and arrange for a carriage to take them home.
Oh, and Richards? Find out how they got in."

He bowed to the two ladies, dashed back to his dressing room to grab the clothing already laid out for him, pulled on his pantaloons and shirt, and grabbed the rest. He could shrug into his waistcoat and coat and tug on his boots while she told him what the problem was. It was a little late to worry about appearing in front of her improperly dressed.

In his sitting room, Lady Charlotte was striding to and fro, turning at each end of her path in a swirl of skirts. Her brows were drawn together and she was biting her upper lip. She became aware of his entry and stopped to face him. "You said I was to ask you if I needed something." The edge to her challenging tone hinted that she expected him to reject her. *Never.*

"I told you I was at your command," he reminded her. "That hasn't changed. Will you permit me to sit, my lady, to put my boots on?"

She gave a huff of displeasure. "We don't have time for drawing room manners."

Nonetheless, she dropped into one of the chairs by the window, releasing him to sit on a footstool to tug on his most comfortable boots. "Perhaps, while I get ready, you could tell me what you require from me?"

She regarded him solemnly for a moment, then blurted, "I want you to take me to Devil's Kitchen to rescue a boy I have been sponsoring. I believe he has been kidnapped by the villain who calls himself the Beast. I believe the man wants him… Has an unhealthy purpose… Is interested…" She blushed, unable to voice her suspicions.

Aldridge nodded. "I understand. The 'Beast' has a certain unsavoury reputation for preferring young children." He paused, his mind focused on strategy. Talking Lady Charlotte out of her mission wasn't going to work, and nor was going into a neighbourhood like the Devil's Kitchen. Not even with an army of thief takers. Or militia, for that matter.

Aldridge had waited two and half years for her to ask something from him. Why did she want something so impossible?

"Who is this boy?" he asked. 'I believe', she had said. She was a clever and competent woman. She wouldn't assume the boy had been kidnapped without evidence, but even so, she might be wrong. He hoped. "Are you sure he has been taken? Might he have gone of his own accord?"

Charlotte's glare was withering. "No," she said. She relaxed her indignation sufficiently to explain. "Tony said the man was after him. He came to beg me to take him out of London. He was afraid, Aldridge. I told him we would leave tomorrow, but I came back from a meeting this evening, and he was gone."

She grimaced. "The man calling himself the Beast is Wharton, the man who attempted to kidnap my cousin Ruth and the Earl of Ashbury's daughter. A friend of Tony's is the Beast's 'pet', and Tony knew full well what the Beast had in mind."

Aldridge frowned. "Wharton has gone. He was arrested and held for trial, but managed to escape and get away. The West Indies, I heard."

Charlotte shook her head. "That is what we believed, but my uncle has discovered that he is still here, hiding out in the slums, his appearance disguised."

Aldridge opened a cabinet on his wall and fetched out his duelling pistols. After a moment's thought, he added a knife in a sheath he could strap to his wrist, and another larger one that belted around his waist. "I don't suppose you have any of your scary East-erners with you?"

"Three," Charlotte said. "I hope that makes you feel better."

"Certainly," Aldridge agreed. "Four—" he caught her eye and bowed "—five people against hundreds is much better odds than two." He opened the door into the passage and called out, "Richards! I want James and Matthew, armed and with me in one minute flat."

Two of the warriors who had accompanied the Winderfields from their Central Asian mountains were leaning against the wall and straightened to exchange bows with Aldridge. He called back over his shoulder, "Lady Charlotte, do you have a carriage or horses?"

"Horses." Charlotte joined him and her men in the passage.

Aldridge's usual reaction to her proximity was untimely. He ignored it.

"Richards! Horses for three! And ready another carriage for the two ladies in the next room. I'll be needing the one that is waiting." Poor Richards would have to keep Lady Thirby and Mrs Meecham from tearing the house apart while their transport home was prepared. "If we can find the boy," he told Charlotte, "hiding him in a carriage is probably a good idea, and we don't know what his condition will be."

The senior Winshire retainer nodded approval.

"Can we hurry?" Charlotte tapped one foot, impatiently, as two of Aldridge's most competent footmen hurried up. Both had been soldiers, and both could be trusted to defend the lady with their lives.

"This way." Aldridge waved Charlotte ahead of him down the stairs and out of the door that let on to the mews courtyard. "I am pleased to be of service, of course, but may I ask why you sought my aid?"

"Uncle James is out of town and Drew has a meeting in Southampton and won't be back until tomorrow. Yahzak refused to… Well, I needed someone who understands London slums." She passed him as they came out into the courtyard, where another Winshire retainer sat on one of their magnificent horses while holding the reins of three more. Grooms held three of the Haverford steeds, and a driver and groom clambered up onto a blank anonymous carriage.

It had languished at the back of the carriage house during Aldridge's celibacy, until tonight. Well, there was another with only minor decoration and no scutcheons. The ladies upstairs could take that.

Lady Charlotte paused beside her horse and looked back over her shoulder. "Besides, I think Tony might be your son."

4

———

E ven before she disturbed Aldridge at his pleasures, Charlotte had expected to be turned away. When she walked in on him entertaining two naked women, she had almost turned around again and left immediately, certain her interruption would secure her immediate eviction. Only her pride kept her in place, allowed her to demand his help.

Her pride and her howling panic at what might be happening to Tony.

Aldridge had confounded her expectations by immediately agreeing to come with her. Thank goodness. She needed someone who knew the underbelly of London, and Aldridge was reportedly an expert. Or had been. Again, rumour said he no longer frequented the brothels and gaming kens.

Though clearly, he brought those same activities home. She should not care what he had been doing. What was it to Charlotte, after all, if Aldridge had two women in his bed? Two! To think Charlotte had nearly been taken in by the stories that he had given up his tomcat behaviour. To find the gossip wrong should not have been a surprise. But it was.

Not a disappointment. It was not her place to be disappointed.

Her next stop would have been the Ashbury household. Her cousin Ruth's husband had been a soldier, but he lacked a hand and didn't know London at all. Besides, she wasn't even sure the Ashburys had arrived back from a visit to Sussex. They were due this week, but no message had been sent to the Winshire mansion to announce their arrival.

She didn't have a third option—no-one else she could depend upon to support her, and to attempt to rescue a child from the slums just because she cared. How annoying to find out that Aldridge was the only man outside of her immediate family that she trusted.

"If you and I ride in the carriage, Lady Charlotte," said Aldridge, "you can tell me where you think the boy has been taken and we can work out who we need to talk to in order to find him. I am thinking that my brother Wakefield might be useful, so I've instructed the coachman to take us there first."

It was a small detour and a good idea. Aldridge's base-born half-brother and his wife were successful thief takers, and had been very helpful to the Winshires during the troubles with Wharton last year. Come to think of it, they were probably the source of the latest intelligence.

Nonetheless, Charlotte fretted about the delay and Aldridge's arrogant assumption of command, even while she told him as succinctly as possible about Tony and her reasons for fearing he'd been taken.

He asked few questions, and nodded at her conclusions. "So. We need to find out if the Beast has him at Heaven and Hell, or whether he is being held somewhere else."

"Heaven and Hell?" Charlotte asked.

"He is master of a gambling den called Hell, which contains a—er—a place of assignation above, which he has called Heaven. Good L—gracious, I wonder if the bawd upstairs is his sister, Lady Ashbury? Word in the clubs is that she speaks like a lady, but is always masked. Her customers say she is haughtier than a duchess. They think it a fine joke."

"Lady Ashbury? As the madam in a brothel?" Charlotte tried to imagine the proud countess, widow of the Earl of Ashbury's

brother, in such a role. The lady had also been sentenced to trans-
portation for the plot to kidnap Ashbury's daughter and the
attempted murder of Charlotte's cousin, now Ashbury's wife.
Wharton had found a way to stay in England. Why not his sister? *I
will need to tell Uncle James. And Ruth.*

Aldridge shrugged. "Wakefield might know. We'll be there in a
minute, Lady Charlotte. Before we arrive, you mentioned that this
boy might be my son? Is that what he claims?"

Charlotte bristled at the term. "He does not 'claim' anything,
except that his father was an aristocrat who was his mother's
protector at one time. Or at least her lover. I suspect the relationship
was over before Tony was born, since he says he never met his
father. She wouldn't tell Tony much about him—said she had been
paid to stay away."

Charlotte growled the last bit. Whether the funds given to the
poor woman when she reported her pregnancy were inadequate, or
whether she wasted them, the fact remained that Tony was living in
the worst sort of slum when Charlotte met him. No man should
wipe his hands of a child he had engendered, however unintended
and unwanted.

Aldridge was frowning, so Charlotte gave him her best evidence.
"I guessed him to be yours because he looks just like the painting of
you and your brother that hangs in your mother's private sitting
room. Also, there is the name." Aldridge had been baptised
Anthony plus a string of other names, as had his father, though she
had never heard either of them called anything but their title.

The marquis lifted an eyebrow, but didn't comment on the coincidence of name. "It was a good likeness, my mother says, so I
imagine he is of Haverford blood. I would need to know more
about the circumstances to venture a guess as to which of the
Haverford men might be responsible. I can assure you that I am not
in the habit of abandoning my responsibilities, but he might still be
mine. If she approached my father instead of me… It would not be
the only time that he dismissed a child or a grandchild born on the
wrong side of the blanket."

The carriage pulled up, and Aldridge leaned forward, then

stopped with his hand on the door's latch. "How old did you say the boy was, my lady? I was eleven when that portrait was painted, so around that age?"

The door opened, and one of the footmen let down the steps.

Charlotte leaned forward as Aldridge descended and turned to hold out his hand. "Twelve, he says," she replied, as she put her hand in his. "He lived with his mother until he was nine, so I expect he knows."

The other footman was knocking on the door of the tidy town-house before them. It opened as Charlotte and Aldridge mounted the steps. "Claridge," Aldridge greeted the servant who stood in the gap. "Lady Charlotte and I are here to see Mr and Mrs Wakefield. Are they receiving? It is a matter both professional and personal."

The butler bowed. "If you and the lady would care to wait inside, my lord?"

"Also, Yahzak Beg, my guard commander," Charlotte insisted. Yahzak was at her elbow, his nostrils slightly flared and his eyes shifting from shadow to shadow as he kept watch on the street around them.

He nodded his approval even as the butler stood to one side to let them enter. Charlotte awarded the proper Englishman and the mountain warrior equal points for imperturbability, as each pretended to be completely at ease.

The butler showed them into the room where the Wakefields met with clients and occasionally, when they brought work home, interviewed witnesses and suspects. Aldridge had been taken upstairs to the family parlour last time he had called, but presumably Claridge considered his companions not worthy of that privilege.

He and Charlotte took seats opposite the desk that dominated one end of the room. Yahzak chose to prowl the room, examining the objects on the chimney piece and lifting one corner of a drape so he could peer outside.

David Wakefield ushered his wife Prue ahead of him into the

room, and Aldridge stood to greet them. Prue's gaze moved from him to Charlotte and back again, her eyes lively with curiosity. "Prue. David," he greeted them. "My apologies for intruding on your evening. Lady Charlotte, have you met my brother David and his wife?"

He waved a hand in the direction of Charlotte's escort, his eyes on Prue. "And this is the head of Lady Charlotte's guard detail, Yahzak Beg. I understand that 'Beg' is an honorific; something between our 'mister' and our 'lord'." Yahzak inclined his head, some slight crinkling around the outside of his eyes indicating amusement.

"We have met in the company of my godmother, the Duchess of Haverford," Charlotte said to Prue. "Thank you for seeing us this evening, Mrs Wakefield."

David clearly felt enough time had been spent on social trivialities. "Professional and personal?" he asked Aldridge, as he moved a chair closer to the pair Aldridge had chosen and handed his wife into it.

Aldridge nodded, taking his own seat again. "Lady Charlotte came to me with a problem this evening, and we need your advice on how to solve it. Lady Charlotte? Will you tell them about Tony? And what you think has happened to him?"

David pulled up his own chair and sat beside Prue. Both Wakefields focussed their attention on Charlotte.

One of the many things Aldridge loved about the lady who wouldn't be his was her clear, incisive mind. She started with a summary: that her protege had been kidnapped by the Beast and was in immediate danger of abuse, and that she intended to rescue him. She then listed the reasons for her conclusions.

David interrupted once, to comment that he was aware of the Beast's identity, as his firm was the source of the Duke of Winshire's information. Prue grimaced and nodded at the reference to the Beast's proclivities. Otherwise, they sat silent and watchful until Charlotte was finished.

"You'll want to get into the club Wharton and his partner run," David deduced, after a thoughtful silence. "It is larger than it appears. The buildings in the next street are connected, and the principals have apartments there, but they are extremely well guarded."

"A likely place to keep the boy, though," Aldridge suggested.

"What part of this is personal?" Prue asked. When the other turned to look at her, she explained, "Aldridge said the matter was both professional and personal."

"Ah." Aldridge nodded, his lips pursed. "Lady Charlotte tells me that young Tony looks very similar to my own portrait aged eleven, the one in my mother's sitting room."

"I know the one," Prue agreed. "A Fitzgrenford, you think?" She addressed the question to Charlotte, who was looking from Aldridge to David.

"His eyes are identical in shape and similar in colour," Charlotte observed.

Prue also looked at one brother and then the other. Their colouring differed, as did their build, and Aldridge was a good half a head taller, but they shared their hazel eyes with the duke their father.

"A likely motive," David suggested.

Aldridge nodded. Stanley Wharton had been at Eton with him, a senior classman in his final year when Aldridge's younger brother, barely eleven and young for his age, had arrived at school and been assigned to do chores for Wharton. "Wharton is obsessed with my brother Gren."

Even as a young man, Wharton had been known for pressing his attentions on unprotected boys from the junior classes. Gren had come to Aldridge in distress after Wharton had made advances. Wharton soon found that a Grenford was never unprotected. "He hates me and David," he told Charlotte. "That may well be his motive for going after your young Tony."

He turned to David. "How does that help us?"

"It doesn't change what we do next," David said. "We need to get into Heaven and Hell. Not you, Lady Charlotte. Me and Aldridge, I think."

"Wharton will know us," Aldridge warned.

"Wharton will know you, but he won't know you know him. And I'll be in disguise."

Aldridge nodded. "No one would believe David Wakefield was brothel crawling. Or gambling, for that matter." They would believe it of Aldridge, though he hadn't darkened the door of a brothel since his salad days. His damnable reputation.

Prue, bless her, acknowledged his pain, though with a sting in the tale. "Those who know you are aware you are not so promiscuous now, Aldridge. And you know perfectly well that you've maintained the reputation to keep matchmaking Mamas at bay."

Charlotte looked as if she was bursting to share how she had found him not an hour ago, but mercifully kept her opinion to herself.

"We are agreed?" David asked. "Lady Charlotte, Yahzak Beg, my wife will explain where you'll need to wait. If we find the boy, we'll break out, and we may need help to escape. I'll go and change. Aldridge, if you'll come with me, we can plan our strategy while I get ready."

5

From behind the goat's head mask he wore as master of Hell, the Beast's mind seethed with plans and hatred as he watched the Marquis of Aldridge. *Look at him, surveying the room with that curl to his lip, his nose in the air. Thinks he is better than me, just because he is wealthy, and the son of a duke.*

The whoreson golden boy had always been the same, always interfering with the Beast's pleasures, since they first met at school. The Beast had hated him for two decades. Aldridge rejected the Beast's overtures of friendship, showed disdain for the group the Beast gathered around him, and insisted on standing between the Beast and those who attracted his anger or his desire.

The beautiful Lord Jonathan Grenford could have been Wharton's, but for Aldridge. The Beast's mind darkened at the memory. Lord Jonathan Grenford had been a lovely child when he arrived at Eton, and was assigned to do chores for Wharton. Wharton had so many plans. They would have been happy together; he just knew it. Gren—it had been Wharton who had given him that name—was a little jumpy, but Wharton was working on him, and he would have surrendered in the end. Wharton would have taken care of him after that, made him happy.

Then Aldridge had Gren assigned to another senior classman. Worse. He sent someone—a grown man—to growl threats in the dark, threats reinforced with a dagger to Wharton's throat. Cowardly bastard.

Aldridge had interfered, too, a decade later, sending his base-born brother to destroy Wharton's fledging export business. And surely it was not coincidence that the man who cut off the supply of girls for that business was Aldridge's cousin, another sodding peer?

The boy tucked away in the Beast's private chambers would not be a full replacement for the lost Gren, though the appearance was uncannily like. Gren at eleven had been a pampered princeling, all softness, humour, and charm. The boy Tony was a slum brat, gristle and sinew, sharp of tongue and wit.

Good food would put some weight on him, and a few beatings would teach him to obey. The Beast would smooth off Tony's rough edges and recreate him in the image of the boy he had never been able to have or to forget.

Is Aldridge here to stop me?

Panic jagged sharp shards through the roiling bitterness. Almost, the Beast gestured to his bully boys to seize his enemy and throw him into the street, but sanity prevailed. Aldridge couldn't possibly know about Tony. The boy had been taken from the garden of the Winderfield mansion, and the Winderfields and Haverfords did not speak.

Rumour had it the Duke of Haverford and the Duke of Winshire had been rivals for the same woman. Haverford had married her and Winshire—only a third son then—had been sent away overseas and declared dead to his family. Haverford's duchess must have preferred the exiled suitor, for all these years later, Haverford still hated Winshire. Indeed, he'd hired slum assassins to kill the man, as the Beast knew full well, since he'd been the one to procure them.

Aldridge's presence here could have nothing to do with the Beast's new pet. Aldridge needed—deserved—to be dealt with. However, the Beast could not attack a man of Aldridge's rank in the midst of the high-bred crowd who thronged his Hell.

Wait until he is alone.

Yes. That was the way. If he stayed here in Hell, the Beast would make sure he was fleeced of a few thousand pounds and then followed once he left and beaten. Him and the man with him. The Beast had barely noticed the companion, but examined him now. No one the Beast knew: a plump fellow with grey hair and thick-rimmed glasses, somewhat older, quietly dressed. A secretary, perhaps.

Best if Aldridge chose to go up to Heaven, and he probably would, the rutting whoreson. Once he was alone with one of the girls, the Beast could make sure he suffered. Away from Heaven and Hell. Hatred for Aldridge could not be allowed to spoil his business or his cover. But easy enough to slip him laudanum or the like, and have him carried elsewhere for his punishment.

His companion, too.

Aldridge had made his way around the room, had spoken to one of the servants (they were dressed as demons, which the Beast considered a fine conceit), and was now heading for the stairs.

Good. He is going to Heaven, then.

The Beast slipped through the door behind him and headed for the private stairs that led to his sister's office. At last, Aldridge would begin to pay.

"The decoration is rather obvious," Aldridge murmured to Wakefield, out of the corner of his mouth. The place had been done up to match the name. From the moment they handed over their coats and hats at the door of Hell, everything followed that theme: furniture, fittings, adornments. Even the clothing of servants and employees—such as it was.

The girl who took their outerwear had small horns emerging from her hair, goats' ears, and dark paint shaping a cat's eye outline around her eyes. Her costume was mostly gauze in shades of red— an assortment of scarves that left her breasts bare but provided enough of a cover at hip level to hide whatever anchored a long lizard tail.

The broad passage leading from the entrance was painted with a long mural on either side—well-dressed partygoers in riotous procession, at first sight. But a closer look showed they were indulging every imaginable vice, flames licking their heels, on their way to the arches at the other end, which echoed the real arch ahead of Aldridge and Wakefield.

In the mural, a devil stood at the side of each arch—a tall golden figure with goats' horns and a leering grin, arms open in welcome. Beyond the arch, the artist had painted a bonfire, all flames and smoke, but for the hints of an orgy within the conflagration—a bare arm or a foot or a face or other less socially acceptable parts.

Devils, or servants costumed as devils, stood on either side of the real entrance, and opened the double doors to allow Aldridge and Wakefield to enter.

The room beyond was a typical gambling salon, except for the lurid scenes painted on the walls and the extravagant costuming of the demons, imps, and devils who were there to serve the scores of so-called gentlemen out for a good time.

"One room leads into another, my lords," one of the door devils murmured. "Please continue through until you find something to please you."

"I seek Heaven tonight," Aldridge responded. "Which way—?" He broke off. He had just seen the staircase leading up to the side. Again, the imagery was obvious. The same crowd of partygoers marched up the wall, but this time the flames had died away by the third step, to be replaced by clouds.

By the fourth step, the multitude of vices diminished to the most obvious, with each other and with winged beings whose skimpy costumes and voluptuous bodies made the term 'angel' a blasphemy. An obscenity, too, Aldridge decided, his sharp gaze taking in some of the detail.

"Indeed, my lord," the other door devil agreed. "Please follow the stairs. Our heavenly beings wait to serve you."

Aldridge looked around as they walked down the side of the room to the stairs. Across the floor, beyond the gaming tables, raised up above the crowded room on a dais, the original of the painted welcome figure sat on an ivory throne.

Naked from the waist up, his lower half was clad in gilded fur, or perhaps tightly curled wool. His face was covered by a gilded mask —a goat's head with large curled horns—except for large apertures through which his eyes glinted. He was staring at Aldridge, who inclined his head but continued towards the stairs.

"The Beast, I take it," Wakefield murmured.

Presumably. The man stood as Aldridge and Wakefield started up the stairs, then disappeared between the curtains behind his throne. Aldridge put the villain out of his mind. The Beast was not the immediate target tonight.

Upstairs, they found the usual lounge, and by now the variety of skimpy goddess, god, and angel costumes came as no surprise. No sign of the Madam. Aldridge had expected the companion throne, ebony rather than ivory, and more delicately carved. It was empty.

One of the women approached. "What is your pleasure, my lords?" The neckline of her white gown plunged to her waist, and the skirt that hugged her swaying hips was split strategically so that glimpses of thigh showed as she walked. Her face was classically beautiful, marred by the vacancy of her smile, the weary distance of her eyes. "Heaven prides itself on meeting all appetites," she assured them.

Wakefield took the lead, pointing. "That girl and that one, and one room with a large bed," he ordered. Aldridge nodded in agreement. Wakefield had contacts among the women who earned their living in the world's oldest trade; presumably he'd recognised the ones he'd chosen.

The two selected approached, their smiles professional and meaningless. One was dressed in skimpy Grecian robes with her brunette curls dressed high and bound with gold cord—Artemis, from the little toy bow and arrow she carried in one hand. The other wore her fair hair down, flowing over her upper body. Other than her hair, a bright scarf was her only covering, cinched at the waist by a circlet of flowers that echoed the one on her head. Gauzy wings hinted that she was, perhaps, intended to be a fairy.

"Artemis," the greeter confirmed with a wave, and, "Ariel," with a second. "Something to drink or eat, my lords?"

"Perhaps later," Aldridge said. He slipped an arm around the blonde fairy and sniffed at her flowers. Silk, but he ignored that detail. "Come on, sweet thing. Show me to a bed."

"The India room," the greeter decided. Wakefield offered the brunette a raised hand. "Shall we, your divinity?"

She giggled as she placed her hand in his, and raised her nose in the air, slanting a glance to the others in the room to ensure they noticed. Aldridge allowed the woman he was holding to lead the way down a passage.

They stopped at the fourth room on the right, where a partly opened door gave entrance to a room decorated with richly embroidered silken wall hangings and what looked like copies of Hindu temple paintings in a frieze around the walls. The main feature of the room was a circular bed at least ten feet across.

Aldridge gave Ariel a gentle push on her bottom to propel her further into the room so he could disengage, then put out a hand to catch her wrist as she reached for her belt. "Don't disrobe," he said, as Wakefield escorted Artemis inside and turned to shut and secure the door.

The fairy attempted to rub herself against Aldridge as he held her away from him by the wrist. "How may I please you, my lord?" she asked.

"Information, Sukie, and an alibi," Wakefield said, drawing the attention of both women. Their poise slipped as they narrowed their eyes at him. He had been examining the walls, and now led them all to the corner of the bedchamber nearest to the window.

With his back to the room, Wakefield removed the glasses whose tinted lenses disguised the colour of his eyes and ejected the pads that puffed out his cheeks into his hand.

"Gor blimey!" The goddess's refined accent devolved into broad slum in her surprise. She lowered her voice at Wakefield's urgent gesture. "Sukie, it's Shadow."

The fairy looked from the enquiry agent to Aldridge and back again.

The goddess declared, "You're never here for a poke. Him, maybe, but not you. Your missus would feed you your bollocks."

Wakefield laughed softly, and whispered back, "True, Bets. Ladies, may I make known to you the Marquis of Aldridge, my brother. Aldridge, Saucy Sukie and Bouncing Bets are old friends."

Aldridge bowed as if being introduced to a couple of dowagers, and the two prostitutes giggled and flushed like debutantes.

Wakefield continued to take the lead. "You're right, Bets. We're here to take back… Well. Before I get to that, how do you like working here? Are conditions good?"

Bets screwed up her face in disgust. "Good? Not bleedin' likely. Never been any place worse. Can't leave the house without a bully-boy tagging along. Can't make any money till we've paid for our costumes, and our food, and our anything. Twelve cullies a night or we get fined, unless the cully pays double for more than forty minutes, and ain't nobody going to pay twelve times as much for a whole night."

Sukie added, "And that's not the worst, Shadow. La Reine, the madam? She sells everything and anything. Don't care if it damages the merchandise. One of the girls got beaten so bad she couldn't come to work again, and then she just disappeared. Gone back to her mother, La Reine said. Bullshit, I say." She shuddered.

"Even kids," Bets agreed. "I don't hold with that. I wouldn't have signed on if I'd known they sold kids."

"We're here to rescue a boy," Wakefield said. Aldridge shot him an alarmed glance, but presumably his brother thought these women could be trusted.

At that moment, someone tried the door handle, and then there was a knock.

"This room is occupied," Aldridge called out, allowing some of his anger to colour his voice.

"Drinks!" came the reply. "Compliments of the House."

Wakefield nodded at Sukie, but Aldridge said, "Wait." He pulled the scarf off her shoulder leaving her upper half bare, and tipped her floral coronet sideways. "Here." He drew a heavy bag of coins from his belt. "Tell them we want the next three hours, and no interruptions."

Sukie carried out her commission, barely opening the door, handing over the bag and taking the tray.

"The money is not going to help much," Wakefield whispered to Aldridge. "If they're not already watching through the walls, they'll be on their way."

"Then we'd better be on ours," Aldridge whispered back, though he was kicking himself for forgetting that they were probably being observed. Disrobing Sukie just so she could answer the door might already be counting against them.

With the door bolted again, all four of them retreated to the corner by the window, where Wakefield and Aldridge laid out their reasons for being there and what they hoped to achieve.

"If we help you find the boy, will you take us with you?" Bets asked, and Sukie nodded.

"It's going to be dangerous," Wakefield warned. "I can't give you any guarantee that we'll get out safely."

Sukie snorted. "For certain sure, we're not getting out on our own."

"Then we'll take you," Aldridge decided. "Whether we find the boy or not."

He crossed to the tray of drinks and reached for one of them. "I wouldn't," Wakefield warned.

Aldridge pulled back his hand as if scalded. "Drugged?"

"A drink given to you free in Wharton's brothel? What do you think?"

Aldridge shuddered and followed the others from the room.

The first part was the most fraught. With Sukie at the entry to the passage and Bets at the next corner, keeping watch, Wakefield did something to jam the lock while Aldridge stood over him, his pistol at the ready.

No one came. So far, then, they had not established watchers in the hidden passages.

Soon, they were following Bets up a flight of stairs, along a passage, and then up another flight of stairs. "The Beast has his rooms in the next building. There's a way through from Heaven, but we're taking the bridge from the attics. All the workers are downstairs. It should be safe enough."

In the attics, Bets lit a candle and led them past a series of small rooms, with side passages running off at intervals. "We girls sleep up here," Sukie explained. "The men sleep across the bridge in the other attic. The Beast is on the floor below, and he keeps his pets close. If he has the boy you're looking for, it'll be there."

Bets hesitated at an intersection "Can we stop and get our stuff?"

"One small bag," Wakefield replied. "Something you can carry while running."

"Better get changed," Aldridge suggested, "into something you can wear in the street."

Wakefield agreed. "You'll not only attract the wrong kind of attention dressed like that; you'll freeze. Be quick. We don't know how long until they raise the alarm."

Bets led them down the next side passage, and handed Aldridge the candle. Both women fetched stubs of candles to light, and disappeared into their rooms.

Listen as he could, Aldridge could hear no sound of alarm, but that didn't mean their absence hadn't been discovered. For one thing, they were now in another building. For another, Wharton and his minions would keep any pursuit as quiet as possible, so customers were not alarmed.

He frowned at the door behind which Bets was presumably changing and packing a bag. What was taking so long? Even as he had the thought, Sukie let herself back out into the passage, and Bets was only a few seconds behind.

From the bulky look of them, both of them had decided to wear as much of their wardrobe as they could, layer on layer. All to the good. It wouldn't slow them down, and they'd be all the warmer.

Again, Bets took the lead. Aldridge followed, with Sukie behind him and Wakefield bringing up the rear.

Along the narrow passage, down a few steps, and on to a

broader passage that led to double doors. Bets eased one of them open, and shielded the flame of her candle with her palm. This must be the enclosed bridge that led to the other building. No windows, but Aldridge could feel the wind whistling in from outside through gaps in the floor and walls.

Betts saw his hesitation. "It's solid enough." She slipped through the door and Aldridge followed, then the other two.

A few paces brought them to another pair of doors. Aldridge opened one enough that Bets could lead them into another warren of rooms and then down another staircase, this one a single flight ending at a panel that opened into a far more opulent passage.

"There will be guards," Betts whispered. "The Beast always has guards."

There were, but they did not expect an invasion from the servants' quarters. Two men stood within view of the main staircase, discussing a prize fight while watching over the apartment's main entrance. Aldridge and Wakefield studied them from the shadows. Several minutes passed and they heard no one else. They withdrew around the corner to where they'd left the two women sitting in darkness, and decided their strategy in whispers.

Aldridge was the better bowler, and a small stone carving on a side table made a suitable projectile. As planned, it sailed silently over the heads of the sentries, hit the wall of a cross passage with a thud, then clattered on its way until it ran out of momentum. It worked even better than they planned. Both men ran after it, and by the time they re-emerged from the passage, Aldridge and Wakefield were one either side of the egress ready to fell them, one with the cosh Wakefield pulled from his pocket, the other with a twin to the impromptu cricket ball in a stocking donated by Bets.

They were checking their victims when a voice called, "What was that?" They had only enough time to tug the first two men out of the way before a third rushed through the doorway and met the same fate.

With help from Bets and Sukie, they bundled all three into a linen room which handily provided sheets to tear up for bindings and gags.

"This way," Wakefield suggested, leading them into the cross passage from which the third guard had emerged. It continued the opulent theme of the foyer, and was lit by glass-shielded candles in wall sconces.

Sure enough, halfway along, a chair sat in front of a door, a half-eaten meal on the floor beside it.

The door was locked.

Wakefield went back to search the sentries for keys, while Aldridge tried the other doors. The rest—all empty bedchambers—opened easily. Each had two single beds, a washstand, and a tiny mirror on the wall. None of the others had been locked and guarded.

"No keys," Wakefield said. "I'd be prepared to bet that Wharton keeps them."

"Don't know this Wharton," Sukie commented, "but the Beast and La Reine carry all the keys."

At that moment, they heard breaking glass from within the room. Wakefield knelt, pulled a kit from his pocket, and began an attempt to pick the lock. Aldridge ran into the next-door room and pulled open the window, to see a slender fair-haired boy climbing the sheer and near-smooth wall.

"Tony," he hissed.

The boy looked down in alarm and lost his grip with one hand. Aldridge held his breath as the climber recovered and shimmied another couple of feet until he could reach over the top of the façade. A quick scramble, and he was gone. Aldridge returned to Wakefield.

"Our boy was here," he said. "He has gone out of the window and over the roof. Can we set up a diversion, do you think?"

"You are sure it was him?" Wakefield asked.

"I couldn't see much in the dark," Aldridge admitted. "Fair hair, right size for the age, smart. The face, maybe."

Wakefield nodded. "And the door was locked and guarded. Very well. Let's go down a level, sort out an escape route, and make a racket."

6

____

Aldridge and Yahzak had tried to convince Charlotte to wait with the carriage. Their plan set her teeth on edge— to go into the brothel and hire two harlots, so they could get them alone and pay them for information. As if that was all Aldridge wanted from women like that!

She didn't have a better plan, so she kept her opinion to herself. In any case, she was being ridiculous. It was not, after all, as if she wanted his attentions, or those of any man.

Even so, she insisted on being with those who watched to give whatever support they could. She pointed out they would have to split their strength to make sure she was well guarded. She was better to stay with the men all in a group, she insisted. She kept to herself the burning need to be as close as she could to Aldridge as he put himself in danger on her behalf.

Probably, she could do no good. Probably, she was just as useless here on the rooftop of a nearby building as she would be hidden away three blocks closer to civilisation in a mews that Wakefield said was safe with the driver and one man to watch the horses. "As safe as this part of town can ever be," he'd qualified.

Yahzak watched her fidget, hugging herself against the cold, leaning forward a little to see if she could detect a change in any of the windows in the next building. "The waiting is the hardest part," he acknowledged.

He and his cohort did not seem to be restless. Even Aldridge's two footmen were more patient than Charlotte, though she supposed their work required a lot of waiting. It was one of them that saw the drapes twitch back in a room on one of the upper floors, and a face at the window.

"Lord Aldridge," the footman said.

Charlotte could see little more than a pale blur outlined by lamplight and distorted by the small thick panes, but she waved, and the person must have seen them in even in the dark, because he or she waved back before retreating out of sight.

They continued to wait, but nothing further happened for long minutes, until a racket broke out loud enough to be heard even from this distance and through walls. Shouting. A crash. The light in the room they'd been watching went out. Lights moved in and out of rooms accompanied by more shouting.

"What is happening?" Charlotte asked, but, of course, none of them had an answer.

"We need to get closer," Yahzak decided, and sent his men along the parapet and across a sloping roof to the next building. The two footmen followed, and then Charlotte, with Yahzak bringing up the rear.

"There," one of the guardsmen said, pointing. From this new angle, they could see where the two main buildings were joined to those at the back, with a narrow alley barely an arms-reach across, bridged at multiple points with box-like passages.

On a balcony on the closest rear building, two shapes—little more than darker shadows against the grey—bent over the balustrade focused on something Charlotte could not, at first, see. Another shadow. No. Two. A woman, by the skirts, being dropped on a rope to someone who waited below.

As she reached the ground, one of the two on the balcony climbed over and began the descent. None of the shapes were small enough to be Tony.

The rumpus had moved to the rear buildings. Charlotte could hear it approaching the escapees, see the lights flickering from one window to another. "Hurry," she whispered.

Yahzak snapped a couple of orders, and his men unshouldered their rifles and knelt to steady the barrels against the stone wall that divided this roof from the one next door. "My lady, we go down now. That is Lord Aldridge, I think, needing our help, perhaps."

Aldridge's footmen, their own weapons in their hands, took the rear as Yahzak led Charlotte through a trapdoor, dropping down to catch her, then hurrying ahead down a narrow flight of steps that stank of unmentionable things. Fortunately, the gloom protected her from confirming the noxious substances her nose suspected.

From above them, they heard the bark of rifles. Yahzak lengthened his stride, taking three steps at a time. Charlotte allowed one of the footmen to thunder down the steps in his wake, though the other insisted on staying with her as she hurried as fast as her shorter legs and her skirts would allow.

They were disappearing into an apartment as Charlotte and the footman reached the ground floor. She followed, apologising to the family who sat frozen as they traversed to the open window that Yahzak and the other footman had just used to exit.

It was a courtyard between the buildings, a sparse rectangle that trailed away into pathways in four directions. One was the narrow alley where they'd seen the people escaping from the balcony, though from this angle they could not see the balcony itself.

Charlotte took a step in that direction, but the footman who had followed Yahzak waited at the mouth of another way, gesturing them to follow. The path took them out between another two buildings into the back alley beyond the Heaven and Hell complex.

Aldridge was waiting. Farther down the street, two women hurried after a man. Wakefield? There was no sign of a boy.

Before she could ask, Aldridge said, "We found the room where we think Tony was being kept prisoner, but he has escaped. Come, we need to get out of here before they follow us."

"I will cover," Yahzak declared.

Wakefield beckoned from the corner, and Aldridge took Charlotte's hand, breaking into a run. The carriage and the string of horses waited. The two women from the brothel were just clambering into the carriage.

"Who are your friends?" Charlotte asked Aldridge.

His eyebrow twitched at the sourness she couldn't keep from her tone, but his reply was mild. "Let's put some miles between us and pursuit, and I'll explain." He made a step with his hands and tossed her up into her saddle.

Yahzak and the footmen came around the corner, and the remaining guards dropped down into the street from the rooftops. In moments, the entire party were mounted and on their way northwest to Bishopsgate Street, and then up Sun Street and from there through Crown Street to cut across to Finsbury Square.

There, they paused. "Where next," Yahzak asked.

"Let's talk." Aldridge dismounted and came to offer Charlotte his assistance.

They gathered next to the carriage, where they could see one another's faces in the flickering coach lamps. The two women opened the door and leant out. "Lady Charlotte," Wakefield said, "may I present Sukie and Bets?" The two women bobbed, as much of a curtsey as they could manage while seated and canting forward.

Charlotte nodded in return, trying not to wonder whether Aldridge had got his money's worth, and if so, with which one. Perhaps both. After all, Wakefield was purportedly besotted with his wife.

Wakefield continued, "They helped us this night, and in return asked our help to escape."

"Wakefield explained our intentions," Aldridge added, "and the ladies took us through the attics to the place the Beast keeps his prisoners. Just as well, because he had guards on the main stairs. There was only the one prisoner, and he took advantage of the disturbance we made to break his window and escape—I saw him climbing the wall. A boy of about eleven or twelve, slender, fair haired. I couldn't pick up more than that in the dark."

"So, we made a disturbance to give him time to get away," Wakefield added, "and then left."

A brief explanation covering the hour or more that they'd been in that place. Charlotte instructed her prurient imagination to behave. What Aldridge did was none of her business.

"Do you know of anywhere young Tony might go for shelter?" Aldridge asked, oblivious to the direction of Charlotte's seething thoughts.

Charlotte wrenched her mind back to her purpose for being here. "Back to Winderfield House, I hope. Failing that, the school."

"Then we'll check the school, since that is closer, before returning to Winderfield House," Wakefield decided. "Sukie? Bets? Do you have anywhere to go? Somewhere the Beast and his sister cannot find you?"

The two women exchanged uncertain glances. "Can't think of a place, guv," Bets offered with a shrug, but her eyes spoke of her fear, and Sukie was weeping silently. They were young, Charlotte realized. Younger than her. Victims, perhaps, of the fate women suffered when men took what they wanted without concern for the consequences.

It could have been her. It could have been Sarah. They'd had a strong aunt with her own wealth, plus a mother with connections. Otherwise, they might have been thrown out to fend for themselves, as the duke their grandfather threatened more than once.

In her jealousy, Charlotte had lost sight of compassion, for a short time. "Then we shall have to find you a place," she said. "You shall come home with me for tonight, and we shall talk about what you want to do after that."

"Lady Charlotte!" Aldridge exclaimed.

"Lord Aldridge!" she responded, mimicking his tone.

Wakefield intervened before Aldridge could burst out with whatever arrogant remark was on the tip of his tongue. "Thank you," the enquiry agent said to Charlotte, and then, to the two women, "I would like your help to make a drawing of Heaven and Hell. I also have a few questions about the routine, and what you've heard about the owners. May I call on you later in the day? If that is acceptable to you, Lady Charlotte."

"Of course." Charlotte contented herself with casting a

triumphant glance at Aldridge before adding, "We should be moving on, now we have a plan. We are attracting attention."

Lights had gone on in several of the houses, and curtains twitched. Charlotte crossed back to her horse and accepted Yahzak's help into the saddle before Aldridge could get to her side. He mounted and guided his horse alongside her to make the expected protest.

"Lady Charlotte, it cannot be suitable for you to bring women like that into your own home. Wakefield should not even have presented them to you. What will your uncle say?"

Men were such hypocrites. "They have helped us, and now they need our help. It would hardly be appropriate for you to take them into your own home, Lord Aldridge." She shot him a considering glance and couldn't resist adding, "Though I don't suppose it would be the first time. Still, they should have a choice about whether to continue in this life, do you not think?"

Aldridge opened his mouth, thought again and closed it, then opened it and closed it again, his mouth set in grim lines. Finally, he let his horse drop back.

Insufferable man. The carriage peeled off, heading west, with one of the guards in escort. The other horsemen rode south, on the familiar route to the school. Charlotte followed close behind Yahzak with one of Aldridge's footmen on each side and Wakefield, Aldridge and the other guard bringing up the rear.

The sky was paling in the east by the time they reached the school. Yahzak's men dismounted to prowl the perimeter, checking any hiding places, but found nothing beyond some smears of blood on the front steps. Whoever left them was gone.

"Where else could he have gone?" Charlotte wondered.

"We'll find him," Wakefield assured her. "I'll put some people on to it this morning. For now, though, there's nothing further we can do. I suggest home for breakfast and a sleep."

7

Aldridge sent his footmen home. "Get some food into you then sleep," he told them. "Tell Richards I've given you the rest of the day off."

"I will do myself the honour of escorting you to Winderfield House, my lady," he told Lady Charlotte.

She put her chin up, her nostrils flaring as she took in a deep breath to wither him.

"It is my duty, as I'm sure my mother would insist."

"I need no other escort than Yahzak and his men," Lady Charlotte said, looking to her fierce guard captain for his support.

"Nonetheless…" Aldridge said, not wanting to explain—barely wanting to acknowledge to himself—his burning need see her safe inside her own home before he surrendered to the fatigue that was his reaction to the night they'd spent.

Especially the moment when he had stood by the mouth of that alley expecting Wharton's hirelings, only to see Charlotte emerge, putting herself right in the path of danger when he had thought her safely out of the way observing from the rooftops.

Yahzak backed his horse a step, his face impassive, saying nothing. Her statement was undoubtedly true from the point of view of her physical safety, but the Easterner was implicitly refusing to come between his master's niece and her…what? Friend? Champion, perhaps? Fool, probably.

Aldridge's moment of heart-stopping fear had given way to anger when they'd ridden beyond the reach of the slum boss, and he'd been fighting ever since to contain his temper, to speak with her and the others with calm and civility.

Her obstinacy over the prostitutes had nearly defeated his control. Didn't she understand how her own reputation could be tainted by association?

His civilised self knew that Saint Charlotte was nearly as well known for her virtue as for her works of charity, and that wouldn't be changed by housing a pair of refugees from a brothel, especially two witnesses who could help bring down a dangerous criminal.

Actually, the value of the investigation was a good point to make if anyone dared criticise her ladyship in his hearing. Not that it soothed his irritation in the slightest. He was being irrational and he knew it. But he couldn't seem to stop himself.

On the ride back through the steadily brightening streets, she ignored him. Probably as well. He didn't trust himself to speak without disclosing more of his feelings than was consistent with dignity.

She had clearly been stewing, however. In the forecourt of the Winshire mansion, when he dismounted and reached her stirrup ahead of Yahzak, ready to help her down, she allowed the privilege, but stepped out of his reach while his body still hardened from her touch, turned both barrels of her ire on him and let fly.

"You take too much on yourself, Lord Aldridge. I am grateful for your help this past night, but that does not give you the right to dictate my behaviour or comment on my decisions." She didn't sound grateful.

Aldridge managed to keep his reply courteous, even pleasant, despite his pathetic emotional state. "I want only to protect you, my lady."

"Because I am not capable of protecting myself?" she

demanded, with heavy irony. "Because I don't have a family of my own to support me?"

"No!" He clamped his mouth shut on the next words on his tongue. *Because you are mine.* She would kill him. Or castrate him.

She jabbed him in the chest with her forefinger, and kept jabbing to reinforce her points. "You have no right to tell me what I should and should not do. Furthermore, I am astounded that you have the sheer audacity to judge those poor women for their lives, given how you have benefited from their availability. Let alone your own reputation and the way I found you last night."

Aldridge sucked in his breath at that low blow, unable to think—let alone speak—for the pain of it.

She was only getting started. "Women can be ruined for as little as a kiss out of place. Even less! But a man can have a score of women in a night, and still be accepted everywhere. Admired, even!" She stamped her foot and let out a frustrated growl. "It makes me so cross."

Paradoxically, her general anger at Society's rules and the entire male gender helped him back on his mental feet. "I am sorry I offended you, my lady. I did not mean to be judgemental. I was only concerned that you might suffer for your generosity."

She was still glaring, but he noted a slight softening and played to it. "It was not my place to comment," he agreed. He couldn't promise he wouldn't do the same thing again, though.

"That's… Very well, then." She let out a long sigh. "I hate that women are exploited in such a way and then decried for it, even by the very men who enjoy their favours."

Aldridge nodded. He hated it, too. "I don't," he offered, and then had to explain. "Enjoy their favours, that is." He regretted starting down this conversational line, but somehow it seemed important to continue. "I haven't been to a brothel in a decade."

To be fair, he'd given up casually purchased sex only in part because he'd come to realise that most of the women he swived would have preferred almost any other way of life. The other reason was a case of Venus's Curse and the mercury treatment that followed, though he wouldn't wish to explain that to a gentlewoman.

He'd been careful ever since, keeping a mistress sworn to faithfulness for a number of years, and using a French letter even with aristocratic lovers. Still, the indiscriminate habits of his youth continued to cling to his reputation. And yes, Lady Charlotte was correct. Continued to be part of his mystique, which was as outrageous and as unfair as the lady suggested.

Lady Charlotte had been silent, examining him with her eyes narrowed in thought. "Do you mean you didn't… Last night, I mean… Never mind. Forget I asked."

She thought he'd taken time out during the mission into Heaven and Hell to roger one or more of the women? He was both appalled and amused. "We had a task to carry out," he reminded her. "That was the only reason I was there, and the only thing I did."

Some indefinable tension went out of her. How interesting. Was Saint Charlotte jealous of a pair of good-natured wenches from a bordello? Surely not. The mere possibility, though, dispelled the last of his ill temper.

She put a hand on his arm. "Come in for breakfast, Aldridge. It seems the least I can offer you after making use of you all night and then insulting you this morning."

Aldridge swallowed to control his response to her infelicitous choice of words. "Thank you. I'd like that."

Lady Charlotte looked over his shoulder, and he turned to see a man—a gentleman by his coat and his boots—approaching across the forecourt.

"You are early, Lord Bentham," Lady Charlotte greeted him. "My sister is still away."

Ah. The Earl of Lechton's newly rediscovered heir. One of Aldridge's secretaries had said the man was in town, bride-hunting. Was Lady Sarah in his sights?

"I came to see you this morning, my lady," Bentham replied. "Or at least to leave you a message. I expected to be told you were not available to visitors."

"I have been out early," Charlotte agreed, "and I fear that we must go out again soon. Aldridge, have you met Bentham, Lechton's heir?"

Bentham nodded at Aldridge, heir to heir, but spoke to Lady Charlotte. "I have a message from a boy named Tony."

Everyone stilled, and Lady Charlotte started forward. "Tony? You have seen him?"

"I treated him," Bentham replied. "He will recover. He fell and broke a leg. Bruised ribs. A few bangs and cuts. He is safe and in the Ashbury Clinic in Brightwell Lane just off Wintermount Street."

"Ruth's clinic?" Lady Charlotte asked. Lady Ashford, her cousin Ruth, was not only the founder of the clinic, but also worked there when she was in London. She had trained as a doctor in the far-off mountain kingdom her father had ruled in Central Asia.

Bentham added, "He said to tell you he did not run. He was taken from the garden."

Charlotte turned to him. "There, Aldridge. I told you. Thank you, Lord Bentham. Aldridge, can we go now?"

"Is he awake, Bentham?" Aldridge asked, and when the young viscount shook his head, he said, "May I suggest breakfast first, now that we know he is safe, my lady? I am sure your men are hungry, and I know I am. Why don't you invite Bentham to join us? He can tell us how Tony came to be at the clinic."

"I will dispatch a man to stand guard," Yahzak suggested.

"Dismiss your carriage, Bentham," Lady Charlotte commanded. "We'll see that you get home."

Aldridge argued through breakfast, but Lady Charlotte wouldn't budge. In truth, he knew she would be well guarded, and—in any case—he doubted Wharton was fool enough for an all-out war on the Duke of Winshire. Attacking Lady Charlotte would attract the kind of official attention he couldn't survive, and so would an assault on the clinic founded and sponsored by the duke's daughter.

He tried advocating for his right, as a blood relative, to at least meet the boy. But Lady Charlotte said, and Bentham agreed, that Tony wouldn't be fit for visitors today, and probably not tomorrow, either.

In the end, Aldridge gave in with the best grace he could summon, and went home to Haverford House.

He entered through the centre block of the mansion. Haverford House was built in the form of an H, with the cross bar containing most of the public rooms. The right side was given over to family and guest rooms. Aldridge lived on the left side. The rooms south of the cross bar comprised the Heir's Wing, where adult Marquises of Aldridge had lived since the house was built in the late sixteenth century. North of the cross bar, the same wing contained large entertaining spaces, including a massive ballroom and a banqueting hall, plus further guest rooms.

The work of the duchy was administered and managed through a series of rooms centred on the room always called The Duke's Study. Aldridge had maintained a desk there since he first began to take over the work that didn't interest his father, more than a decade ago.

The rooms housed a dozen clerks and three secretaries, and they and the duchy's agents came and went through a private entrance tucked into the corner where the central building met the Heir's Wing.

Aldridge mounted the short flight of steps from the courtyard and used his own key to let himself into the first office. Early as it was, three clerks stood to mark his arrival. He waved them back into their seats and went through to the next room, and then the next, where the secretaries were holding their first meeting of the day, sorting correspondence into social, estate business, investment business, politics, family business and other. Since the categories often overlapped, the meeting helped to keep them all informed about anything that might affect their area of responsibility.

They, too, would have risen, but Aldridge said, "Don't get up. Just tell me if there's anything urgent I need to deal with. I've been up all night, and want a bath and a sleep."

"Two letters: one from your mother, one from Lady Hamner," reported Edmund Markinson, who kept track of Aldridge's social obligations, managed any business issues to do with family, and maintained oversight of the dower properties he had set aside for his two unmarried sisters.

"Also, a message from Haverford Castle," Edmund added. "It can wait until you are refreshed, my lord."

But will need your attention today, went unsaid. In fact, knowing Edmund, the subtext was probably more like, *but don't read it now or you won't sleep.*

Aldridge raised an eyebrow in question, looking at Erasmus Castle, his investment secretary (commonly known as Rook), and then Peregrine Fitzgrenford (Hawk), whose portfolio comprised all of the ducal estates. Both shook their heads.

"I have the final figures on the Four Hills canal, but it can wait until you have time," Rook commented.

"I'd better be awake for that," Aldridge joked, and the three secretaries rewarded him with a dutiful chuckle.

"Nothing here that can't wait," Hawk confirmed. "We have the last of the harvest figures. I'll need time to finish my analysis and make a summary of the land stewards' recommendations."

"Two days?" Aldridge asked. Hawk nodded. "Block out some time with me the day after tomorrow, then. Rook, I'll catch up with you later today. Edmund, I'll take the letters up to bed with me. Gentlemen, thank you."

This time, they stood to return his bow, and Aldridge let himself into The Duke's Study. The duke's desk, a massive object of carved oak, stood in the bay window, its back to the view out over the pleasure gardens that descended from the house to the river.

Aldridge had thought of taking it over; of shifting it at a right angle to the windows so he could enjoy the view while he was working.

He would certainly enjoy the extra space. His own cadet desk, tucked away in a corner near the door, was a quarter of the size. And, as each secretary in turn had pointed out, his father would never return to this room or even to London. Aldridge was duke in all but name, rank, and title.

It was a final step he wasn't willing to take until he had to. He would take his father's desk when he inherited his father's title.

Refusing the first was, he knew, a symptom of his reluctance to assume the second. If the doctors were to be trusted, he'd be the Duke of Haverford within the next twelve months, and probably sooner rather than later.

None of his secretaries or clerks understood. They thought he was lucky. But then, they and the rest of the population of England thought he was the Merry Marquis; envied him his wealth, his position, the hordes of women keen on an illicit relationship, even the maidens panting for a chance to be his duchess.

The reasons people wanted him had nothing to do with him. He could be a donkey on two legs, and they'd still praise him. The woman would still pant to bed him. The men would still court his favour. And if it was bad now, how much worse would it be when he was duke?

He was a title and a position, not a man. Even those who knew him best—even sometimes his own mother--couldn't see past the marquis, the heir. Just a clever automaton, smartly dressed, with a repertoire of motions and words to fool people into thinking he was a real person. On days like today, when he had given the one lady he wanted to attract yet another reason to despise him, when he'd been unable even to protect a boy who apparently bore his blood, he wondered if they were right.

He gave a short laugh. How the rest of the world would mock and marvel to know he was feeling sorry for himself. A bath and then a sleep, and he would be able to face another day.

He collected the letters from his desk, and left by the door into the hall that led to the main house in one direction and the Heir's Wing in the other.

8

___

The Beast was in a rage all the more potent for being suppressed as long as he had to be in front of customers. His men had searched all night, but the boy Tony was nowhere to be found, and no one admitted to seeing him.

The searchers brought back many reports about the intruders, and the two whores that had run off with them. They'd taken off on those odd-shaped horses the Winshires bred. At first, the Beast had assumed Tony was in the carriage they had with them, but several reports insisted that the escaped females were the only occupants.

Beyond a doubt, the boy had gone out the window. The glass was broken and the door was still locked. But if the intruders helped him, why wasn't he with them?

The guard said he'd not heard the breaking window. The guard was an idiot. He let himself be distracted and overwhelmed by Aldridge—a *ton* clothes horse, a pretty boy, an overbred mummy's boy who had never done a lick of work in his life.

Aldridge. Here he was again, sticking his nose where it wasn't wanted.

Wharton had been looking for someone like Tony ever since he lost the lovely Gren. His latest pet was a Grenford get, beyond a doubt, but all the Grenford males were so randy it could have been the father or either of the brothers. Or perhaps just a by-blow from an earlier generation.

Tony either didn't know, or wasn't saying.

No matter. He was unacknowledged, which meant the notoriously soft-hearted Aldridge didn't know about him, which meant the Beast could have him without Aldridge's interference. It was his reward for twenty years of suffering since Gren was taken from him.

The Beast sulked on his throne. He'd refrained from throwing things or screaming at people all night, lest he frighten those whose money was fast replenishing his coffers. Now the edge had gone off his temper, though he was likely to find it again if no one brought him news that allowed him to retrieve his property.

How had Aldridge found out about the boy? He came for Tony; the Beast was certain. He may have left with a couple of harlots, but light-heeled girls were ten a penny, and Aldridge was, in any case, too fastidious for brothels. He didn't come for the girls.

The Winderfield chit, who was harbouring the boy, must have told him. The Beast glared at the stairs to the upper floor, where his sister reigned. This was her fault, too. She had assured him that Aldridge and the Winderfield female were at loggerheads.

He shouldn't have trusted her, not after last year, when Aldridge's mother put all her weight as a duchess behind another Winderfield female. The Beast hated the Winderfields, too. Most of what followed was entirely their fault. They dared to bring their foreign troops to attack him, and instead of objecting to such a clear breach of the law, that fat freak in Brighton deputed his own troops to support them!

That fiasco had ended with Wharton having to once again change his name and start again. He had lost several lieutenants and a reputation he'd taken years to build. For that, the Winderfields would pay.

Being no fool, the Beast had long ago realised the value of holding his assets and investments under more than one identity. He had several that had no connection to activities the law frowned on. He and his sister had been able to hide while he built a new base. It had taken time, and he'd needed to shelve his plans for those who had opposed him.

No longer. The Winderfields had taken Tony out of the slums, away from the Beast. Then, when he retrieved what should be his, they had come into his territory to steal the boy back. The Marquis of Aldridge had dared to invade his home, make off with two of his harlots, and at least provide a distraction so Tony could escape. It was time for revenge.

"Master?" Harry the Scar approached, bowing. Harry the Scar was currently chief of his enforcers, having fought his way to that position over the dead body of his predecessor. "We found someone who knows where the boy went last night." Or, at least, that's what the man's dialect meant.

Scar beckoned, and one of the bullies he commanded dragged a woman out of the shadows. "This here bint works at the sawbones' place off Wintermount Street. The boy got took there."

The Beast felt a clutch of alarm. "Tony is hurt?"

The woman stood mute until the bully shook her. "Broke 'is leg, din't he?" she whined. "Doctors found 'im in the street and brung 'im in."

"So." The Beast stood. Tony would have the best of care, and a broken leg would soon heal. "Fetch him home," he ordered Scar.

"'E's gone," the woman offered. "Some fancy lady come in a carriage. Good as a parade, it were. Foreign men on 'orses, an' all."

The Beast spun around and felled her with a blow, roaring, "No!" The Winderfield bitch had forestalled him. With great difficulty, he reined in his anger. They would pay. They would all pay. "Out!" he roared. "Everyone, out." He needed to think. He needed to come up with a plan to punish them all, but not bring the army down on him.

In moments, the room was empty, his people having scurried for their holes. There would be a way. He would have the boy and his revenge.

Charlotte heard Sarah moving around their private sitting room while the first light of a tardy November dawn was still struggling to filter through the fog. She'd been awake early herself, though her sleep during the day yesterday had been barely enough to take the edge off her fatigue.

Sarah had arrived home yesterday morning just as Charlotte and Bentham were arriving home from the Ashbury Clinic with Tony. Charlotte knew that Bentham was anxious to talk to Sarah, but it was not the right time. Bentham was focussed on his patient and Sarah had just arrived home after an early start and a half-day's journey. But the looks each bent on the other when they thought themselves unobserved suggested that Sarah's husband hunt was over.

Sarah continued to avoid Bentham when he returned later in the day to see Tony, staying hidden upstairs. "I cannot face Lord Bentham today," she told Charlotte. "Please ask him to call at eleven tomorrow morning."

The boy had a broken leg and two cracked ribs. He'd escaped out of the window of the room where he had been imprisoned, and climbed the building to take the rooftop route to safety, clambering up and down slopes and jumping across gaps.

One such gap defeated him. "My foot slipped," he grumbled. "Would've made it easy, else."

It was a simple fracture, Bentham said, and they could expect Tony to make a full recovery. In the meantime, they could treat the pain with cold compresses and low doses of laudanum for a few days.

Aldridge also wanted to call, to talk to Tony. Charlotte had sent him away yesterday, but he would come back today, beyond a doubt. Charlotte's mind fed her images of Aldridge, no matter how much she tried to rip it back to something else. Anything else.

He had been magnificent yesterday. She had gone to him in desperation, with no one else to turn to, and he had dressed immediately and come with her. Her mind replayed the scene she had walked in on, and her mouth dried before she forced her thoughts into a different path.

As Charlotte pretended to sleep on, the maid crept in as silently as possible to stir up the fire so that the room would be warm for Charlotte to wake in.

Sarah was back early. From what Sarah said, the house party had been a disaster. But her son Elias seemed far keener to talk about being invited to call Sarah 'Mama' than in sharing the bullying he'd suffered.

Aldridge said that he hadn't been to a brothel in a decade. He'd had a mistress, though. The whole world knew the Rose of Frampton had been in his keeping for three years, and he had worn a black armband for her when she died.

"Argh!" Charlotte flounced out of bed. Better to make an early start than to go on fighting her errant imagination.

She opened the door to the bedchamber and called out a good morning as she retreated back towards the bed to pick up the robe that lay ready.

"You are up early," Sarah said, appearing in the doorway. "Shall I send for your hot chocolate?"

"A coffee this morning, I think," Charlotte told her.

Sarah retreated to speak to one of the footmen who waited in the hall to run messages. Charlotte followed her into their shared sitting room. "Could you not sleep, dearest?" she asked.

"No more than you, I think, and for similar reasons." Sarah sighed. "Are you sure that you cannot marry Aldridge, Charlotte? One has only to see him watching you to know he cares."

Did Aldridge watch Charlotte when she wasn't aware in the same way that Sarah and Bentham looked at one another? That combination of appreciation and hunger?

No point in pretending that she was not affected by the man. Sarah knew her too well. "I have given him no encouragement," Charlotte pointed out.

Sarah raised an eyebrow. "Which makes it all the more remarkable."

Charlotte shrugged. "Have you forgotten how I found him when I went for his help?" She had told Sarah the whole story the last night. Charlotte blushed at the memory of Aldridge's barely clad body with the two naked women on the bed behind him. How was she going to look Lady Thirby and her friend in the eyes ever again? Mind you, at least *she* had been clothed.

Sarah laughed. "You know as well as I do that the Thirby woman has been chasing him these past two years. He is not made of granite, Charlotte. He has been a rake, after all, and you have, as you just said, given him no encouragement."

"Nor will I," Charlotte insisted, reining in her errant imagination. "You know I can't, Sarah. After the incident, I do not know if I can bear to let a man—even Aldridge—do…that. But even if I could, he will need an heir."

"You could tell him you are probably barren," Sarah replied, naming the problem with brutal precision. "You want him; I know you do."

"The chief role of the duchess is to bear an heir," Charlotte reminded her sister. "Whatever I feel about Aldridge, I cannot burden him with a barren wife."

Sarah shook her head. "Should you not let him decide whether what he would lose is more important than what he would gain?"

A knock on the door heralded the maid with their morning beverages. Charlotte contented herself with a glare at her sister. When the door closed behind the maid, Sarah showed she'd understood the message. "I am sorry, Charlotte. It is just that I wish you happy."

"And am I to wish you happy?" Charlotte asked.

Sarah blushed. "I do not know, sister. Uncle James says that I must listen to Nate's explanation of his disappearance all those years ago, and I know he is right."

Nate was Lord Bentham, whom Sarah had loved and lost when she was a girl, and who had suddenly reappeared in London just last week.

Sarah's voice softened. "I do not dare hope, but I find myself doing so, anyway."

Whereas Charlotte had no hope at all. Only a yearning that could never be fulfilled, and a grief for the life that should have been hers.

Lady Lechton, the Earl of Lechton's young wife and Bentham's stepmother, gave Aldridge an address for her husband's son: serviced rooms in a block of apartments for well-to-do young men. The building's doorman, however, said that Lord Bentham had gone out, and was not expected back until evening.

Aldridge stopped at the top of the building's steps and waved to his groom, who was walking the high-strung pair harnessed to Aldridge's phaeton. Aldridge wanted to know how the injured boy was, but beyond that, he'd hoped to consult Bentham about the report from Haverford Castle. After all, the man had been a doctor in the navy, so must be familiar with the condition that had driven the Duke of Haverford insane.

Three different doctors had three different opinions about treatment, and the steward whom Aldridge had left in charge of Haverford's incarceration was appealing to Aldridge to make the decision.

He needed advice from someone he trusted to keep the consultation secret. His father's deterioration would make fine scandal for the gossipmongers, and his mother and her wards, his half-sisters, had suffered enough over the years from the rumours that swirled around the evil old man.

There must be dozens of doctors who served London's upper classes, and perhaps every one of them was a pillar of moral rectitude. Or perhaps any of them would succumb to the temptation to let their closest confidants bask in the reflected glory of knowing the details of the medical history and condition of the notorious duke.

Bentham knows how to keep a secret. Aldridge had once been part of the wild pack of young rakes with whom Viscount Elfingham, the Winderfield twins' brother, ran. The young viscount had done his best to keep up the acquaintance even after Aldridge lost interest in constant drunkenness and whoring. The young viscount was indiscreet when in his cups, which was most of the time, and had told Aldridge a couple of strange stories not long before he died. One was about a vicar's son who dared to run off with his sister—Elfingham was proud of his contribution to breaking up the mésalliance, as he saw it. The other—Aldridge had always hoped the other was a drunken fantasy.

Aldridge had already known about the young lovers. They had run away the same summer that Aldridge met Charlotte, when she and her sister had been convalescing at the Somerset estate from mumps. Charlotte had sworn her new friend to secrecy then told him about her sister's romance, which was the reason that Charlotte spent so much time alone.

Aldridge remembered her story years later when Lechton inherited, and people speculated about the son who had gone missing. Lechton had been a vicar. He'd held his living in Somerset from the Dukes of Winshire through their Somerset estate.

When Lady Sarah suddenly acquired a ward earlier this year, Aldridge had done the maths. And now Bentham had reappeared, and immediately began courting the lady. *He loves her still.* Aldridge knew the symptoms. But Bentham had not said a word to embarrass Lady Sarah or to force her hand.

Which gave Aldridge another reason to approach Bentham—befriending the man might be a service Aldridge could offer to Charlotte. If she would accept nothing more from him, she had come close in this last twenty-four hours to giving him her friendship, and he yearned to cement his gains.

Perhaps the man had gone to the Ashbury Clinic? Aldridge leapt up into his phaeton, and his groom ran from the horses' heads to clamber up into the perch behind. "Where next, my lord?" the man asked.

"Do you know where the Ashbury Clinic is, Henry?" Aldridge asked.

"Somewhere near the slums, my lord?"

Aldridge guided the pair around a stopped carriage, neatly avoiding a curricle coming the other way. "An actual address?"

"Sorry, my lord."

"No matter." He made the necessary turn, barely slowing. "Someone in the Ashbury household will be able to tell us."

Lady Ashbury was another person who could give him a perspective on the duke's treatment. She had her medical training in the East, and—according to his mother—would have the title 'doctor' if English medicine were not so resolutely convinced that women were not intellectually and emotionally capable of the role.

That said, Aldridge couldn't see himself discussing third-stage syphilis with a lady, which—he supposed—made him as hidebound as the rest of the establishment. Perhaps he could talk things over with Bentham and ask Bentham to talk to Lady Ashbury?

When Aldridge was announced, he found Ashbury sitting cross-legged on the drawing room hearthrug, a little girl leaning on each knee, his single hand busy with charcoal over paper. The earl glanced up and smiled. "I'll just be a moment, Aldridge. Help yourself to a seat."

Aldridge felt one eyebrow rise. He had seen fathers who enjoyed their children's company —his brother David Wakefield, for one. But he'd not before been in a home where children were permitted to make themselves at home in the drawing room, let alone where attention to them took priority over guests, even unexpected ones. Watching the vignette on the hearthrug left him charmed and wistful.

A short time later, Ashbury folded the sketch he had been working on as if it was a fan and handed it to one girl child, and picked up another folded paper from between his knees to give to the other. "There, my sweets. Make your curtsey to Lord Aldridge before you begin, if you please. Aldridge, my daughters, Mirabelle and Genevieve."

Both girls stood to curtsey. "Good morning, Lord Aldridge," they chorused, as their father clambered to his feet.

Aldridge bowed. "Lady Mirabelle, Lady Genevieve. May I enquire what your father has been drawing for you?"

The smaller of the two girls approached, holding out the paper. "Paper dolls, Lord Aldridge. Look. We cut out around the lines and then we can paint and dress the line of dollies."

Ashbury had a talent. The front fold of the fan showed half a fine lady, her hand and skirt remaining uncut on the fold on one side, the rest of which had been cut away, one dainty toe stretched to the bottom of the page, the tip of her half bonnet touching the top. The details of the lady were lightly sketched in, a row of ringlets, one fine eye with lush lashes, half a Cupid's bow in a sweet smile, the neckline of a morning gown and its high waist, a hint of lace at cuff and hem.

Aldridge smiled at the child and handed her back her paper. "Your father makes a fine sketch," he commented.

"Now up to the desk with you, ladies," said Ashbury. "I'll come and admire your work after I've talked to Lord Aldridge. Aldridge, can I offer refreshments? An ale, perhaps?"

Aldridge demurred. "I did not mean to interrupt your day, Ashbury. I was just seeking direction to the clinic your wife supports. I'm hoping to find Bentham there."

Ashbury had crossed to the door to speak to someone in the hall. "Possibly," he said, as he came back into the room. "It is clinic day, and several of the doctors attend, including my wife, as it happens."

Aldridge had heard that the lady still worked as a doctor, though he hadn't been sure whether to believe it. He certainly didn't know of any other peer who would allow his wife to do such a scandalous thing as provide medical services to slum dwellers.

Ashbury went on, "But do join me for an ale, if you have time. Ah!" He turned back to look at the door, as a pair of maids came in with trays. "Thank you, Sally, Maud."

He sent the maids away and again broke protocol by serving his daughters with a slice of seed cake each, and pouring drinks for them from one of the jugs. He then poured the sparkling amber contents of the other jug into two tall tumblers and passed one to Aldridge along with another slice of seed cake.

"Cook's specialty," he commented.

Aldridge took a sip. "Nice brew."

"Our own. We shipped barrels by canal from Leicestershire. I hear you have an interest in several canal companies."

"Haverford does," Aldridge agreed. "They are useful, but if you are looking for investment opportunities, you might want to consider railways."

Ashbury nodded. "The Middleton Railway appears to be working well."

Aldridge sat forward. "I think it has potential for passengers, as well as freight," he commented.

They were deep in a conversation about the problems and possibilities of steam engines and rail, and onto their second tumbler of a very palatable ale, when they were interrupted by the butler, who ushered in a panting dishevelled footman with a note.

"The clinic is on fire, my lord," the man gasped. "My lady wants you to send help."

9

Ashbury sprang up, dropping his tumbler. "Brown, every able-bodied man servant, and prepare as many carriages as we need for transport."

The butler nodded, and hurried out the door, shouting names and instructions. Ashbury was questioning the footman. The fire had started in several different places at once. They were focusing on moving all of the patients. Her ladyship was unharmed.

"Ashbury, my phaeton is outside," Aldridge offered. "Tell me where I am going, and I'll get you there before your own horses can be harnessed.

In moments, Ashbury had farewelled his daughters and left instructions for his men. They took off at a controlled trot, speeding whenever the roads were free enough. Ashbury was in the seat beside Aldridge leaning forward as if that would make their passage faster, and one of Ashbury's servants squeezed into the groom's spot instead of Henry, who was running as fast as he could to the insurance company Aldridge sponsored to fetch equipment and manpower to help fight the fire.

They swung out of Wintermount Street onto Brightwell Lane, and the way was blocked by a crowd of onlookers, who shifted reluctantly out of the way of Aldridge's team. The stink of smoke filled the street, and had the horses twitching nervously.

He drew them to a stop. Ashbury and his man Crick tumbled from the phaeton and raced into the melee ahead of them, where Lady Ashbury could be seen giving directions as pairs of stretcher bearers hurried out of the clinic building and other men hurried in with heavy buckets.

Aldridge looked around. Though most of those in the street were watching the action ahead, one boy was gazing longingly at the team. "Boy!" he called, and when the lad ran closer, he asked, "Think you can manage them?"

The boy's dirty face lit up. "Cor. Aye, m'lord." He ran to the horses' heads, and in moments had the spirited pair sniffing at him as he whispered to them.

Aldridge dismounted and slipped the boy a florin. "A guinea when you're done. If you walk them in Wintermount Street, my groom will come and find you. Name of Henry. You can turn them over to him, but stay with him. Tell him I told you to stick to him like glue and help with the cattle until I come."

He waited no longer, but threw himself into the action. Ashbury had already organised a second bucket crew to a further pump, and was commissioning another, recruiting bystanders with a ruthless and liberal hand.

"They've cleared the ward upstairs," he told Aldridge, "but my lady says they had a clinic full of patients when someone threw a fire pot through the window, and they scattered in all directions. Might still be people inside."

Lady Ashbury was occupied with the hospital evacuees and with casualties of the fire. "I'll organise a search," Aldridge told Ashbury.

He found some volunteers to enter the building, working in pairs to hunt room by room, looking for any person who might have been left behind. The building was by turns deceptively calm—but for the overriding stench of smoke—and a hellish inferno, as the fire creeping along within the walls and under the floor broke out unexpectedly in yet another room.

Nonetheless, they worked methodically through the ground

floor, finding a couple of boys trapped by a beam that had blocked the door in what was probably a consultation room and a mother nursing the head of her injured son under a table in what looked like some kind of waiting room.

The boys scurried out of the building on their own once freed, and the other pair of searchers carried the unconscious boy out on the sheltering table, his mother hovering anxiously.

"We'd better try upstairs," Aldridge said to his helper, but the man backed away, shaking his head. "They took out the patients from the hospital, my lord," he said. "Did that first. No point in risking the floor caving in or the roof coming down."

Aldridge acknowledged the point, and followed the others from the building, stopping on the doorstep to examine the scene outside. Ashbury's crews were focusing on damping down the surroundings so the fire would not spread. A fire engine had arrived and was being dragged into place by men in the distinctive livery of his insurance company.

Bentham had joined Lady Ashbury, and was currently bent over the boy that Aldridge's men had rescued.

Aldridge could see some of Winshire's foreign guard, too, riding the magnificent horses they had brought with them from their faraway home. They delivered a pair of waterskins apiece to a group of footmen in Winshire livery and rode back in the other direction. Lord Andrew Winderfield was in the midst of the footmen, lugging a pair of skins and directing his team to pour the water into the trough of the engine so the pumpmen could fill the cloth hose.

A shout, "Watch out!" was Aldridge's only warning, and enough for him to shift sideways, so that the flaming mess of timber shingles and wooden beams that crashed down from the building's pediment only struck him a glancing blow.

He clawed at whatever it was that entangled his face and head, as hands grabbed his arms and dragged him several steps. Other hands pulled at the blinding obstruction. "Hey!" he protested, as someone slapped at his head.

"Hold still, my lord. Your hair's on fire." The voice was familiar.

The blinding obstruction cleared, and he looked down into the anxious face of his groom, Henry. Two other men were stamping on the remnants of what must have been the cloth banner that hung over the pediment.

Ow. He could feel the burn, now. One side of his head stung with it. "My thanks, Henry," he said. It could have been much worse.

Charlotte's eyes widened as she entered the drawing room. Aldridge's hair had been trimmed so close to his scalp that, fair as he was, it was near invisible.

"Lord Aldridge. I didn't expect you after I heard of your injury. Should you not be resting?"

He smiled and bowed. Even shaved like a convict off a hulk, with one side of his scalp pink and already peeling, he was temptation personified, all elegance and charm.

The fire had not affected the low hum of his voice. "The injury is more to my self-esteem than my physical well-being, Lady Charlotte. My valet has done the best he could to remove the singed bits and even up the sides so I can appear in public, but I present an odd appearance, I know."

"Startling, let us say," Charlotte offered. "I suppose you are anxious to speak with Tony. I shall show you up."

He inclined his head, and followed as she led the way to Tony's bedchamber. "You will find him alert, and the distraction of your visit is just what he needs," she confided. "He has refused the laudanum, but I am sure the leg and rib must be paining him."

The boy was sitting up in bed, supported by pillows, two other pillows elevating his leg. Charlotte had organised a tray table and a variety of activities to keep him occupied. He was currently frowning at a wooden puzzle. It had come apart easily enough, and now needed to be rebuilt in precisely the right order.

He looked up and smiled as they entered. Charlotte carried out the introductions. "Meet Tony Tweedy, Aldridge. Tony, this is Lord

Aldridge, the gentleman I spoke to you about." Charlotte nodded to the footman who had been sitting with the boy. He put the book he had been reading into his pocket and slipped out of the room.

"You knocked out the guard and gave me the chance to escape," the boy said.

"I am glad I could help." Aldridge pulled up a second chair beside the one the footman had occupied. "My lady?"

Charlotte sat so that Aldridge could do so, and Tony shifted awkwardly to face them, wincing as he did so. He narrowed his eyes. "Her ladyship thinks you might be my father." His tone was threaded with resentment.

Aldridge inclined his head. "I have no doubt we are related, Mr Tweedy. You look too much like the men of my family for doubt. Which means you can be assured of my help, whether we are distant cousins or the closest of kin. What did your mother tell you about your father?"

Tony rewarded Aldridge's promise with a cynical glance but answered the question. "He were—*was* a nob. A nobleman's son, she said. Not a sailor died in the wars, like I always thought. He bought her the shop she ran till she got sick. She said I was old enough to know the truth, and sides—*besides*, I mean—I was going to meet him when we got to London." His jaw tightened and his eyes glistened as he forced out the next sentence. "'Cept she died, din't she? And I din't know who the dandiprat was or 'ow to find 'im."

Aldridge nodded calmly. "Then let's talk about what you do know, and work it out." He pursed his lips, then continued. "I have four children of whom I am aware. I keep track of their well-being and I have made provision for each of them and their mothers, but I have never purchased a shop."

Charlotte blinked and turned her face away to hide her blush. Not that Aldridge's bland recital was particularly shocking, when she thought about it. The man had been a notorious rake while she was still in the nursery, and it would be more surprising if he had no offspring at all. And, of course, he was kind, as well as fabulously wealthy.

The only surprising thing was that she had never heard mention of any of them. He must have acted with amazing discretion. To further cover her reactions, she went to the door and ordered refreshments. Aldridge, without taking his attention off the boy, stood when she did, and sat again when she resumed her seat. He and Tony kept talking, Tony thawing slowly as he shared his story.

He had grown up in a village in Kent, where his mother ran a drapery, claiming to be the widow of a navy man. Charlotte gained the picture of a close pair— a mother who doted on her son and a boy who adored his mother. "We were not rich, my lord, but we had enough. And then Mam got sick."

It was consumption, the village doctor said. She needed rest. Tony left school and took over the shop, but his mother continued to decline. That was when she told Tony his true history, and planned a trip to London, "as soon as I feel a little stronger."

But the hoped-for improvement never came. "Galloping consumption," the doctor said. And before she could do more than write a letter to the man she said was Tony's father, the illness caught up with her.

"After the funeral, I had to sell everything to pay the doctor's bill and the rest. Had enough for a coach fare to London, but when I got here, the man at the place Mam sent her letter whipped me away from his door. Anyways. The landlady said the whipping man had only been there six months, and she hadn't owned the house herself ten years back, so she didn't know who had lived in those rooms."

That had been several years ago. Tony had been surviving somehow, doing odd jobs whenever someone would employ him. Honest or not, Charlotte assumed, and certainly wouldn't blame him.

Aldridge asked more questions. Tony's birthdate brought the comment that Aldridge had been in Scotland for a year around the time Tony was conceived. But the marquis reacted to the address where Tony had sought his father. "But surely… Tony, what did your mother tell you about your father?"

"He was right young, she said. But kind and he made her laugh.

She was working for a milliner in a village called Windsor, and the old lady was a besom. They kept company till he had to go home for the summer holidays, and Mam didn't know she'd caught a baby till after he left. Then the besom fired her, so she took the coach up to London and found him, and he bought her the shop."

Windsor? Charlotte knew the Haverfords well enough to leap to an unlikely conclusion. "He was only fifteen!" she objected.

Tony looked from her to Aldridge. "My brother Jonathan was at Eton in Windsor," Aldridge explained. "And yes, he did have a London apartment." His voice dried. "The duke our father thought that young men should have a place to spend time away from their mother."

"My second name is Jonathan," Tony offered. "Anthony Jonathan Tweedy."

Aldridge smiled. "The name is a further clue. Even Tweedy. Tweede means 'second' in Flemish. Gren is Haverford's second son. We'll write to Gren to confirm, but I believe you are my long-lost nephew, young Tony."

Charlotte served them both with tea and cake as Aldridge explained that Jonathan had been overseas for the past seven years, and two years ago had married into one of the principalities between Russia and the German states. "I expect your mother's letter went astray," he said. "He would have written to ask me or our brother David to help you if he'd known you needed us."

It was a long visit; longer than Tony was really well enough for. But he was intrigued as Aldridge shared some stories from Lord Jonathan's childhood and youth, and she kept putting off turning Aldridge out.

In the end, he made the move. "You need to rest, and her ladyship and I have to prepare for a ball. If Lady Charlotte permits, I will return to visit you tomorrow."

10

For once, Aldridge was looking forward to a ball. Lady Charlotte had promised to dance a set with him—the set before supper, at that. She had come to him when she needed help, and this afternoon when he visited Tony Tweedy, the icy defences that had won her the name North Wind were nowhere in evidence. They had talked more easily than in all the years since he first showed an interest in courting her.

Even better, he would be escorting her for the first part of the evening. He'd gone from visiting Tony to consulting Bentham about his father—Bentham had concurred with the dissenting voice among the three doctors. Nothing could be done at this stage apart from making the duke as comfortable as possible.

Lord Andrew had arrived as Aldridge was leaving, on an errand for his father to question those who'd been at the fire and take the information to David Wakefield. When Aldridge had mentioned his need to leave in time for the ball, Lord Andrew had asked him to pass on the message that he would be there in plenty of time to conduct his cousins home.

Since Aldridge would be escorting his mother the duchess, he offered to ask her to chaperone the Winderfield sisters as well as her ward, Jessica. Jessica had returned early from a house party yesterday but would say nothing about her reasons beyond a wish to do some shopping in London before the family retired to the country for Christmas.

Aldridge expected she had been snubbed and gossiped about. When they were babies, Her Grace of Haverford had taken three of her husband's base-born daughters into her own nursery as her wards. His Grace never countermanded her decision, but he retaliated by pretending they did not exist. Jessica and her half-sister Matilda had made their debut three Seasons ago, though rumours about their origins made would-be suitors wary. It would have helped if the Duke of Haverford, their father, acknowledged them.

In the carriage, Jessica diverted his questions by teasing him about his new haircut, and Aldridge let her. Both Mama and Aldridge had warned her not to go to the house party without them present to demand that the other guests treat her with the respect due to a young lady, but she had insisted on going with only an elderly cousin as her chaperone, and Cousin Maude was far too ineffectual to defend Jess from the cuts and insults Society offered those of questionable birth.

He'd not insist on answers; let Jess keep her pride. But he would find out. No one hurt his sister and got away with it.

Perhaps by the time the youngest, Frances, was old enough for a Season, Aldridge would be duke and able to lend her his consequence. Meanwhile, Matilda had made a spectacular and unexpected match at the beginning of this year, and Aldridge had hopes this would encourage those interested in Jessica.

The carriage eventually made its way up to the head of the queue and stopped at the steps up into the house. Aldridge descended and helped his ladies down and saw them into the entrance hall before returning outside to wait for the Ladies Charlotte and Sarah.

The stars were aligned in his favour this evening, he concluded as he conducted the Winderfield sisters to his mother's side. Once they were in the ballroom, Her Grace gravitated towards the older ladies while the younger ladies crossed the room to talk to their own friends, Aldridge trailing in the same direction.

Charlotte noticed and smiled. She was relaxed and friendly tonight, which was a gift Aldridge intended to enjoy. Sarah, though, was on edge about something. Then Bentham entered the room. His eyes sought and found Sarah, whose tension shifted up another notch.

Charlotte took her sister's hand. On the whole, Aldridge was inclined to like Bentham, but if he upset Sarah, that would upset Charlotte, which Aldridge wasn't about to allow. But the man approached and both sisters greeted him politely.

Other gentlemen came to claim the sisters for the first dance. Aldridge took Jessica out on the floor, making it clear to the assembly that she was the precious sister of the almost Duke of Haverford. He handed her over to the Earl of Colyton. Hadn't he been courting Lady Sarah last time Aldridge noticed him?

To keep himself from standing to one side glaring at the earl, a sin for which Jessica would not easily forgive him, Aldridge set off for the wallflower corner to seek partners for the two sets that stretched like a desert between now and the supper dance.

It was one of his stratagems for enjoying an evening. The less favoured maidens did not develop expectations from a single dance, and Aldridge enjoyed making the unseen ladies visible to other gentlemen. If a girl was graceful, and if she managed to converse and look as if she was enjoying herself, she was sure to get other invitations onto the floor.

And if she continued to be clumsy and tongue-tied, no matter how Aldridge exerted his dancing skills and his charm, then it was a mere thirty minutes of his time, soon over.

Tonight, the first wallflower partner was plain and a little plump. However, she danced like a dream and her smile at Aldridge's humorous comments on the other dancers transformed her into passably pretty, though she didn't manage much in the way of conversation.

The second was a bluestocking, his favourite kind of wallflower, since all he had to do was find a topic that fascinated her, and she carried the burden of conversation from that point. Some of them were even eloquent, and Aldridge had whiled away many a set learning about topics as varied as Sapphic poetry, the construction of automatons, and the wildflowers of rural Shropshire.

Sadly, this partner's genuine interest in archaeological digs was not enough to overcome her flat delivery of a crushing volume of measurements and dates that obscured the very real human stories that made such investigations come alive.

Still, she was a graceful dancer, which beguiled the minutes until he was able to deliver her back to her chaperone with thanks for her company.

Then, at last, it was time for the supper dance. Thanks to a heavy dollop of charm to the hostess and a bribe to the musicians, it was a waltz. Possibly a mistake, since holding Charlotte in his arms struck Aldridge speechless for several minutes.

Aldridge gathered himself when he realised that Charlotte was stiff and awkward, holding herself as far apart from him as the dance allowed, her hand trembling in his. It occurred to him then that he had never seen her waltz.

How could he put her at ease? She broke the silence before he found the right words. "Does your burn pain you?"

A teasing smile might lighten the mood. "I am well, my lady, but pleased to know you are concerned for me."

She lifted her eyebrows, fixing him with an admonishing glare. "Do not make light of it, Aldridge. Of course, I am concerned." Her eyes slipped sideways, focusing somewhere over his shoulder. "Our mothers are friends."

"We are friends," he dared to insist. "You came to me for help, remember."

She stiffened still further. For a moment, he thought he had pushed her too far. Then she relaxed a little, sweeping into the next figure of the dance with more ease than she had shown so far. "Yes, I suppose we are." Her smile was a benediction. "Have I thanked you, Aldridge? I do thank you."

He had been prepared to argue his case, and her sudden capitulation took his wits away, but he gathered them in the next turn, saying, "I served my family, Lady Charlotte. Tony is a Haverford responsibility."

She shook her head. "You came immediately, without questions, without knowing what I wanted. I will never forget." The colour rose in her face, hinting that the situation in which she'd found him was part of what she would not forget. Aldridge was very tempted to probe that tender memory, but he'd be a fool to risk their truce.

"I will always come without question," he assured her, only hearing the more salacious meaning after he'd said the words. Fortunately, the lady merely gifted him with another smile.

Charlotte seldom waltzed. She loved dancing, but the waltz required too much touching, too much trust in her partner. She hated being at the mercy of a larger stronger male beast, and if she had known that the supper dance would be a waltz, she would never have agreed to Aldridge's invitation.

But they were on the floor before the music began, and she could not leave without embarrassing Aldridge, so she gritted her teeth and stayed.

At first, he had been silent, and she had been waiting to suppress the usual sense of panic. But it didn't come, and she relaxed enough to start talking. And then still further.

For the first time in her life, she was enjoying the waltz; enjoying being in the arms of a man. This man. Aldridge was a masterful dancer, but they were partners in the dance. He led, but he didn't haul her around. He indicated his intention with the lightest of touches, and she chose to follow.

Would he be like that in bed? The thought shocked her, not so much for its impropriety as for how unusual it was. She never had thoughts like that. She would never have a chance to find out. She was *not* disappointed at that fact. Was she?

Inevitably, the dance drew to an end. From the raised dais where the musicians sat, their host called for the guests' attention, saying that the Lords Tremaway and Lechton had an announcement to make. The Earl of Lechton was Bentham's father. Aldridge and Charlotte were at the far end of the ballroom, with a crowd between them and the three lords on the dais. Even standing on tiptoes, Charlotte couldn't see them, but she had a bad feeling about this.

"Excuse me," she told Aldridge. "I have to find Sarah and Lord Bentham."

"They went into the supper room," Aldridge told her, offering his arm and leading the way along the side of the ballroom, forging a path with polite words and taps on obdurate shoulders. *There they are.* Sarah and Bentham had just emerged from the door leading to the supper room. Sarah stopped, her eyes on the crowd. Bentham dived into it as Lord Lechton continued to ramble on about family heritage and the importance of securing the succession.

Charlotte let go of Aldridge's arm and slipped her own around Sarah's waist. "Do you know what is going on?"

Drew and Uncle James came up on Sarah's other side. Whatever Lechton was up to, Sarah had the support of her family. The four of them moved back away from the crowd, to improve their view of the dais, and Aldridge followed.

Tremaway took over from Lechton, announcing the betrothal of his daughter to Bentham. Charlotte cast Sarah a concerned look as Uncle James murmured in her ear. Charlotte couldn't hear what Sarah replied—the assembled guests were talking and clapping— but she looked irritated rather than angry or mortified.

Then Bentham's voice was raised at storm strength, shouting, "No." In the silence that followed, everyone in the ballroom must have been able to hear him deny any knowledge of the betrothal and refuse to be part of it. "My word is already given elsewhere."

The disputants moved to another room and Lady Framington announced supper.

Since Sarah had no wish to be part of the gossip that would spread from this ballroom like wildfire throughout the ton, the Winshire party decided to go home. Aldridge was hovering, and Charlotte took a moment to speak to him while Drew was ordering the carriage.

"I am sorry. I was looking forward to having supper with you."

He smiled: not the Merry Marquis's charming and practised smirk, or the watchful but gracious spread of the lips with which he wooed his business contacts. Not even the indulgent look he kept for the youngest of the wallflowers and the oldest of the dowagers. No, this was the tender expression he turned only on his sisters, but with something extra. Something she didn't understand.

"Look after your sister, Cherry. You can owe me supper another time. I'll remind you. May I call on Tony tomorrow?"

Charlotte agreed, and allowed him to take her hand, lift it and mime a kiss just above the gloved fingers. She then hurried after her family. She struggled to listen to Sarah's story in the carriage on the way home and later in their private sitting room. Her thoughts were on trying to understand what it meant: that dance, that smile, the old nickname he had given her during their illicit afternoons together when she was turning sixteen.

Illicit but innocent. Aldridge had been drunk. He'd been enjoying the favours of most of the women at Rockford's house party, on the estate next to Applemorn. But for some reason, he'd treated the girl he met at the pond on the border between the two estates with courtesy, respect, and affection.

He had named her for the cherries they were eating, picked from the cherry tree that arched over the folly on Applemorn's side of the pond. And perhaps for other reasons, for his eyes whenever he called her Cherry hinted at other, hidden, meanings.

Then, the following year, came the event that had shaped her life. The rape, and then the loathsome disease that followed and left her barren—or so the doctors said. She had not wanted to marry after that, and especially not to a man who was known at as a libertine. But Aldridge was more than she had imagined, and his touch… his touch disturbed but did not repel her. She cupped the hand he had almost kissed in her other.

Which changed nothing. She was unfit for marriage. She wrenched her mind away from Aldridge and what might have been, and focused her attention on her sister.

As it was, Sarah did not need Charlotte's support. She assured Charlotte that Bentham had explained his disappearance, and that she was determined to give him a chance to woo her again. He came knocking on the door before they had finished discussing the evening, and Sarah went down to talk to him. Afterwards, she floated upstairs. "I have not decided what to do," she assured Charlotte, but Charlotte knew her twin. Sarah was dreaming of a future with the man she had always loved.

If what Bentham said was true, his leaving was none of his doing. He'd been abducted and thrown aboard a naval ship, his enlistment papers signed. The navy had owned him right up until his father claimed back his heir. Bentham—no, Charlotte would have to get used to calling him Nate—Nate wanted to be a husband to Sarah, a father to Elias. Charlotte was thrilled for them all. Really, she was.

Sarah said she was going to be cautious; was going to take the time to get to know Nate again. But the following morning they had all made a trip to the park. Nate brought his little half-sisters. One look at Elias side by side with Nate's eldest sister, and nobody would doubt that they were related. Their courting time was running out. It was a scandal waiting to happen.

11

"**I** don't like this unrest in the slums," Aldridge said to his brother, David Wakefield, as they rode side by side to Winshire house to visit their newly discovered nephew.

"It is bad," Wakefield agreed. "Arson attacks, riots, assaults—all seemingly unrelated, and all against philanthropic organisations."

"Supported by the Haverfords, the Winshires, or both," Aldridge pointed out.

"Which is not necessarily a link," Wakefield cautioned. "The ladies of both families are heavily involved in many different charitable ventures."

Aldridge raised an incredulous brow. "Are you telling me that you don't see Wharton's hand in this?"

Wakefield shrugged. "So far, the incidents appear to trace back to widely disparate sources. Individuals with a grudge, such as the chimney sweep who broke into the orphanage on Fairview Street with ten of his mates, purportedly to find boys to replace those he claims the trustees stole from him, or the brothel keeper with a grudge against the Theodora Foundation's mission to offer alternative occupations to sex workers."

"It's Wharton," Aldridge insisted.

"You could be right. But I can't prove it, Aldridge. It may be a series of coincidences."

Aldridge shook his head. "I don't believe in that level of coincidence."

Wakefield grimaced. "Whether it is a plot or coincidence, those behind the attacks have overstretched. The little people of the slums have been hurt, and my agents can scarcely keep up with all those wishing to slip us bits of information."

They broke off the conversation as they moved into single file to pass a stopped cart that blocked most of the street, and only resumed once they had turned the corner into a wider avenue.

"A dozen people have been taken into custody, all of them linked to at least one of the crimes, none of them to all of them. And none of them are known to be working for Wharton. I have to follow the evidence. I'd hate to miss something by concentrating on him when something else is going on—or someone else is behind all this turmoil. But if there is a link, I'll find it."

"I've suggested that Mama and the girls leave early for Christmas with our sister Matilda, but Her Grace insists they have accepted several invitations for the next week." Aldridge sighed, then shook his head. "At least she has agreed none of them will go anywhere without armed footmen in attendance."

"Your men are well trained," Wakefield agreed, "and if the ladies stay out of the slums, they should remain safe. So far all of the attacks have been in areas no lady should visit."

Aldridge's response was a rude noise, which drew a smile from his brother. Like the Winderfield ladies, the Haverford ladies took a hands-on approach to philanthropy, and several of the institutions they supported were based in areas Aldridge would prefer his ladies to stay away from.

"It could not come at a worse time," he told Wakefield. "I have to leave in the next couple of days if I am to get to Haverford Castle and back in time to escort the duchess to the Hamners'. I need to see the duke's condition for myself and make sure the doctors are very clear about what I expect. If I don't go now, while the weather is reasonable, it could be a month or even two before I am able to make the trip."

"What do the doctors say?" Wakefield asked.

Aldridge snorted again, this sound closer to disgust than laughter. "Three of them, and all of them with a different opinion. One wants to dose him with mercury. One insists on a scalpel to remove the worst of the growths. One counsels leaving him to his well-deserved misery."

He nudged his horse closer to Wakefield and lowered his voice. "His mind is all but gone, David. This time last year, he was reliving times past, when he was still one of the foremost rakes of the *ton* and a power in the realm. Now—or so my people say—he's little more than an animal, and a wounded animal at that. A dangerous, nasty animal driven by constant pain."

"How long?" Wakefield asked.

"How long can he last? None of the three doctors in attendance is prepared to give an opinion. The disease will kill him, but Bentham says he could survive a long time in this condition. Or his heart might give out tomorrow. You'll look in on Tony while I'm gone? He should be safe with the Winderfields, and Lady Charlotte says they will take him to Shropshire with them when they leave for Winds' Gate."

"The broken leg will slow the boy down for a while, and even someone as crazy as Wharton is not going to make a direct assault on Winshire's mansion," Wakefield reminded him.

"True. I take it you'll be telling Winshire what you've told me about the turmoil in the slums?" Aldridge didn't mind Wakefield working for the Duke of Winshire, but it amused him to let his brother know that he knew about it.

Wakefield didn't rise to the bait. "Of course. And I'll keep you both informed as I find out more."

When they arrived at the mansion, the butler agreed they were expected, and showed them straight up to the guest room where Tony was sitting up in bed using one hand to slide parts on a wooden puzzle box. Charlotte sat at the window, her pen busy over a lap desk, which she put aside on their entry.

"Lord Aldridge, Mr Wakefield."

Aldridge bowed. "I hope you do not mind me bringing my brother with me, Lady Charlotte. I wanted Tony to meet his other uncle." His letter might take a month to reach his brother, perhaps longer, given the winter where Jonathan's Grand Duchess ruled in north-eastern Europe. Aldridge had heard enough from Tony, though, to have no doubt that his precocious brother was the boy's progenitor.

Lady Charlotte directed them to the chairs by the bed with a wave. "Not at all. You are welcome, Mr Wakefield." She resumed her perch on the window seat.

"How come he's a lord and you're a mister?" Tony asked, with an edge of belligerence.

Wakefield took a seat as he answered. "I am half-brother to Aldridge and your father, but our father was married to his mother and not to mine. We also have three half-sisters. There are other brothers and sisters who prefer not to be acknowledged by the family."

"Don't know as I want to be acknowledged." Tony drew the unfamiliar word out into a sneer. "Don't sound like it's a family what takes care of its own."

Aldridge's eyebrows twitched but Wakefield showed no reaction. "The duke our father is an evil man," he said calmly, "but Her Grace your grandmother believes that family should look after family, and I daresay will have a word or two to say to Lord Jonathan about failing to give her direction to your mother in case of emergency."

Aldridge leaned forward in the chair he'd chosen. "Her Grace would like to visit you, Tony, if you have no objection, and if that is acceptable to Lady Charlotte." He'd spoken with his mother yesterday, and Wakefield was right. Her Grace had been cross that Gren left Tony's poor mother without a way to reach Gren's family if anything happened to him.

"Aunt Eleanor is always welcome," Lady Charlotte agreed, pulling Aldridge's mind back to the present.

"I don't mind," Tony allowed. He was frowning, though, and he added, "But she's a duchess, right? I'm a slum rat. Why would she want to meet me?"

"Your Uncle David is right," Aldridge told him. "Mama doesn't care about such things. You are Gren's son, and that makes you her grandson. She is very much looking forward to getting to know you."

Tony shook his head in bewilderment, but made no further objection.

Wakefield began telling Tony some stories about Gren in France, which led to explaining about Gren and Wakefield's wife Prue being kidnapped. Wakefield didn't say, and Aldridge wasn't going to, either, that the man behind those abductions was also responsible for Tony's. It wouldn't help Tony to know that Wharton had been obsessed with Gren since his Eton days.

In mentioning his own mad flight into Napoleonic France to retrieve his wife and their brother, Wakefield commented he was an enquiry agent, which set Tony to questioning him eagerly about his work. "I could do that," the boy kept insisting.

Aldridge left them talking and crossed to a chair near Lady Charlotte's window seat. "Will your family object to my mama coming to visit Tony? I would suggest taking him back to my place, but I don't think he should be moved until the bones have started to knit."

"He is welcome here, and well protected if that madman Wharton tries anything. Aunt Eleanor may visit at any time. I'd be glad of it, actually. It is nearly a year since your father dropped out of Society. With him gone, there is no reason for a continued rift between our families."

"True." Trust Charlotte to get right to the heart of the matter. Two and a half years ago the Duke of Haverford had decreed that the Winshires did not exist. His dependents had honoured the command to ignore an entire ducal family and all their connections more in the breach than the observance even while they were under the man's eye. In the nine months since his incarceration, only Her Grace continued to even pretend that she was obeying the duke's strictures. Aldridge wondered if Charlotte was aware that her uncle and his mother had been meeting in secret this whole time.

"The gossipmongers will make a meal of the Duchess of Haverford visiting the Winshires, but this is a good time to get it over with. The *ton* are already beginning to leave London. When we return next year, it will be old news."

"Are you going to Haverford Castle this year?" Charlotte asked. "For Christmas?" She was examining her hands as intently as if she wished to memorise them.

"We are spending Christmas with Matilda and Charles, but I have to go to Haverford Castle first. Just a quick trip, and I'll be back in time to escort Mama and my sisters to Gloucestershire. I'll probably leave tomorrow."

She glanced up and a sound escaped her before she changed her 'Oh' into a polite tip of the head. "Tomorrow," she repeated.

Senses alert, Aldridge fished for whatever it was that bothered her. He kept his voice casual. "Or the next day."

Charlotte nodded, her eyes returning to her hands. "I imagine you will not be going to the Bowkers before travelling the next day."

"If I can redeem the promised supper with you, Cherry, I will be at the Bowkers. I can leave late in the morning or even the day after. I have time." He struggled to keep his voice friendly, light. Don't rush your fences, he reminded himself, and was rewarded when she met his eyes again and smiled.

"I would like that," she said, hastily adding, "as a friend. You have been a good friend to me, Aldridge, even when I have been sharp with you."

A friend, was it? He reassured her that he always had been, and always would be, her friend, keeping to himself the pain of yet another rejection. Pathetic fool that he was, he would take whatever she would allow.

Charlotte would not have come to the ball tonight had it not been for her promise to Aldridge. Now that she was in his arms being swept around the floor, she couldn't settle to enjoying it. That had been the plan, but plans had changed. Everything had changed.

In part, it was her physical reaction. Her chest clenched when she saw him; butterflies took up residence in her digestive system when he smiled at her; her most intimate parts softened and ached when he touched her. How could anyone enjoy that?

Then, too, she had the dull throb in her temples and the aching drag in her lower torso that hinted at a few uncomfortable days with Eve's curse. Her courses had been irregular and painful ever since the infection that followed the incident. Her body seemed to have the knack of letting her down at the worst possible time.

Honesty compelled her to admit, though, that Sarah's situation bothered her most.

"Can I help?" Aldridge asked.

Charlotte looked up at him, startled out of her own morose thoughts. "I beg your pardon?"

"You are unhappy about something," he said. "Can I help? Whatever you need. Even if it is just someone to listen."

Charlotte shook her head. "Just a touch of the headache," she told him. The rest was none of his concern.

Aldridge wouldn't leave it there. "I wondered if something was wrong with Sarah. I have not seen her this evening."

"There is nothing wrong," Charlotte insisted. "In fact, it is very right. Sarah and Uncle James went to spend the evening with Bentham and his family. You may have realised that Bentham is courting Sarah?"

It was too fast. Just two days ago, Sarah was promising to take her time. Then came the outing yesterday. Even Charlotte had to admit Bentham showed to advantage with his half-sisters. They went out together this afternoon, too, just Sarah and Bentham, and came back smelling of April and May ready to plot with Uncle James to announce their marriage.

Even without their marriage lines. Even without the witness Wakefield and his agents were seeking alongside the more urgent work of stopping the attacks on any Winshire or Haverford initiative to help those in the slums.

Something in the shift of Aldridge's eyebrows suggested he knew more than he should. "I suppose you know they are old friends," she guessed.

"That summer, you told me Sarah had a sweetheart," he pointed out. "I guessed the rest."

She remembered, now he mentioned it. Had that been how her brother Elfingham had found out? But she didn't tell even her glamorous new friend when Sarah eloped. Besides, even as she looked at Aldridge in alarm, Charlotte knew he would never have broken his word to keep their secrets.

Again, he demonstrated his uncanny ability to read her mind. "I was not easy in my mind about my promise to you, so I made a point of meeting the boy, and asking about him. He was a good person then, Charlotte. He planned to speak to your father, to seek for Sarah's hand." Aldridge shrugged. "I can't imagine that went well."

Charlotte shuddered. "Not well at all. He ran away with Sarah in part to save her from the husband my father and grandfather had chosen. But that was then, Aldridge. He has changed."

"Not in the essentials, I think. I believe him to be a man of honour, and I saw him with young Tony. I know he has compassion."

"You are right," Charlotte agreed. "And that is why all is happening as it should." Elias would have a father; Sarah a husband. And Charlotte would be alone. She set her jaw and firmed her resolution. She would not be so selfish as to let Sarah know that she was feeling abandoned. Again.

As lonely and as lost when her twin turned away from her now as in that long-ago summer when Aldridge had become her friend. Her only friend, it seemed, at the time, though now the same feeling came pounding back, she was adult enough to know it for maudlin self-pity.

She would dance at the end-of-season ball that Uncle James was already talking about giving to announce that Sarah was, in truth, Bentham's wife, and had been so for seven years. She would wave them off to their new lives together with a smile on her lips.

She changed the subject to the attacks in the slums, and Aldridge obligingly followed her conversational lead. The topic carried them through the rest of the waltz and on into supper, helping Charlotte to keep her headache at bay and distracting her from her mournful reaction to her sister's happiness.

Indeed, if she could just manage to get past the uncomfortable quiver she felt whenever Aldridge was near, they could be company to one another in these interminable social events, which he hated as much as she did.

I can do it. No. I can't. Spending time with Aldridge hurt too much. It made her yearn for the dreams she had put away after the incident.

12

The Beast, her brother Stanley, had run mad. He was calling in favours all through the slums: expending credit that had taken him a decade to build. Revenge, he said, but Elspeth could not see the point.

Certainly, she had not objected to the fire at the Ashford Clinic. She could not deny her satisfaction in doing an ill turn to that cold foreign bitch who had married her brother-in-law, who had stepped into her deceased husband's shoes to become Earl of Ashford. But Stanley hadn't stopped there. He'd stirred up brothel-keepers, kid kens, upright-men, arch-rogues, night-walkers, and dimber-dambers. He'd convinced them all they were under attack, that the charitable ventures of the Haverford and Winshire ladies threatened their livelihoods.

Yes, it was true it hurt to lose a kinchin-cove here, a whore there. But there were always more where those came from. The pain would be a lot greater if the Haverford and Winshire families turned their formidable resources to cleaning out the slums.

Oh, they wouldn't succeed, or not for long. Others would rise where the criminal kings and queens had fallen. As long as people were willing to pay for sex, for power; to scramble over one another for more and better, crime would be there to serve them.

But the current hierarchy was doomed to fall, and she was not going down with them.

Elspeth had been brooding ever since Stanley kidnapped the protégé of a duke's niece. She needed to decide the best time, the most effective way, to change sides. But his latest start made her defection a matter of some urgency. Not only did she need to get out before the wrath fell upon them, but the information she was taking with her could be enough for her to bargain her way out of the hangman's noose.

When Kit, her current lover, returned with the news that Stanley had retired to the wing where he kept his boys, she handed him the bag she had packed and led the way downstairs. At this time of the morning, few of the staff were about, and none high enough in her brother's esteem to risk disturbing him at his play.

She gave the guard on the door to the alley a regal nod of acknowledgement when he opened the door for her. The trips she had made on previous mornings paid off; he did not even ask where she was going.

She let the veil down from her bonnet as Kit hurried ahead of her to find a hire carriage. The sooner they were out of this district the better, not just for their own safety, but for the success of her mission.

Aldridge was in the ducal offices, giving instructions to his secretaries, when Richards came to find him. "A visitor, my lord. A lady. She will not give her name. She says it is a matter of some urgency."

"Tell her that I am about to take a trip, and ask her if she will make an appointment for my return," Aldridge instructed.

"My lord, she says she has information about Stanley Wharton and his intentions."

"Tell Henry to walk the horses," Aldridge instructed a hovering footman. "Where have you put this lady, Richards?"

The most formal of the parlours in the heir's wing had not been much used in more than seven decades, since the tenure of the last ducal heir to have a wife and family before ascending to the title.

Richards, who had a butler's discernment about social rank, had seen fit to leave the visitor there, and to have her supplied with refreshments. It is not often the man is wrong, Aldridge mused, observing the visitor for a moment before she noticed his entry. Indeed, he could not blame Richards. The vicious she-devil had been raised as a lady and had the title and the manners, if not the morals or the ethics.

The boy with her, Aldridge dismissed at a glance. Even when she was still accepted in Society, she had kept such accessories. Pretty youths with little spine and only the ideas she had planted.

"Lady Ashbury," he drawled. "To what do I owe the singular pleasure? Or should I address you as La Reine?"

He had to give the hellcat credit. She turned her head and inclined it in greeting, her countenance unruffled, for all the world as if she were in her own parlour and not a wanted fugitive from justice. "La Reine is no more, Lord Aldridge. After I tell you what I can of my brother's plans, returning to that persona would be… injudicious."

If she intended to startle, she succeeded, but he managed to control his reaction, instead, crossing the room to sit opposite her, and pouring himself a cup of tea from the pot before her.

"You seek to exchange information for your freedom, I assume?"

Again, the gracious inclination of the head. "I do, of course. You may ask me any question you wish, and I will answer. However, there is some urgency in the matter of Lady Charlotte Winderfield, and you may wish to see to her safety and question me later."

A few minutes later, Aldridge was giving instructions to his butler as he hurried to the mews. "She is to remain here, guarded at all times. No visitors. She is in danger, but she is also a danger to others. I'll be back as soon as I can."

He had time for no more as he reached his phaeton, and leapt aboard. "Let them go," he told the groom, and with a flick he had the horses trotting out into the street.

The Winshire mansion was closer to Westminster than Haverford House, and away from the river. At first, Aldridge was able to gallop, but he took a shortcut through Hyde Park. On the other side, he met the clutter of morning traffic, and had to drop his pair to a walk. It seemed to take forever, though the light vehicle was able to weave around larger drays and carriages, and was seldom stopped entirely.

He pulled up in front of the main entrance and called to a groom to hold the horses even as he leapt down to take the steps two at a time and thunder a knock on the door.

"Is Lady Charlotte home?" he demanded of the man who opened the door.

"Lady Charlotte is not receiving, my lord," said the butler.

"Yes, fine. I do not need to see her; just to know if she is at home."

"Charlotte is not well, and is still in her bedchamber, Aldridge," said the Duke of Winshire from the stairs that descended into the entry. Bentham and Lord Andrew followed behind him. "Is there a problem?"

Aldridge felt weak at the release of tension. He was in time. "If a message arrives for her from a sewing workshop in Clerkenwell, tell her not to go. I have been warned that it is a trap."

"Sarah!" Lord Bentham clutched the duke's arm. "Sarah ran the errand for her."

The duke didn't hesitate. "Drew, run upstairs and ask your cousin for the address in Clerkenwell. Aldridge, tell us what you know. Who plans to trap her, and why?"

Aldridge took his first deep breath in half an hour as Bentham descended the stairs ahead of the duke, his face blanched of all colour, his eyes wide with shock and burning with anger. "Quick, man. We have to go after her." He forked his fingers through his hair and grimaced. "She left perhaps forty-five minutes ago, Uncle James. We may already be too late."

His Grace put a hand over the distressed viscount's. "Whoever it is must get through Yahzak and John, and your wife is not helpless, Nate. She has a knife and a pistol, and is trained to use them."

His wife? It was true, then, what Elfingham told me, so long ago. And if that, then probably the other. Aldridge put the thought from his mind to focus on the immediate. "If Lady Charlotte has the address, we will be close behind them," Aldridge promised. "The men sent to take her at the workshop work for a brothel owner who is, according to my informant, being rewarded for the abduction by someone who hopes to marry Lady Charlotte. They will have to transport her from the workshop to somewhere else. We have time to catch up."

The duke must have given a signal, for one of his foreign retainers hurried out from behind the stairs. "Yousef, I want horses ready. Assign four men to guard the house with the footmen. High alert. No one comes in or out until I return. Everyone else will come with me."

"I have my phaeton outside," Aldridge said. "I'll go on ahead, and you can catch up."

"I am coming with you," Bentham stated. And he had a right. If Charlotte had fallen into their hands, as they intended, Aldridge would not leave the rescue to anyone else.

Lord Andrew came clattering back downstairs, buckling on a sword as he came. Behind him, Charlotte appeared at the balustrade wearing a housecoat, her hair in a plait over her shoulder, her face pale and drawn. "Little Potter's Alley, off Mutton Lane, which leads off the northwest corner of Clerkenwell Green," Lord Andrew reported.

"It is the fourth house on the right, the attic floor," Charlotte told them. "The proprietor, Mrs Wilton, lives on the floor below the attic. This is my fault. I should have gone."

"It is their fault, Charlotte," Aldridge assured her. "We will bring her back."

Bentham was already on his way out the door. "Come on, Aldridge."

<hr>

They were too late at the seamstresses' workshop. Sarah had already been taken, though they arrived in time to prevent the murder of her footman and her guard. The workshop's proprietor had betrayed Charlotte for money, handed over Sarah instead without a qualm, and—to save her own skin—was easily convinced to betray the client who purchased the trap and tell them where Sarah had been taken.

Another wild dash across London, this time to Whitechapel, took them to a backstreet brothel in a once fine townhouse. The duke had sent a couple of his men to the magistrate with a request for constables, but he did not plan to wait for them. Bentham was all for storming in the door immediately, but the duke proposed a bit of caution, since they had Sarah as a hostage.

Aldridge suggested that he, Bentham, and Lord Andrew enter as clients to do a reconnaissance. They were still discussing refinements to that plan when he felt something sting his cheek. Looking up, he saw Lady Sarah, waving to them from the roof.

Bentham was beside himself with joy. "She escaped from that window," he insisted, pointing to one with bars on the lower half. Sure enough, she'd left scraps of lace or some such substance from her dress as she climbed the building. Aldridge was glad he hadn't been there to watch the perilous climb!

"Find a way up through the building next door," Winshire told Bentham. "Take your wife home. We'll storm the building once you have her free and once the constables arrive. Meanwhile, Aldridge and Drew will go in and keep them entertained while we wait."

Aldridge nodded. *An even better plan.* "Take my phaeton and pair," he offered. Winshire sent one of his men with Bentham, and the rest split to fade to one side of the building or the other, while Lord Andrew hammered on the door, carolling in drunken tones, "I need a skirt. Open up, my lovelies. My friend and I have lots of lovely money."

<hr>

In the end, taking down the brothel-keeper was an anticlimax; just something that had to be done. The duty magistrate had arrived with the constables, and the Duke of Winshire stepped back to let the man make the arrests, but stayed close at hand to guide the questioning.

At first, the bawd argued that she'd merely been facilitating an elopement, but Winshire put a stop to that by repeating what the woman had said to his niece. "Lord Bentham took his wife back to Winshire House to have her injuries tended," he told the magistrate. "She will be available to talk to you whenever you wish."

After that, the magistrate had no problem with answers to his questions. The whole plot poured out of the bawd, who put all the blame on the gentleman who wanted Lady Charlotte for his wife, on the Beast, who had come up with the plan with Wilton as a tool to execute it, on the Winderfield twins, whose work in the slums interfered—so said the woman—with the private affairs of business people by giving their employees expectations beyond their station.

Aldridge interrupted to ask the identity of the gentleman. Lady Charlotte might still be at risk. The woman claimed not to know. Winshire said nothing, but when Aldridge declared that he was going to walk a couple of streets over to find a hire carriage, Winshire walked out with him.

"The Duke of Richport," he said, as they stood in the brothel's doorway. "How well do you know him?"

Aldridge examined the duke's face, but his expression showed nothing beyond polite interest. "You suspect Richport, Your Grace?"

Winshire twitched his eyebrows upwards. Aldridge found himself answering the question. "We were friends when I was young and wild. Of a sort." Not that Richport had friends. Tools, companions in debauchery, even allies, if it suited his purposes. Aldridge had never been the first, had become sickened by the second, and was not interested in the third.

"He withdrew from polite society a decade ago, and his path and mine diverged at least six years gone. He is capable of ordering such an abduction, if that is your question." And Aldridge would call him on it, and damn the scandal.

As if Winshire heard the thought, he explained, "What I am about to tell you is in confidence, for I do not wish word of this to become public. Sarah is married, and therefore somewhat protected. If it had been Charlotte locked up in a brothel, her reputation would be shredded before we could make it back home."

"You believe it was Richport." Aldridge would kill him. Slowly.

The duke began to stroll down the alley. After a beat, Aldridge caught up to walk at his side. "He made an offer for Charlotte earlier this year," the duke said. "He did not believe her, at first, when she refused him. Once we convinced him she meant it, he was offended, though he did his best to hide it."

The anger burned higher. Arrogant, self-centred, conceited shit sack. "And that makes you think he decided to force her into marriage?"

"Not that alone. One of the men who locked Sarah up told the other man with him that he should leave Sarah alone or 'his grace' would slice out his gizzard. It could be a foreign duke, of course, or one of the royal dukes who thinks he might be able to get his father's approval for marriage to a Winderfield. But if we assume it is an unmarried non-royal duke of this realm…?"

"Richport," Aldridge agreed.

"Richport. Go and see him, Aldridge. Tell him what has happened. Tell him we know what he did, and that I and my sons will make it our personal mission in life to see that he pays for it."

"Why warn him?" Aldridge asked. Just slam him with it. Take him apart piece by piece. He and Winshire between them could easily bribe the authorities to look the other way; even the Prince Regent. In fact, the Prince Regent was in debt to Richport, and would be pleased to see him brought down.

They had reached the end of the alley. The duke stopped and took Aldridge's hands, looked him straight in the eyes. "I want no gossip, no scandal. When he asked for her hand, Richport said something that leads me to believe he has knowledge that would hurt Charlotte badly."

The duke must have seen something in Aldridge's face, for he nodded. "You know it, too. You know what happened to her six years ago, and you know it must never be made public. You want revenge, Aldridge, but you want Charlotte's safety and happiness more. That is why I am trusting you with this. Tell Richport we are giving him one chance to leave England and to do so without further repercussions. If he does not, we'll move to punishment."

The man was right, dammit. They couldn't take Richport down without giving him time to smear Charlotte. Not unless they killed him outright, before he knew they suspected him. Even in his rage, Aldridge knew he couldn't order an assassination or kill the man himself in cold blood.

He nodded, reluctantly. "I do not like it. But you are right, Your Grace. We cannot let this touch Lady Charlotte."

"He will go into exile, Aldridge. It will be enough."

It would have to be. Charlotte came first.

13

———

The cramps bit hard, but Charlotte could not rest. She ensconced herself on a chaise in the window of a parlour that looked out over the street, hugging a hot brick wrapped in a towel and cursing herself for being unable to join the rescue.

She cautioned herself to be patient. They had to go all the way to Clerkenwell and who knew where else after that. But still, time should not be moving so slowly. The minute hand of the clock on the mantel took aeons to creep from one mark to the next.

A carriage stopped at the front steps. From her vantage point, all she could see was a foreshortened view of two top hats and two sets of shoulders in overcoats, one black and one navy. She had told Grosvenor, the butler, that she was not home to guests, and everyone else in the house was off rescuing Sarah, so she waited for these two to be turned away at the door.

However, they disappeared under the portico and did not reappear. After a couple of minutes, a knock on her door heralded Grosvenor. "Forgive me, my lady, but Mr Wakefield is here with a Mr Beauclair. I told them I would enquire whether you would receive them, my lady, since everyone else is out."

Beauclair was Nate's family name. Was this the cousin who had witnessed that long-ago wedding? "Bring them up, Grosvenor, and arrange for refreshments, please."

Arthur Beauclair was a thin man with nothing distinguished about him: medium height, fair hair in a neat cut, light blue eyes, neither particularly handsome nor decidedly plain. Undistinguished, that was, until he smiled. It was no mere polite movement of the lips. His face lit, and his eyes warmed, and he was suddenly quite beautiful.

Charlotte, unsure of how much Mr Beauclair knew, had intended to keep the conversation to polite nothings, but he preempted that intention as he took her hand and held it for a moment in a firm clasp. "Lady Charlotte, I am so pleased to meet you at last. Your sister spoke of you so warmly when I knew her. But are you ill, my lady? There is something wrong, is there not? Or you would be in bed where you belong. Is it my cousin? Your sister, who is also my cousin by marriage?"

Charlotte found herself telling him and Mr Wakefield about the message from the seamstress and Aldridge's discovery of the plot. "They were not much behind her; not much more than half an hour. And they would have been faster through the streets than the town carriage. But if they caught up with her at Wilton's, I would have expected them back by now."

Mr Beauclair bowed his head, shut his eyes, and moved his lips in silent speech. It took Charlotte a moment to realise he was praying. *An unusual sight in a Mayfair parlour.* Charlotte's relationship with God, for all that half the *ton* called her Saint Charlotte, had been distant since the incident, but prayer seemed a good idea, and she shut her own eyes.

Please, bring her home safe.

She opened them as the maids brought in the makings for tea. Mr Beauclair enveloped her in another benign smile. "They have her," he said. "She is on her way home."

Charlotte returned the smile, hoping hers didn't show too much of her disbelief. She had to suppose the man meant well. She busied herself making the tea. She had barely finished when an excited buzz of greetings in the hall alerted her to another arrival, and in moments, Sarah entered on Nate's arm.

Nate leapt forward to greet his cousin, and Sarah watched them, smiling. She was pale. Her clothes were crumpled and marred with dirt. She looked ready to drop. But she was whole and safe! "You look as if you could do with a cup of tea," Charlotte said to her.

"I could murder a cup of tea," Sarah agreed. She came to sit beside Charlotte, and took off her bonnet. Her hair tumbled down and she looked ruefully at her garments. "Oh dear. Perhaps I should go up and make myself tidy."

Charlotte was about to suggest that they both go up, and Charlotte would organise a bath for her, when Nate turned from his cousin and took over. "I need to see to my wife," he said. *Which is quite right, and his place.* Charlotte nodded when Nate asked her to organise accommodation for Mr Beauclair, and managed a smile for Sarah as she let her husband set aside any objections she made and sweep her off upstairs to bed.

Sarah and Nate had each other, now, and Charlotte was really happy for them. *Truly, I am.*

Only Aldridge's rank and his previous association with the Duke of Richport prevented the butler from shutting the duke's door immediately after announcing that the duke was not at home. Faced with the marquis's insistence on knowing Richport's whereabouts, he capitulated to the extent of allowing Aldridge into the grand entrance hall while he went to fetch 'his grace's man of business, who is overseeing the packing'.

Aldridge paced the length of the hall, noting through doorways that ornaments and paintings were being crated and furniture wrapped in covers. The man of business found him peering into what would have been a parlour in a household run along more sedate lines. In his youth, he had attended a few wild parties in which that room had featured. He shook his head. *What fools we were.*

"Lord Aldridge?" The man at his elbow was short, serious, and bespectacled. "Lord Aldridge, his grace left a message for you. Now let me see. What is the tide, my lord? Do you know?"

Aldridge brought to mind his glimpses of the river on the ride from his home. "It is close to full now, I think. What does it matter?"

The man frowned. "I suppose I had better give you both messages, then, my lord, since by the time I have sent to find out whether the tide has turned, the first may be irrelevant."

The packing. The turn of the tide. *Richport is leaving England.* "Hurry, then, man."

The little man intoned, "Message one," and then puffed out his chest and deepened his voice into an excellent imitation of Richport's drawl. "Well done, Aldridge. You were quick. If you hurry to Flinders Wharf, where I moor my yacht, you may be in time to wave me goodbye. I am leaving these shores for a space. One jump ahead of several scandals that would have amused you before you became so sober and so righteous. Come and wave to me for old times' sake, my once-upon-a-time friend."

He blinked earnestly at Aldridge, and added, in normal tones, "Those were his precise words, my lord. Message two." He stiffened again. "You are too late, Aldridge. I have gone. If you are receiving this message, I am alone, sadly. If my plot to capture my lovely intended had been successful, my faithful Watkin would have been told to have you refused the house, and to answer none of your questions when you insisted, as I know you would. I apologise for attempting to take what you wanted, but you have been too slow. She is too delicious a fruit to wither on the vine, no matter what happened to her before she was ripe. She would have made me an excellent duchess, and taming her would have entertained me in exile. I doubt I'll be back. My son's guardians will do a better job of making a duke out of him than I could, and England has become boring now that my old friends are all either dead or sober."

Aldridge nodded his acceptance of the message as the man fell silent. "Thank you. Flinders Wharf, you said?"

But when the hire carriage reached the wharf, those lounging around its vicinity told him that the Black Arabella, the yacht Rich-port said was named for his deceased wife's heart, had left its mooring thirty minutes before.

14

Charlotte threw herself into the campaign to shape the story about Sarah's and Nate's romance. The couple had powerful allies. The twins' mother and aunt came to town to put their weight behind the marriage, as did the Suttons, the duke's heir Jamie and his wife Sophia. The Duchess of Haverford added her voice.

Meanwhile, the men of her family organised with other peers and powerful influencers in the government to quell the troubles in the slums. Aldridge wasn't part of that activity. He left the notorious former Lady Ashbury to be interrogated by his brother, David Wakefield, and departed for Haverford Castle near Margate in Kent, where his father was incarcerated due to the madness that had descended upon him.

Mr Wakefield also spent time with Tony, and brought his wife and children to meet him. His other visitors were the Duchess of Haverford and her wards, who must be Tony's aunts if their brother Lord Jonathan was his father. Mr Wakefield and Aldridge were satisfied of the truth, though it was too early for Lord Jonathan to have received their letter asking whether he'd known Tony's mother.

Her Grace was convinced enough with the identification to

invite Tony to join her and the rest of her family for Christmas, and Mr and Mrs Wakefield also extended an invitation. Charlotte wanted him to come to Winds' Gate, with her. But it would be Tony's decision.

Nate moved into Sarah's bedchamber, *as is only right when they have been apart so long*. When Sarah asked if she would mind, what was Charlotte to say? "Nate will be welcome, dearest. He is your husband, after all, and I must love him for your sake."

"You shall love him for his own once you know him," Sarah promised, and Charlotte was determined to do so. Certainly, Sarah and Elias did, and both were thrilled to be planning their new life. A life as the family they were meant to be.

Charlotte had to be very careful not to venture out of her bedchamber until she was fully dressed. No more breakfasting in their private sitting room in a robe and slippers. It wouldn't have been the same, anyway, with Nate there, as well as Sarah.

For a start, the conversation was three-way, instead of two, and Sarah would often interrupt something Charlotte was saying to explain the context to Nate.

For another thing, the couple usually took only their morning drink (chocolate for Sarah and coffee for Nate) before going up to break their fast in the nursery with Elias, leaving Charlotte to breakfast alone.

And during the remainder of the day, they were uncomfortable for a third party to live with. They could not be in the same room without touching. They had a tendency to retire to the bedchamber at all kinds of odd times during the day, only to emerge an hour or two later looking smug.

Charlotte was happy for her sister. She really was. Her reaction to the couple's absorption with one another was her own problem. She would not hint by word or action that she was feeling abandoned. Nor that their evident delight in the physical aspects of marriage had her yearning to understand, and thinking of Aldridge, his nakedness poorly covered by his untied banyan, far more often than was comfortable.

When Winshire held a ball a week after the kidnapping, and

joined Lord Lechton in toasting Sarah and Nate as Lord and Lady Bentham, the *ton* was ready to embrace the couple and their son. Even the Earl of Sodfield, that most conservative of lords, was heard to say, "Winshire was injudicious, I must say. Abducting a gentleman's son and throwing him into the navy as a common soldier. Sad about the little boy, too. Very injudicious." The more sentimental members of Society declared the former duke a wicked old man, who was probably roasting in Hell.

On the day after the ball, the Winshires and the Lechtons met at Fournier's pastry shop—a last outing before leaving London. Charlotte was standing with Tony just inside the building talking to Sophia and Ruth, when they heard a woman shriek, followed by shouting. Several of those still inside tried to get through the door at the same time. Before Charlotte could take her turn, she heard a loud bang followed immediately by another.

"That sounds like gunshots," Ruth commented, even as another retort was followed by a woman's shriek. She called, "Has someone been shot? Let me through."

Charlotte was one of the last to exit, and was immediately deputed to help look after the children while Nate and Ruth attended to Lord Lechton, who had been shot protecting Elias with his own body. Most of the other men had pursued the sharpshooter, and Jamie and Drew came back to report him caught. It had all been a tragic mistake. The Beast had paid him to shoot Tony. "The gunman didn't know there were two boys," Drew said. "They simply shot at the first to exit."

The earl's death meant a change of plans, of course. The family stayed on to support Nate and Sarah through the coroner's inquest, and then travelled to Lechford for the funeral.

Charlotte would have stayed on for Christmas if she'd thought Sarah needed her, but—on the contrary—she rather thought she was in the way.

Sarah was absorbed in learning her new responsibilities as Countess of Lechton and mistress of Lechford Hall. The dowager countess, Libby, confessed she had never truly taken up the reins, and had allowed herself to be intimidated by the husband-and-wife team who were butler and housekeeper. She and Sarah were well on the way to becoming friends, and she was delighted to be able to hand over supervision of the staff.

Further, Sarah turned to Nate (as she should) when she was excited about something, or worried, or in need of a listener so she could talk through a plan or a problem. The first time it happened, Charlotte had been caught out.

It was early afternoon. They were all in the room that served as both library and study, the sisters and Libby restoring order to the much-neglected books, which had been sorted by no known system, while Nate worked at the desk set up in the bay window.

Sarah had been called away and was gone for some time. When she returned, she began talking as she crossed the room. "I am sorry I was so long. Just a minor crisis, but it had its moments. Darling, do you have a moment? I'd like to show you..."

Charlotte finished sliding in the book she was shelving and turned to answer her sister only to realise that she wasn't the darling addressed. Nate had already risen, and was saying, "Of course, my love," as he crossed the room to his wife.

After that, when Sarah used an endearment instead of a name, Charlotte checked to see who she was looking at. Nine times out of ten, it was Nate.

As a result, Charlotte was packed and ready when, with a week to go until Christmas, the Winshire party took their leave to make the trip from Oxfordshire to Shropshire.

"We will be there before Twelfth Night," Sarah promised, hugging her sister as if she was reluctant to let her go. Nate enfolded her in a hug, too. "I will look after Sarah and Elias, sister," he promised. "You don't need to worry about them."

She kissed his cheek, and thanked him, conscious that he was giving her more credit than she deserved. It was not Sarah she was worried about but herself. She could see the years stretching lonely ahead of her, even as she berated herself for being selfish and melo-dramatic.

She had intended to be single all her adult life. But she had always assumed that her twin would be single alongside her. She settled into the carriage and pasted a smile on her face for the benefit of her maid. Thank goodness Drew and Uncle James had chosen to ride. She was not up to making cheerful conversation.

The Duke of Haverford was gone, leaving behind only a monster, grotesque in body and mind—what could be seen of him between the bands of cloth that wrapped him to the bed on which he lay. "You keep him bound all the time?" Aldridge asked the nurses—or warders might be a better description.

The larger of the two currently on duty sounded apologetic. "Except for washing him twice a day, my lord, and that takes at least four of us. Had to, after he near killed himself banging his head against the walls."

"The binding was at my instruction, my lord," said one of the two doctors Aldridge had retained. "He was violent and uncontrollable. It is in our report, my lord." The other doctor had been dismissed after loftily informing Aldridge that his colleagues and the London doctors Aldridge had consulted did not know what they were talking about.

Aldridge had read the report in London. A litany of injuries to the warders and even one of the doctors. Multiple attempts to break out from the tower rooms to which Haverford was confined, three temporarily successful. And repeated self-inflicted injuries as he fought even his own body.

The words on paper had not prepared Aldridge for the deterioration in the three months since he last visited. He had hated and feared his father for most of his adult life. Despised him, too. But this miserable animal was not that man.

Haverford might have reacted to the pity in Aldridge's eyes, or perhaps some lingering intelligence sensed Aldridge's authority over the others in the room, for he strove mightily to reach the son he did not recognise, struggling to break free from his restraints, his eyes burning with hatred and his mouth spewing barely intelligible imprecations.

"It would be best to leave, my lord," the doctor suggested. "We have made him as comfortable as we can, but he will hurt himself if he keeps fighting the bindings like that."

"I'll sing to him, my lord," the largest warder offered. "Soothes him sometimes, it does." And he began to sing a sentimental ballad in a pleasant tenor.

Aldridge led the doctors from the room. In the outer room, another warder sat watchful, waiting until he was needed. He leapt up and knocked on the door that gave access to the stairs. "It's me, Frank," he called. "His lordship is ready to leave."

The bolts on the outside of the door rattled as they were disengaged. It was kept locked and bolted from the outside, and always attended by someone whose job was not only to allow authorised comings and goings but to act as a last line of defence should Haverford somehow manage to break out again.

Aldridge supposed the monster the duke had become might overwhelm all four of the warders during his wash, but four inches of solid oak fastened with iron must defeat him? Still, Haverford had broken out a number of times.

"Brandy, gentlemen?" he suggested to the doctors. He certainly planned to have one.

He had another later with the estate's steward, Auberon Fitzgrenford, the grandson of an indiscretion of a former duke.

"The doctors will keep His Grace dosed with laudanum, on my instruction," Aldridge told Auberon. "It will make his care easier and reduce his suffering. If it shortens his life, as the doctors warn it might, I take full authority for the choice."

Auberon shrugged. "No argument from me. I would rather not have more injuries amongst the staff. If the old man was a dog, we'd have put him down months ago, either out of mercy or to avoid bites."

"He is not a dog, however," Aldridge said. "We will do what we can to keep him comfortable and under control, Auberon, and that will have to be enough."

He sat over his brandy after Auberon said good night, staring into the fire. The old man would continue to breath for another few months, and give his reluctant heir a brief respite before he had to step up into the spotlight.

Aldridge had been under scrutiny all his life, as the notorious son of a scandalous duke. He'd learned to ignore it, to do what he wished or what was needful regardless of what people said. The increased attention would not make a difference. Still, he felt as if a cage was hovering, ready to drop and imprison him for the remainder of his days.

It was this place. He could vaguely recall Haverford Castle being a wonderful place to be a child, when Jonathan was a baby in the nursery and David Wakefield lived in the west tower. David was Haverford's son by a gentlewoman who had died shortly after Jonathan's birth. Mama had defied her husband and taken him in.

Halcyon days, those. Mama would come up to the nursery every day to spend time with the baby, and would read to Aldridge or play games with him. David treated his two younger half-brothers with amused affection, and let Aldridge follow him around like a puppy.

Then came the hard years. When Aldridge was just turned twelve, David fell afoul of His Grace's temper and was exiled. And the governess came. Looking back as an adult, Aldridge understood her strategy. Seduce the heir and control him, and then wait. Unfortunately for her, Haverford discovered her in Aldridge's bed a couple of years after she started, and put paid to her games by installing her in his own. Aldridge was given a willing maid to play with, someone nearer his own age. At the end of the summer, he was sent off to Eton.

After that, visits to Haverford Castle were usually brief and unpleasant, Haverford having decided that his son was old enough to be moulded into a man after Haverford's own image. These walls had witnessed many beatings, both verbal and physical, every time Aldridge failed to come up to the expectations Haverford never specified.

Enough brooding. He rose to his feet and put down his empty glass. He had a busy day tomorrow, out with Auberon to take Christmas boxes to tenants around the estate. The following day, he'd give the servants their Christmas bestowals, and then he'd be able to leave for Gloucestershire, to join his mother and sisters to celebrate the season. He'd be out of this gloomy old place soon enough.

Though it wasn't the place itself he hated. Perhaps, once Haverford was gone, he'd be able to make new memories. Unbidden came an image of Charlotte with his baby in her arms, smiling at him from the chair on the other side of the hearth.

Bad enough to be haunted by memories, but if things that had never happened were bedevilling him, it was high time to go to bed.

15

In March, Charlotte came up to London to support her sister and brother-in-law. In April, she and Sarah sat in the public gallery of the House of Lords as Nathaniel Miles Thomas Beauclair, Earl of Lechton, resplendent in his parliamentary robes and flanked by two other earls, made his formal presentation of his credentials to the clerk.

The next day, Charlotte and Nate waited in one of the outer rooms of St James Palace while the Dowager Lady Sutton, the twins' mother, presented Sarah Elizabeth Beauclair, Countess of Lechton, to Queen Charlotte and the Prince Regent, at the Queen's Drawing Room—the first in ten months, and therefore very crowded.

Lord and Lady Lechton hosted a ball the following week at the Winshire mansion, the Lechton townhouse being too small. This rounded out the events that marked Nate's and Sarah's full ascension to the honours and duties of their new position.

Aldridge came to Charlotte to solicit a dance. She had not seen him for months; not since he left London for Haverford Castle, but the old uncomfortable feelings rose stronger than ever. And when he bowed over her hand in greeting, a powerful tingle ran from the fingers he touched so lightly to her core.

She managed to hide her reaction, to ask after his family. The duchess had been late arriving in town, since she waited for Matilda to be well enough to travel after the birth of her child. Aldridge had been to Haverford Castle again, and had only just returned to London.

Her own family news mostly circled around Sarah and Nate, who were just taking to the floor as the musicians tuned up for a new set. Aldridge led Charlotte out, and they took their places for a country dance too vigorous for speech, but not so energetic that Sarah and Nate didn't spend it lost in one another's eyes.

"They seem very content," Aldridge commented, as he and Charlotte took their turn to stand out of the line in the set.

"They are," Charlotte assured him. "I have never seen Sarah so joyous. When she found Elias, she said she had all she needed in life, but there was always an edge of sadness—and now it is gone. She and Nate complete one another, I think."

And now Sarah was with child again. Charlotte didn't mean to sigh. She hoped Aldridge wouldn't think her jealous of Sarah's happiness. His comment showed he understood, as he turned his head to watch his half-sister Lady Hamner skip down through the pattern of the dance, her eyes fixed on her husband. "I see Matilda and Charles, so absorbed in one another and their new baby the rest of us might as well not exist. And I am happy for them, of course. It makes me wistful, though, Cherry."

Wistful described her feelings perfectly. Longing not for the husband her sister had found, but for one of her own. She was so pleased with his understanding that she accepted his request for another dance, this one a waltz, and then regretted it when he put his hand on her back, just above the waist, and the uncomfortable sensations that only he inspired possessed her again.

She hunted around for a topic of conversation to cover her confusion. "I see Jessica is dancing with the Earl of Colyford. Didn't I see her in his curricle in the Park yesterday?"

Aldridge pulled a face. "My mother says he is courting her, and he is certainly assiduous in his attentions. He even brought his daughters over to visit us while we were in Gloucestershire—his own place is just the other side of Cheltenham."

"That certainly sounds as if he is serious, Aldridge," Charlotte commented.

"If so, he is taking his time about making his intentions known. He has not spoken to me, or to the duchess." He sighed. "Nor to Jess, either. I asked her."

Charlotte turned her head to watch the other couple as she and Aldridge passed them. "He doesn't seem to be paying his addresses to anyone else. I wonder what he is waiting for."

Aldridge grimaced again. "Who knows? I suppose it will fall to me to ask his intentions, Cherry." Another deep sigh. "And once Jess is settled, Frances will be making her debut, and it is all to do again."

Aldridge is lonely, too. In some ways, he is lonelier than I. Charlotte might no longer live with Sarah and see her every day, but they were still friends. She had also become close to her cousins and had other ladies she could discuss things with, including Aldridge's sister Jessica.

Who did Aldridge have? He was friendly with his half-brother, but there was always a constraint between them—a carefulness from both sides, as if each feared they could destroy the relationship with a false word. His brother Jonathan was much younger, and had made one short visit to England since leaving in 1807.

As for friends who were not related, she remembered hearing that Baron Overton from northern Lancashire and Aldridge had once been inseparable, but he seldom came to London. Aldridge had broken with Richport long before her botched kidnapping. At social activities such as this one, he talked cheerfully to all sorts of people, but relaxed with none.

I am his friend.

Her mind kept turning that over as he walked her back to her sister and those of her cousins who were present. *A friend, yes, but this attraction between us. It gets in the way.*

What would happen if she acted on these physical urges? After all, what would it matter as long as no one knew? She would never marry. And it could not mean much to Aldridge, after all the women he had been with. She was afraid, of course. But how wonderful it would be to overcome that fear, and to know, if only once, what made her sister and cousins appear to melt when their husbands looked at them with heat in their eyes.

It could never be enough. She wanted a husband, a family. She was ruined and barren, so barred from both, but perhaps she could have a lover. No. Not just a lover, for other men still repulsed her. But Aldridge. Perhaps she could have Aldridge.

The thought, once it occurred, would not go away. An affair with Aldridge. Or, if not an affair, at least a single night. Could she manage it without anyone finding out? Did she dare?

The manager of the bank in Alvechurch did his best to talk Wharton out of withdrawing all his funds. Wharton allowed the impertinence. In some of his earlier personas, he would have crushed the man like a bug, but as Stephen Wheeler, a manufacturer of buttons, he was a mild, even placid man.

The Beast would be glad to leave Stephen behind.

His next persona awaited him, and the funds that had been deposited in Wheeler's account were now needed. They had come first from overseas and later from the Duke of Devil's Kitchen followed by the Beast, proprietor of Heaven and Hell. All against the eventuality that he would need a bolt hole. And he had.

It had been boring. Stephen Wheeler was a boring man, which was part of the disguise, but also meant that Stanley Wharton was not able to indulge his tastes as he preferred.

The next persona, Stirling Whailand, who owned property in Whitechapel and was about to take up residence there, would enjoy much more scope for the games that Stanley liked to play.

Particularly the game of revenge. The Winderfields and the Grenfords were back in London, and Stanley's, or, rather, Stirling's, spies were already in place, ready to report.

Wharton had been collecting information about his enemies for years. His treacherous sister—who would be dead by now if the assassin he sent after her had done his job—had kept meticulous notes about the information her harlots collected from their garrulous clients.

He had thought he could bring Sarah Winderfield down with what he knew about her. Who would have expected that her marriage was valid? But what he knew about Charlotte Winderfield was even more explosive. And better still, Aldridge loved the bitch. If Wharton destroyed her, he would strike a blow to the heart of the man he most hated.

The Duchess of Haverford thought Aldridge should come with her. "It is only as far as Oxford, Aldridge, and we need only stay a few days."

"Mama," Aldridge pointed out, "I barely know the people who have asked you to be godmother to their baby daughter."

"The Fisherhams, Aldridge. Marina Fisherham was one of the organisers of the Frost Fair auction early last year. A lovely girl. Of course you would be welcome, dear, invited or not. You are handsome and charming and practically a duke."

So that was what this was about. "A lovely girl with a younger sister, Mama. No matchmaking, remember."

The duchess shook her head, her eyes wide and innocent. "Of course not, dearest boy. But it wouldn't hurt to look the field over, you know. Fisherham also has several sisters, and there is an unwed cousin or two. Such a clever family, too. I know you need intelligence as well as beauty and breeding in your bride."

"No, Mama."

"And a baptism! Such an innocent sort of an event, I always think. Everyone would be so pleased to have you, dear. Your presence always adds lustre to every family occasion."

Aldridge just barely refrained from gritting his teeth. "Thank you, Mama, but the answer is still no. Do you take Jessica?"

The duchess made a *moue*, but did not press the matter further. "No, dear. I am leaving her with Cousin Evangeline as chaperone. Jessica has arranged to have some of her friends to stay. A ladies' night in, she said."

Evangeline Grenford was a spinster from one of the outer branches of the family tree. Old enough to be responsible and young enough to enjoy the evening with Jessica's friends. Aldridge would make a note to keep out of the family wing that night.

Mama was not one to give up. "Aldridge, my dear boy, I would be failing you if I did not point out that your task as duke will be greatly lightened with the right wife. Do think about it, dear."

"I have hopes, Mama," Aldridge confided. "Lady Charlotte and I are becoming friends again."

He thought Mama would be pleased. Charlotte was her goddaughter, the daughter of one of her oldest friends, a close friend of Aldridge's half-sisters. She was well-born, too: granddaughter to a duke and niece to his heir. And she was as passionate about education as Mama was.

Instead, the duchess's face froze, and she veiled her eyes with her lashes before pasting on a smile. "I am glad you are becoming friends, Aldridge. Charlotte is a sweet girl. But she has sworn not to marry, dear."

"I think Sarah's change of circumstances may be changing her mind," Aldridge explained.

Mama frowned. "Yes. I can see that it might. Perhaps I should have a word with her, Aldridge."

"No matchmaking, Mama," he warned.

"Of course, Aldridge. How can you doubt it? In fact, if you wish, I give you my word that I shall do nothing to promote a marriage between you and Charlotte Winderfield." She beamed at him, a guileless look that he recognised of old. His father had always taken it at its face value. Aldridge wondered what she was really up to. Planning to ambush him and Charlotte both with wedding plans, perhaps.

"If you are to reach Oxford today, you had better be on the road, dearest," he said. She would bear watching, but at least he had a few days before she would be back in London to interfere with his courtship.

It was absurdly easy for Charlotte to carve out a night for herself. She was the only family member in residence, which meant no one to ask awkward questions. Mama had left for Leicestershire to attend Ruth in her confinement. The married couples of Charlotte's generation, Sarah and Nate, Jamie and Sophia, had taken townhouses for the Season.

Rosemary was visiting Aunt Georgie and her companion in the country. A legacy from an aunt had made it possible for Charlotte's aunt to defy her father's plans for a dynastic marriage and set up house with another woman. It was an open secret in the family that Georgie and Letty were more than friends, and the pair of them always had a warm welcome for any female of the family.

Some event was on at Eton, so Uncle James and Drew were staying in Windsor overnight to show their support for Barnabas and Thomas, Uncle James's two youngest sons.

Charlotte admitted no one in her confidence. Not her maid, who packed a small overnight bag at her direction. Not the coachman and guard who conveyed her to Haverford House, to visit her friend Jessica.

Jessica had invited several friends to stay the night under the chaperonage of a cousin of Aldridge's, Aunt Eleanor being away. Charlotte didn't plan to stay overnight. She had sworn Jessica to secrecy, saying only that she had another obligation, but would come to her in the late afternoon and would leave before the other guests were expected.

Jessica was pleased to have her. "I need to talk to somebody, Charlotte, and you are so sensible." Jessica might withdraw that opinion if she could see what Charlotte intended to do after their meeting. If she had courage enough.

Perhaps Aldridge wouldn't be alone. She kept remembering him half naked before that enormous bed with Lady Thirby and her friend. A dozen times on the carriage journey from the Winshire mansion to Haverford House, she made up her mind to give the coachman orders to return for her in two hours, which was what she intended to tell Jessica she had done.

And a dozen times, she determined to go ahead with her plan. When they arrived, she allowed her guard to escort her to the door. When it opened, she sent him away with the coach.

She kept her cloak on, her bag concealed underneath them, saying to the butler, "The halls are beautiful, but cold at this time of year. Besides, if I keep my cloak and bonnet with me, I need not disturb the household when I leave."

"It is always a pleasure to serve you, my lady," he assured her, as he conducted her up to the floor where Jessica had her rooms. *Put the rest of the evening out of your mind and focus on your friend*, Charlotte instructed herself.

Refreshments had been set in Jessica's pretty sitting room. Over tea and cake, they kept the conversation light, sharing news about their families and commenting on others that they both knew. Jessica seemed to have as little appetite as Charlotte. Was Charlotte meant to ask what the problem was? She always had trouble deciding the best thing to do in intimate settings, perhaps because she and Sarah understood one another so well that she had never had to learn the rules of private interaction.

Before she could make up her mind to speak, Jessica took the initiative. "Colyton has asked to marry me," she blurted.

"Do you wish to marry Colyton?" Charlotte asked, cautiously.

Jessica's reply was equally cautious. "He is pleasant company. I would be a countess, and I would immediately be a mother. His daughters are very sweet."

Not a declaration of whole-hearted commitment. "What does Aunt Eleanor say?"

"That he is of good family and good character, and that neither of these things matter if I don't like him. But I do like him, Charlotte, as far as I know him. We have been for drives and walks. We have danced. We have sat together, in company, at tea and at dinner. Always chaperoned. Always observed."

She tossed one hand up in the air, as if throwing her frustrations to the corner of the room. "How is anyone to decide whether the man they are considering is who he appears to be? We are never allowed to even speak alone, except in a dance. How is he to know who I really am? I have to behave at all times with the utmost circumspection. If I laugh too loud, or ride too fast, or flirt even a little, I am a wanton, like people suppose my poor mother to have been."

Charlotte nodded, thoughtfully. She had often thought the same about traditional courtship. Still, what did Charlotte know? She would never marry. "Perhaps you would be better discussing this with Matilda. Or Sarah. Someone who has been through a courtship."

Jessica's comment was a deep sigh.

"Perhaps not Sarah," Charlotte amended. "Hers was hardly a traditional courtship."

"The problem is that all the people I know well enough to talk to about this have love matches," Jessica said. "I am not in love with Colyton, nor he with me. Matilda would tell me to wait for love."

"That is not an infallible guide, either," Charlotte observed. "Remember Margaret Warrington? She loved Lord Semple, and we all thought he loved her, too. But a year later, they could barely stand to be in the same room, and how they managed to produce two sons, I have no idea."

Jessica nodded. "Yes, and everyone knows that the third child is Mr Barclay's, and that two of Lady Fletcher's children look remarkably like Semple. But Charlotte, that rather proves my point. They met at a ball, courted through the Season, and married at the end of it. A traditional courtship, with chaperones and in full view of all the world. Perhaps if they had known one another better, they would never have married."

"I don't know what to say," Charlotte said. "I have no advice, Jess. How can I? I have no plans to marry. All I can offer is a pair of ears."

Jessica reached for Charlotte's hands, and gripped them, her hazel eyes so like her brother's, intent on Charlotte's. "That's exactly

what I want, Charlotte. Not advice. Just someone to listen to me."
She paused, frowning, then continued, "Charlotte, this is my sixth
season. I shall be twenty-four this year. If I was going to fall in love,
surely it would have happened by now? I want to marry. I want children. I want to use the skills I have been taught to manage a household and do my duty by my husband's servants and tenants."

Charlotte felt the same yearning, a desperate ache, a void that,
in her case, could never be filled.

Jessica, flushing, had more to say. "I want to know what the
wives giggle about, Charlotte. Is that wanton? I suppose it is.
Perhaps I should tell Colyton. But if it is wanton, and it gives him a
disgust of me, will he talk about it to his friends and ruin my
chances even more than my birth did?"

She huffed a small puff of laughter. "There. That is part of
what I have been fretting about. Colyton wishes to marry me, but he
has never even kissed me. I have never been kissed, Charlotte. I have
always tried so hard not to be my mother; not to let Aunt Eleanor
down. The only person who attempted a kiss and more—it made
me feel ill. I hope that is because he tried to force me—would have
forced me had Charles and Matilda not come to my rescue. But
perhaps it was me. Perhaps I am one of those women who cannot
enjoy… that."

Charlotte had also never participated in a kiss and hoped to
remedy that this very evening. Perhaps it was her own circumstances
that inspired her with an idea for Jessica.

"Why not tell Colyton that, Jess? That you have never been
kissed, and that you are afraid, for you know marriage requires
more than kissing, and you are old enough to have seen that women
who have a distaste for the marriage bed do not have faithful
husbands. Yes, and that you hope, if you and he marry, the pair of
you will be able to enjoy that part of marriage as well as the friendship and support of one another in other aspects of your lives.
Surely he will not think that wanton?"

Jessica thought about that for a moment, her head bowed, then
looked up, smiling. "Good advice. We have not talked at all about
what we think our marriage should be like, and that was foolish of

me. I imagine he expects me to be a mother to his daughters and to give him a son. But he has not said so. And I have not spoken of my expectations either. I could not, of course, before he asked for my hand. But now… Yes, when he comes for my answer tomorrow, I shall tell him that I wish to discuss what he expects from a wife, and what I hope for from a husband, and then I shall give him my answer. Marriage is for life, after all."

Should I tell Jessica what Colyton said to Sarah last year? Colyton had spoken disparagingly of Elias, whom he thought to be Sarah's ward, and base born. He'd gone on to mention Matilda's marriage to the Earl of Hamner as miscegenation, since Matilda was also a by-blow. And now he had asked Matilda's half-sister to marry him. *He has had a change of heart then, as the Earl of Hamner did. She hoped.*

"But look at the time," Jessica said. "Your carriage will be waiting for you, dear friend. I cannot thank you enough for your advice."

"I hope you receive the answers you want, Jess. You deserve to be happy." She picked up the cloak she had discarded by the door, putting her skirts between Jessica and her bag.

"So do you, Charlotte," Jessica assured her. "I hope the path you have chosen makes you happy."

So do I, Charlotte thought, her mind on the night ahead. "Don't come down with me, Jessica. The halls are cold, and it is hardly worth putting on a cloak just to see me to the door, when I know Haverford House nearly as well as my own home."

For what came next, she needed to be alone.

16

After Charlotte passed the footman on duty outside the family wing, she saw no one during her surreptitious traverse of the main building. Several times, she hesitated at a bend in the passage or a landing on the stairs. Each time, she summoned her courage and kept going.

Outside the door to the heir's wing, she hesitated again. It was not too late to change her mind. A Haverford footman would fetch a coach for her, or send a message to retrieve her own. She took a deep breath and opened the door.

On the other side, a footman straightened from a slouch against the wall.

"You are lost, my lady. This wing is private," he said, politely but firmly. "You will have to go back. I shall call someone to escort you."

"Call Richards," Charlotte instructed him, naming Aldridge's butler. "I have an errand here, and Richards will escort me from this point."

The butler's name fetched a nod and instant compliance, but not trust. Aldridge must have tightened his security since her last invasion. "If you would wait here, please, my lady."

Charlotte inclined her head in agreement.

The footman went only as far as a doorway a dozen yards down the passage, opened it, and spoke to someone inside. Another footman shot out of the door and hurried away into the gloom of the barely lit passage.

Charlotte's footman returned, and took up his post again, this time standing to strict attention. "He will be here shortly, my lady."

Richards was a few minutes, though it seemed much longer. She saw his candle approaching from a distance long before she could see his face, and stepped forward to meet him. His eyes widened when Charlotte pushed back the hood of her cloak enough that he recognised her. He bowed, his butler face back in place. "Good evening, my lady. I'll escort her ladyship, Mullins."

Charlotte resettled her hood so her face was in shadow before turning back to the footman. "Thank you, Mullins."

"This way, my lady," Richards said. Charlotte knew the way, but she didn't argue, following Richards and his light down the long passage, and up the central staircase of the wing to the next floor. This late in the evening, few servants were about, though they occasionally passed another in the light cast by their own candle, working over a task or hurrying on an errand. Charlotte kept her hood up, and averted her face whenever they passed someone.

They reached the door to the heir's private apartment, and Richards let her into the sitting room where Charlotte had waited for Aldridge the night Tony was taken.

"I will tell his lordship you are here, my lady," he said, ushering her through and lighting several candles from his own. He took a flint and tinder from the mantel and lit the kindling that had been laid ready. Once the fire was burning, he exited by the door to the passage, leaving her alone in the room.

Charlotte was too restless to sit. It was a nicely appointed room, decorated sedately in shades of green with brown leather upholstery on the sofa and chairs contrasting in texture and colour with the rich velvet drapes and the cream panelling with its gilded accents. Quite a different furnishing style to the garish scarlet and gold boudoir on the other side of the internal door.

What was taking so long? Was he saying farewell to his lady of the night? If he was with someone else… She shuddered. Perhaps she should just go home.

She put her ear to the door to the bedchamber. Nothing. Not a sound. Carefully, quietly, she opened the door just a crack. Still no sound, and no light, either. Perhaps he was out? Jessica had been sure he was in this evening. "He told Aunt Eleanor that, if I was staying home, he would take a night off himself, and spend it with a good book," she had said.

Perhaps he was downstairs in his library. Or even back in the family wing on the other side of the building, in the library there.

She pushed the door wide open and, when nothing broke the silence on the other side, fetched a candle to explore. When she'd been here last time, she'd been unable to take her eyes off of Aldridge. She blushed every time she remembered his state of undress, and the picture he had made popped up in her mind far more often than she would admit even to Sarah. Indeed, the peculiar excitement the memories invoked had a great deal to do with why she was here.

In the most shocking room she had ever seen. It wasn't just the bold colours, all heat and challenge. The ceiling over the biggest bed she had ever seen was mirrored! *Whoever heard of such a thing?* Her face warmed still further at the thought of being watched, of watching while engaged in intimacy. She should be outraged at the mere idea, not intrigued. Not feeling damp and soft below while her nipples hardened and ached.

And then there was the art work on the walls: lascivious images painted or drawn with great skill, most of them showing coupling— or even tripling, if there was such a word. Charlotte held up her candle to see each one, leaning close to study details. The portrait over the bed startled her for a different reason. At first sight, the person portrayed was dressed almost decently in the styles of the last century, except that the blue fabric of her dress was transparent, so her breasts could be seen. Even so, it was demure compared to the other pictures.

What shocked at first sight was the face—Charlotte recognised it instantly as Lady Overton, wife of Aldridge's best friend, Baron

Overton. But a moment later she remembered hearing—it had been shortly after her father died, and they were in mourning, but someone had written to her with the news—that Lady Overton was scandalously like the Rose of Frampton, Aldridge's mistress, who had died tragically after being thrown by a horse.

This, then, must be the Rose, for whom Aldridge had worn a black armband for a year. Some said he had never got over her, and here she was, in portrait form, above the head of Aldridge's bed, into which he brought other women. *I will never understand men.* Charlotte leaned onto the bed to better illuminate the portrait. "She was very beautiful."

"She was." Aldridge's voice made her jump, and she jerked around, then gasped as candle wax splashed onto the bed.

"Oh! I have spilt wax on the covers. I am so sorry."

"I did not intend to startle you," Aldridge said, the words apologetic though the tone was more reserved. He was leaning against the door, his arms folded, elegant as ever in an evening coat and perfectly tied cravat. He wore pantaloons, however, rather than breeches, and his feet were encased in embroidered slippers.

"Will you step through here, Lady Charlotte, and tell me how I may be of service to you?" he said. "Do not worry about the bedspread. I am sure it can be cleaned."

He gestured to the door she had entered by, and she led the way. She did not believe she had ever blushed as much in her life as she had this evening. "I am so embarrassed," she told Aldridge as he closed the door between them and the bedchamber. "I was curious, but I should not have gone where I had not been invited."

That won her his real smile; the one that lit his eyes. "The saying about curiosity and cats comes to mind, Cherry, except that you are safe in my wicked lair." He spread his hands. "Did I not give you an open invitation when I said you could call on me at any time? What may I do for you, Cherry? Is there trouble? Ask me for anything in my power."

She blurted her answer. "You."

17

―――――

Until that single word, Aldridge had been holding onto his reason by the slimmest of threads. Seeing the woman he yearned for propelled him into a state of frustrated lust; even thinking about her had that effect. But when he found her in his playroom, examining his collection of framed erotica with open curiosity, he needed to step back into the passage, and take several deep breaths under cover of sending Richards away.

Which might have been a mistake, since it left the two of them alone. *Be a gentleman*, he instructed himself, sternly. At least he could trust himself not to frighten her, as he would if he touched her in even the most innocent of the ways that poured through his fevered mind. And, since she would not initiate anything, poor darling, they were both safe, and so Aldridge told her.

But then he asked what she wanted of him and her answer set him reeling. *You? What does she mean, 'you'? As a husband? As a donor for one of her charities? As an escort on a damned-fool errand?* He took a deep breath, blinking slowly, as the most riotous part of him put its own interpretation on the single syllable and signalled its approval.

A gentleman, he reminded himself.

"For what, exactly?" he asked, pleased that he sounded calm. *Or do I sound reluctant?* "Anything you wish, of course, Cherry."

She nibbled at her upper lip, frowning. "I am not sure how to say it, Anthony."

"Think about it while I pour you a brandy," he suggested. He suspected he might need one.

She took the drink he handed her and cradled it in both hands to warm it, as he had shown her late one evening at a house party, when neither of them could sleep and they met by accident in the library.

He smiled at the memory. "Whose house party was it that we drank brandy together?" he asked.

"Was it the Forsdykes? I think it might have been."

That was after he had withdrawn his most recent offer for her hand, and before she began avoiding him. Back when he still hoped she would change her mind. When he still thought that living a sober and celibate life might influence her.

"You frightened me," she said, as if the words burst from behind a dam.

He stared at her, gaping in shock until he realised and shut his mouth.

She shook her head. "Not your fault, Anthony. I misspoke. You did nothing. It was all me. I did not realise what was happening, and that is what frightened me."

Perhaps she meant it as a clarification, but it didn't help. "Can you explain?" he asked. If she couldn't, he might go mad in truth trying to find the sense behind her words. She was among the cleverest people he'd ever known. There must be logic in there somewhere.

Her brows knit together as she frowned, studying the brandy in her glass. "I am not accustomed to my body responding to a man. Not like that."

Aldridge put his brandy down, sure he had somehow had too much and now his dreams were talking.

Charlotte sat down and took a deep gulp from her own glass. "I feel frightened when I am alone with a man. I avoid it even with people I trust, and I shrink away from men even in company. Being touched by a man repulses me. It took me a long time to realise that the discomfort I feel with you is the opposite. Attraction. Not repulsion. I do not understand such feelings. I do not know what to do with them."

Irritation and frustration coloured her tone. She gave a huff of displeasure and shook her head.

"And that annoys you?" It was the least confrontational response he could think of, his brain being otherwise occupied with subduing his libido. It was in rapturous revolt, demanding instant action to show Charlotte what those feelings were for.

"It annoyed me," Charlotte confirmed. "And then I realised what I needed to do."

"And that was?" Aldridge asked. *She cannot possibly mean what I think she means.*

She shook her head again. "I have been dreaming about kisses. Not the ones forced on a person, but kisses a woman participates in. I have had the pecks you have given me, and they were pleasant. But I never wanted anything else. The kisses I have glimpsed from time to time seemed horrible for a woman. They looked as if they were being devoured. And then I shared a suite for a few days with Sarah and Nate." She laughed, but her eyes were sad. "It seems Sarah likes being devoured."

"Most women do," Aldridge observed, "as long as the person kissing them knows what he is doing and is someone they care for."

She beamed at him, as if he had said something clever. "Exactly! That is what I decided. I already like your touch, you are an expert, and you said you would help me. Will you, Anthony?"

Aldridge took a deep breath to calm his racing heart. "Cherry, can you be very specific about what you want from me?" He should have left it there, but hope had him adding, "Are you saying that you have changed your mind about marriage? Have you come to tell me you will be my wife?"

Hope died when she looked dumbfounded. Panicked, even. "Not marriage. Just…you know."

Disappointment made him abrupt. "Specific, Cherry."

She flapped her hands, a frustrated gesture he found impossibly endearing from the always composed, always logical Saint Charlotte. "I don't know polite words. Do you want the phrases used by the women Sarah rescues? I want you to…" she trailed off again.

His resentment insisted that what she was asking of him—the use of his body without benefit of clergy—demanded the crude language of the brothel. His pity had him providing a term more acceptable to a lady. "Bed you? Is that what you are asking?"

Some of his emotions leaked into his tone, despite his best efforts to make his voice neutral, for she cringed, and said, "If you… If you could. If you find me attractive at all. I know I am quite old."

And now he had to reassure her, the woman of his every dream. Though she had just lacerated him to the soul by refusing his honourable offer and instead demanding a disreputable one. *I am being punished for the excesses of my youth.*

"Cherry, I find you attractive. I have for nigh on eight years, since you were so young that my desire for you shamed me, and I will want you when we are both old and wrinkled, should we be so fortunate. In eight years, that hasn't changed."

Wide eyed, she tipped her head to the side and examined him. She looked for all the world like a nervous sparrow, eying up a morsel of bread and trying to decide whether the treat was worth the risk of approaching. "Will you, then?"

He had to try to talk some sense into her. "How can I dishonour you so? You are a lady! Marry me, Cherry, and I will show you all the delights you can imagine." He hoped his smile was not as strained it felt. "Some you have never thought of, too."

Charlotte's blush deepened to a fiery rose. "You cannot dishonour me, Anthony. I am not a virgin." She lifted her glass to take another nervous gulp and lowered it in confusion when she found it empty. Should he refill it? No. Things were bad enough without making her drunk.

"Whatever has been done to you in the past," he said with care, "you are deserving of every honour."

She shook her head, looking at the hands in her lap, twisting the brandy grass, round and round, and her voice was a thread above a whisper. "It is worse than ruination, Aldridge. Much worse."

"It was not your fault, Cherry. Dammit, you were asleep!"

She looked up, then, a tear trembling in the corner of one eye. "Do you know, then? I used to wonder if he told you, since you were his friend, but then you never treated me as anything less than a lady, so I supposed he had not. It would have shamed him, of course, as well as me."

Aldridge cast what caution was left to the wind. "It was Elfingham, wasn't it? Your brother?" Her nod was tiny, and she avoided his eyes again. Aldridge hastened to add, "He said he took a lady unawares. Someone who was not who he thought it was. Even deep in his cups, he never mentioned the name or where it happened. It was years before I guessed the rest."

She was shrinking in on herself, hunching her shoulders against expected abuse. He blundered on, hoping he'd stumble across the right words. "I knew something had happened after that summer we met. At some point between then and two years later, when you were out in Society, you stopped trusting. You had learned to stiffen when you were touched. Your joy had died."

He knelt at her feet and took the glass from her, putting it to one side. With her hands in his, he continued, "Cherry, I guessed someone had betrayed you, because I've known women who were betrayed." He had come close to it himself, as a heedless boy, seducing those who thought he'd promised more than he intended. To be fair, he'd never taken anyone against their will; never, as Elfingham had described, come upon a girl sleeping in a garden folly and forced himself upon her without even waiting for her to wake, without discovering who she was until it was too late.

"You didn't make your debut the year after we met as planned. You were sick, they said, but then you didn't appear the following year, either. Because you were in mourning, I told myself, but your brother did not die until the middle of the Season."

She gasped a deep shuddering breath at that, and the pain of it flayed his lacerated heart, but he could not make his words unsaid so he kept going. "It took me a while to put all the pieces together."

He kept rejecting his conclusion. He hadn't wanted—still didn't want—to believe it.

"I would not have spoken now, except that you sound as if you blame yourself; as if you think Elfingham's behaviour was your fault. It wasn't, Cherry. It was entirely his."

"Elfingham said I was a wanton to be alone where he could come upon me in the dusk. Father and Grandfather blamed me entirely, for the… the incident. And for Elfingham's death."

Elfingham had always been reckless, but after raping his sister he grew even more careless. The stupid accident that killed him had been just the latest in a series of increasingly dangerous escapades. Suicide by curricle, and a team of good horses with him. The other driver had been grievously injured, as well. The boy had been drunk, of course. He'd never been sober.

"You should have been safe in your own garden, and with your own family," Aldridge told Charlotte.

"That is not what they said," she replied.

Aldridge wished he could dig Elfingham up and resurrect him, in order to kill him, slowly. Charlotte had more courage and grace in her little fingertip than her brother, father, and grandfather combined. Elfingham had ruined her life, and her father and grandfather had made things worse.

"So, you see," Charlotte said, returning to her point, "you need not worry about ruining me." She slipped one hand out of his grasp and laid it against his cheek, her gaze not leaving his. "Indeed, I have a theorem, Anthony. I think you can, at least in part, *unruin* me. You have noticed how nervous I am with men? It is not that I am afraid, or not exactly. I know that I am safe when other people are around, but I have bad memories." She was in lecture mode, now, the teacher in her determined to explain things clearly. "The touch and sound of men, their smell, if I might be so coarse—they bring back those memories. Except you. You are the only man I could bear to give myself to. I know you can be trusted, Anthony, not just in my mind but in my heart. If you will bed me, I hope to make new, pleasant memories."

Her hopeful smile trembled on her lips. How could he refuse

when her eyes were so uncertain, when she braced herself for rejection? What she said seemed logical, but was that true? Or just what he wanted to believe?

He mirrored her action, cupping her face with his hand. "If I agree to this, it is not because you are ruined, or in any way deserving of less honour than any other lady we know."

Her smile broadened. "Do you mean it? I have the whole night, Anthony. My family think I am staying the night with Jessica. We can…" She shifted, so she could look towards the bedchamber that he had set up as an erotic playroom when he first moved into the heir's wing as a very young man.

"Not there!"

The idea of taking her in that bed revolted him. He should have had the room redecorated and turned into a sitting room or a guest chamber years ago, when he first realised that his casual encounters left him feeling empty and dissatisfied.

She tensed at his sharp tone, and he softened his voice. "That isn't where I sleep, Cherry. It is—it was—my place for entertaining women. But you are not just any woman. You are my Cherry, and I would be grateful if you allowed me to make memories with you in my own bed." Where the painting he had commissioned of the Rose of Frampton no longer watched over his sleep. He had moved it to the playroom three years ago, before he last proposed to Lady Charlotte.

"Yes," Charlotte said. "Yes, please, Aldridge."

He was overwhelmed by a surge of emotions. She would join him in his bed. He could hardly believe he had agreed; part of him could hardly wait.

Perhaps resolving the internal struggle had freed his intellect a little, for a new plan surfaced in his mind. "One night will probably not be enough, Cherry. I will do my best to ensure you enjoy it, but you have lived with bad memories for a long time. A week of good memories would be better." A lifetime of good memories, if a week in his bed persuaded her to give him a chance.

She trusted him, she said—enough to ask him for this scandalous service. If it was fear of intimacy that kept her from marriage, perhaps a week with him would change her mind. And if she feared the impact should her scandal become known, he had arguments for that, as well.

"A week?" She sounded intrigued, and not dismissive.

"I have a cottage," he said, inventing the plan as he disclosed it. "We would need to look after ourselves to ensure our privacy, but I can carry water and set fires, and a couple of hampers from Fourniers would mean we would not starve."

"A week," she said again, this time thoughtfully. "I will need a day or two to make the arrangements. But I may still stay tonight, may I not?"

Aldridge was unable to resist leaning forward to lay his lips upon hers, his mouth closed, just a tender promise of things to come. "Tonight, and then—shall we say in three days' time? I will send a carriage to collect you?"

"Friday." She closed the gap between them, returning his kiss with one to his cheek. "Yes, I will come to you for a week."

"Excuse me for a moment, Cherry." He lifted her hand and placed a kiss in the palm then left the room to open the door that blocked his personal suite off from the rest of the house. Sure enough, his butler was himself keeping watch over the door.

"Richards, no one is to come into my suite of rooms until I change this instruction, which will not be before tomorrow morning. Who apart from you knows of the lady's visit?"

"Only Mullins, my lord, who was on duty at the door to the main house. And he does not know the lady's identity. She kept her face covered."

Mullins had been with Aldridge for several years, and had served his mother as a hall boy before that. "Very good. Will he forget her presence entirely if you ask?"

"Yes, my lord," Richards assured him. "You and the lady will not be disturbed, Lord Aldridge."

"Only in the event of a dire emergency, Richards. If the house is on fire, or the like. And in such a case, you are to come yourself. No one else."

"Of course, my lord." Not by word or expression did Richards hint at his thoughts on the topic, though Aldridge guessed that he disapproved. He ought to disapprove. But what was a man to do? His lady was resistant to his proposal, and this might be his only chance to persuade her to his point of view.

"I have asked the lady to be my wife, Richards. She does not like the idea of marriage, but I hope she will change her mind."

Richards allowed a small smile to crack his butler's visage. He bowed. "I hope she will, my lord. My fervent wishes for your success."

Aldridge closed and locked the door. Richards had a key, but could be trusted not to use it except in need. It was unlikely that anyone else would even try, but the Lady Thirbys of the world could be cunning as well as tenacious, and his relatives could be unpredictable.

Now that he had decided to do this, his first consideration must be to protect Lady Charlotte's reputation in every way possible. Locked doors and all.

She was staring into the fire, her hands clasped peacefully in her lap, but she leapt to her feet when he came into the room. She was not as calm as she appeared. He took a candle from the mantel and held out his hand to her.

"We will not be disturbed, Cherry. Will you come with me now?"

"I will set the fire guard," she said, suiting action to word. Then she took his hand.

With the sense he was throwing someone else's loaded dice in a wild gamble, with everything he possessed at stake, he led her from the room.

18

Who would have thought that the Merry Marquess had such a sober bedroom? Certainly not Charlotte, who had assumed the boudoir—the playroom, he called it—was where he slept. His actual bedchamber was even larger, but almost spartan in its appointments.

No. Perhaps not spartan, for everything was of excellent quality and in superb taste. Above wooden wainscoting, the walls were papered in a cream and gold strip. Dark blue drapes covered the window, and the colour was echoed in the striped bedspread that covered the bed, which was large, but not massive.

A pair of easy chairs, in a finer stripe using the same blue, cream and gold, flanked the fire, with a two-seater sofa upholstered in a paisley pattern that introduced greens and purples and other shades of blue along with the room's signature colours. A small table sat by the window, where Aldridge perhaps ate breakfast or supper. No. Not Aldridge. She was about to be intimate with the man. For years, ever since he had invited her to call her by his Christian name, she had resisted calling him Anthony in her mind. But it was time.

She allowed Anthony to lead her to the sofa, and twisted to

continue to examine the room while he lit several candles around the room and went to the large chiffonier, which held a tray with a set of decanters and several glasses.

The room had several bookcases, too, with books in an assortment of sizes and covers, so favourites, perhaps, rather than chosen for decor. And perhaps the objects scattered on various surfaces were also personal choices. A dish of coloured rocks. A row of elephants carved from a dark stone. A lacquered box painted with scenes in the oriental style. Scattered miniatures—Charlotte recognised Anthony's half-sisters and his brother Jonathan.

Large watercolours in carved wooden frames hung on the walls. Haverford Castle, set on its cliffs with the sea behind. The house she was in, seen from the gardens that led down to the river. Barlow Hall in Yorkshire, which she had visited once with her mother. The others—or at least those well enough lit by candles to be visible— also showed mansions or manors in their grounds. Other Haverford Estates?

Anthony poured another two drinks and brought them to set them on the low table, then took his seat beside her. "There are some things I need you to agree to, Cherry. Guidelines, if you will."

Charlotte nodded, cautiously.

"First, we do nothing that you don't like. Stop me if I frighten you or go too fast for you."

She nodded, but reminded him, "I am not a virgin, Anthony."

He kissed her, another quick peck on the lips. "Your only experience was horrific. We need to make sure nothing we do is anything like what happened to you, so you will tell me if you are frightened or if you want to stop for any reason. Any reason at all. Will you promise?"

She nodded again, wishing he would just get on with it. Her body was a maelstrom of sensations; her brain seethed with so many conflicting emotions that she found it hard to focus on his words.

"Second," he said, "and it is connected, you will let me know what you like. What you enjoy; what gives you pleasure. Every woman is different, and you and I will discover together the surest and best ways to bring your body to the sweetest of all destinations, that state of bliss the French call *le petit mort*, and that doctors call a paroxysm."

He was stroking her hands as he spoke, long brushes of his fingers, and the tingling he produced was making it hard to think. "I like what you are doing now," she said, and he smiled.

"I'm glad. I like it, too. Third, I want you to remember that the journey is not just about the destination. As we travel this path together, we will take as long as we need, and we will enjoy everything we do together. It does not matter if you do not, this time, reach your paroxysm; if I do not. We will have a memorable journey." He lifted her tingling hands and placed a lingering kiss in first one palm, then the other.

"May I help you off with your pelisse?"

She nodded again, and then grasped her courage and told him, "If I can help you with your coat."

He pressed his next kiss to one corner of her lips. "We shall disrobe one another, then. You start, my angel."

How to do this? His coat was moulded to his form, fitting his shoulders like a second skin. If he turned his back on her so she could ease the garment off from behind, he would have to stop kissing her, running his lips down one side of her face and then up the other.

She slipped her hands out of his, put her palms on his chest and slid them under the coat and up towards the shoulders. He took a shuddering breath at her touch, and nuzzled her ear, which distracted her from her task and set her trembling.

Focus, Charlotte. She ran her right hand over his shoulder, pushing the coat backwards and down his arm. He dipped and twisted that side, then used his other hand to pull the sleeve over his wrist and down. The other side slipped easily, and she caught the coat, folded it by its shoulders, and leaned away to lay it on the nearest chair.

"My turn, Cherry," he said, catching her around the waist and pulling her to him for another kiss, this one full on the lips, his mouth open, his tongue shaping her lips until she gasped at the shock of pleasure that speared through her, and his tongue darted inside. She sank into the sensation, conscious of nothing but his mouth on hers until she felt him easing her pelisse off one shoulder. She turned her head to look, breaking the kiss, grateful for the firm hand around her waist and for the support of the sofa, for all her bones had turned to jelly. She had not even been aware of him unbuttoning her garment with his free hand.

"Too fast?" he asked. She shook her head, her voice having got lost somewhere during that kiss.

The concern faded from his eyes, to be replaced by heat, as he changed the supporting hand and removed the pelisse from her other arm, tossing it onto the chair after his own coat.

She evaded his mouth so she could find his cravat pin, but she unknotted and unwound the cravat blind, as she allowed him to indulge her in another melting kiss.

He pulled her close again, kissing and nibbling down one side of her throat and then the other as his hands deftly undid the buttons of her gown. He pushed it off her shoulders and followed the neckline with his mouth, down to the lace that trimmed the top of her chemise. His tongue swiped underneath, across the nipples that were tight and aching, first on one side and then on the other.

She moaned, and he murmured, "That's right, beloved. Tell me what you like."

More. She wanted more. She fumbled his waistcoat buttons open and stripped it from him, captured one hand after another to unfasten his cuff links, undid the button that closed his shirt. He pulled his arms from the shirt one by one so she could tug it over his head.

Bare to the waist, he was beautiful—an athlete like those immortalised in stone by the Greeks, but in full colour, alive and warm, his skin firm to the touch. And touch him she did, exploring the wonder of his chest and his back with eager hands.

His breath came short, and his muscles twitched with the effort at self-control, but he held still and let her examine his torso, cataloguing its similarities and differences.

When she dipped her head to taste him as he had tasted her, he lay back against the padded arm of the sofa, sprawling so she had to kneel between his thighs and splay herself across him to continue her experiments. She didn't stop even when she felt her laces loosen, and her petticoat slipping from around her waist. In a moment, all she wore was the knee-length chemise and her stockings. And it was his turn to offer up an item of clothing. His doe-skin pantaloons? Or his stockings? She knew all too well what had been pressing into her stomach as she draped herself across his lower torso. She sat back to undo the buttons of his fall, but shied away at the last minute and removed a stocking instead, then leaned back on the other arm of the sofa and offered him a pointed toe.

He supported her ankle with one hand, running the other up the silk-clad leg to her knee to unfasten her garter, caressing the soft skin of her inner thigh as he did so. Gently, slowly, he rolled the stocking down her leg, featherlight touches on the skin he bared chasing the stocking down and sending shocks of pleasure up her leg and into her core. By the time he removed the stocking entirely, she was rocking from side to side, moaning. And then he put her foot to his mouth to kiss and lick the arch, to suck each toe, before placing it gently on his thigh and taking his hands away.

His eyes smiled and his brows lifted in question. He waited. She narrowed her eyes, but she knew a challenge when she saw one, and she would not be defeated. She picked up his other foot, and repeated his actions as well as she could. Well enough, from what she could tell of his reaction.

By the time her other stocking was gone, he had had his revenge, driving her near demented with his teasing touches. "Shall we move to the bed?" he asked, and she nodded. He could still walk, which aroused her competitive spirit but allowed him to lift her in his arms, which was just as well, as her knees didn't want to hold her up.

He placed her gently on the bed, then stepped back. "May I take your chemise off now? Not if you don't want to, Cherry, but I would love to see all of you."

"You first?" It was his turn to remove something, after all, and he had only one garment left.

He raised those expressive brows again, but obediently unfastened his fall and peeled his pantaloons off one leg and then the other. He posed, winked, and did a slow turn, while Charlotte gaped. He was gorgeous. And much larger than she expected. She knew what happened next, and surely it was going to hurt?

Anthony joined her on the bed. She lay back and looked up at him and was confounded when he moved up to sit against the piled-up pillows at the head, and patted the pillows beside him. "For the next stage, we will do better sitting, and side by side," he said.

His move had brought the spectacular evidence of his desire level with her eyes. She shimmied up onto the pillows next to him where she did not have to look at it. "The next stage?" she asked.

"We use our hands and mouths on one another's naked bodies," he explained. "But if you'd like to keep the chemise, I'll improvise."

Quickly, before she could change her mind, Charlotte pulled the chemise over her head. Anthony caught it and tossed it onto the floor, not taking his eyes off her as he did so. His voice hummed with emotion as he said, "You are even more beautiful than I imagined."

"You imagined me naked?" she asked, trying to sound indignant.

"Darling Cherry, ever since I met you. Even when you were a schoolgirl and I imagined what you would be like once you were a woman."

He was curving his hands around her breasts, stroking and admiring. "Dusky rose," he said, and nodded. "I thought so." He dipped his head towards one breast then sat back up again. "This is a game for two, beloved. Touch me anywhere you wish."

She followed his lead, her hands at first tentative, but growing more confident as she became fascinated in the similarities and differences between them. She froze briefly when his seeking hands found her most private places, but he reminded her that she had only to ask him to stop if he did anything she didn't like.

She didn't dislike it. Soon, she discovered she liked it very much, and not long after that she yearned for something more.

Charlotte was so responsive, so passionate, Aldridge lost himself in the give and take, the sharing of physical intimacy, and forgot the need for extreme care. Fortunately, he was so attuned to her that when she froze as he entered her, he knew it immediately. He stilled.

"Cherry? Does that hurt."

She had her eyes screwed tight shut, but she opened them at his words and looked up at him. "Not hurt, no. It just... In my mind, I know it is you, Anthony, but I am having trouble convincing my body."

"Do you want to stop?" He shifted his pelvis and she grasped his buttocks to hold him in place.

"No. Please. Just give me a moment." But she was still tense, all the fire gone from her.

"I have an idea," Aldridge said. "Let's try this the other way around." He shifted again, and Charlotte clutched even tighter, which was a help since he managed to keep her with him as he rolled.

"If you can manage to sit up while still keeping us attached, I will be able to caress your delectable breasts as we wait for you to become accustomed to the sensations," he suggested. His hips wanted to buck. Fighting his physical response while keeping his voice casual and relaxed was a strain, but he managed it.

She worked out how to perform the manoeuvre, slowly bringing her knees up to either side of his hips. The move was sweet torture, and Aldridge barely breathed until she was sitting above him, her brow furrowed. Her eyes had been distraught, but now they were merely puzzled.

"We can do it this way? Is that allowed?"

He resisted the obvious point that 'allowed' was an odd choice of word when their coupling had not been sanctioned by a church blessing, and instead told her, "It is sometimes known as 'riding St George'."

That sparked the intellect he admired so much. "Why on earth—?"

"Because the dragon is on top," Aldridge told her.

When she laughed, he felt her relax, just an infinitesimal amount, so he cast about for something else to amuse her. "You were saying that you didn't know the words," he commented.

"Bedding, you said."

"Here are some more. The beast with two backs, basket making, blanket hornpipe, bed sport, horizontal waltz, at clicket."

Another snort of laughter, and she relaxed still more. He let his hands roam over her breasts as he added, "If you want to be polite, amorous congress or even convivial society. I am enjoying your convivial society, Cherry."

Her giggle sent quivers through her torso. "Anthony, I've heard that one before! I overheard one lady ask another if she had enjoyed a certain gentleman's convivial society, because if so, she would accept his invitation herself! I had no idea it was such a scandalous conversation."

This was working. If he could keep sane long enough to relax her completely with jokes and anecdotes, while bringing her back to arousal with his hands, he might persuade her safely beyond her memories of terror and give her pleasurable memories in their place.

He told her a story about a pair of stupid boastful fellows who had once bet on the number of ladies they could persuade to join them in convivial society in a week, without once repeating positions. He was cautious about describing the positions, until he was sure that it was having the hoped-for effect. His Charlotte was too honest a woman to deny her physical reaction to the mental pictures he was drawing for her.

"But is that even possible, Anthony?" she asked, a couple of times, and he promised, "We shall have to try it some time, Cherry, so I can show you."

He could feel her let go of her fear and lean into the sensations he was invoking. As for him, he was in a space he had never imagined, for all his experience. He felt what she felt, and her arousal not only became his, but also defined his. He could have kept on all night if that was what she needed in order to reach her peak.

He had loved before, but never had he felt as if he and his beloved had fused into one being. He didn't know where he ended and she began. They were one body with two centres but only one heart, one spiralling arousal, one—ah yes, here it came—one trembling, quaking, gushing, sparkling, glorious, all-encompassing release.

19

Having amorous congress with Anthony was a dreadful mistake. Charlotte realised it when he first took her to bed. She fought the awareness, telling herself she had made a commitment. She should have run.

But even then, it was too late. She had come to the heir's wing of Haverford House to seduce him, and instead, his tenderness had seduced her. The gentleness with which he negotiated her fear. The reverence he showed to her body. The love with which he infused every word, every action.

The magical response he aroused in her when the sensations overwhelmed the last of the old nightmare.

He is a rake. This is how they treat their women. She told herself that, but she didn't believe it.

In the pleasant lethargy that followed their first encounter, Anthony spoke, "Time to fuel up, Cherry, my love. Give me a minute. I asked Richards to arrange us a supper, and it should be at the door." He pulled on a silk robe. "In case the footman delivering the food is still there, and embarrassed," he explained, cheerfully.

Did he feed Lady Thirby and her friend? The waspish thought took her by surprise but brought back all her doubts. She climbed out of bed and found another robe, which she belted tightly around herself before returning to her pillows.

"You called it your playroom, the scarlet bedchamber," she said, when he came back with a tray of cold meats, bread, pickle, cheese, and fruit, which he put on the bed beside her. "Explain, please."

She was sorry immediately. His face had been open, relaxed, happy. It closed, became the watchful company face of the remote Marquis of Aldridge. "Never mind," Charlotte said.

He relaxed again. "You can ask me anything, Cherry. Let me get us a glass of wine each to go with supper, and I'll answer your questions."

When they were both settled back against the pillows with a glass of wine and a plate of food, he returned to the subject. "You asked me to explain the playroom. You know that I was given the heir's wing when I was eighteen? Traditionally, it is for Haverford heirs when they marry. Until then, they have apartments in the family wing.

"His Grace my father never lived in it, because he was only twenty-three and still single when he inherited. The last resident before me was his grandfather, who inherited and moved to the main house when my father was an infant.

"But His Grace decided to break with tradition. He thought I was too much under my mother's influence, and he wanted me to have a place of my own; somewhere I would be able to—" he deepened his voice and imposed a sneer that made him look uncannily like the Duke of Haverford "—fornicate with anyone I chose without frequenting low places."

Aldridge grimaced and returned to his normal voice. "He was a nasty old man, Cherry. But when I was eighteen, I still thought he stood at the right hand of God, even though I also knew him to be a bully and a tyrant. Except for that and his disdain for my little sisters, I wanted to be just like him." He sighed.

"That is natural," Charlotte allowed. "You were very young."

"I figured it was my mission in life to have a good time, and I threw myself into every piece of mischief available to someone who is young, wealthy, and titled. My friends were mostly a little older than me, and even more debauched than I was, but apart from me, only Richport had his own house.

"All of a sudden, I had my own place—empty for more than sixty years and much in need of redecoration. It was great fun. I set up a whole suite of rooms in the heir's wing where my friends and I could have parties, including a bedroom to which I and the woman of my choice could retire when we wanted privacy." He wrinkled his nose. "A personal choice. I have never been fond of having an audience when I was at bed sport."

He took a sip of his wine, watching her over the rim.

"It is very…bright."

"Gaudy, even," he agreed cheerfully. "Not to my liking, these days, but I've never wanted the fuss of redecorating, particularly when I do not sleep there. And none of my visitors had the good taste to object. After all, none of them had to live there, either."

"Except your mistress, I presume." She was mortified by the tart note in that statement. Aldridge ignored it.

"I brought the Rose of Frampton here when I first took her as my mistress, while I found a house for her. And she did have good taste, and insisted that I have no part in decisions about the decoration of that house." His voice was warm with affection. "Other than that, no one has ever lived here in the heir's wing with me. I have had visitors, of course. You know my reputation. But I have not had a mistress since I lost the Rose nearly five years ago, and casual encounters no longer appeal; haven't, indeed, for a long time."

Charlotte made no comment, but perhaps her thoughts echoed through the bedchamber as they did in her head, for he answered the question she hadn't asked.

"Cherry, I did not invite Lady Thirby and her friend here. I have been celibate for three years. I hoped to show you that I am a rake no more."

Charlotte felt something in her ease. Anthony never lied. "But I rejected you again," she reminded him.

He grimaced at the memory. "Lady Thirby kept suggesting a liaison, but it wasn't me she wanted. Just the Merry Marquis. Just the notoriety of being able to say she had been with me. I decided it wasn't worth it."

He picked up a cube of cheese on the end of a fork and offered it to her. "And then—Richards was on his half day—she bribed one of the footmen to smuggle her and her friend into the house, and bring me a message that I was needed in the playroom. Told him a tarradiddle about it being a joke between us. He was new and an idiot."

He sighed. "I was fetched from my bath, and was in the process of telling them they had to leave when you walked in. I have never apologised to you, have I? I deeply regret that you saw that, Cherry."

Charlotte was both comforted and annoyed at his recital. Comforted, because her jealousy of the Thirby woman was misplaced; annoyed because seeing him as more than a rake made it even harder to resist him. "I am the one who should apologise. I barged in without an invitation. Anthony, have you really been celibate for three years?"

He grinned; his social mask gone as if it had never been. "Not anymore," he reminded her, waggling his eyebrows. "As I said, I have lost interest in casual encounters. And for anything more serious, you are the only woman I want. It would horrify His Grace, if he was sane enough to know, but it appears I am predisposed to be faithful, Cherry. You are the only woman for me."

Charlotte took a gulp of wine to hide her reaction. She could not afford to believe him. He would have to marry one day, and he deserved a wife he loved.

"If you've had enough to eat, I'll move the tray, and we can snuggle while we finish our wine," Anthony suggested, and he suited action to words.

When he returned to the bed, he sat where the tray had been, and put an arm around her waist to encourage her to shift closer. She leaned against his side, her head on his shoulder, her hip touching his. "There," he said, "this is comfortable. Have you more questions, my love?"

He grinned. "Or are you ready to try another position?"

In the morning, Anthony showed Charlotte to the door by the duke's offices and from there the footman Mullins, anonymous in his Haverford livery, escorted her along the facade of the house to the main portico. Anthony had said goodbye in his own private suite, where he was free to give her another of those knee-melting kisses. "I should see you safely to your coach, Cherry, but people might take note and wonder whether you were visiting me and not Jessica."

"I can walk one hundred yards across a private courtyard on my own, Anthony," she told him, but he said he would worry if she went out into the open alone. "Take a footman, Cherry, to stay with you until your own guard arrives."

As it happened, her carriage and guard were coming through the gate as she and Mullins reached the front steps. "Thank you, Mullins," she said to the footman. He stopped to watch as her guard handed her up into the carriage, and she lifted a hand in half a wave—not to Mullins, but to those windows of the duke's suite of offices that looked out onto the courtyard.

Perhaps Anthony had forgotten about her already. But no. He would be watching. She had underestimated his feelings for her, but last night he had showed her in a thousand ways that he truly cared. His reverent care of her. The private memories he shared. The heat and love in his eyes when she woke from a deep sleep to find him watching her.

Which had prompted a third round of amorous congress before they fell asleep again. They enjoyed one another's convivial society a fourth time this morning, and Charlotte could feel the effects of the night's pleasure. Not soreness, exactly. A certain tenderness in the places that were still soft and puffy. And an ache deep within that she now knew was her body yearning for his.

Perhaps, after all, she could risk telling him the full truth. Even if he rejected her, she was sure he would be kind, and perhaps he loved her enough to marry her, ruined as she was, even if she could not give him an heir. She was smiling and humming to herself as she walked up the steps of her home, thinking of the immediate future. She had some planning to do and some arrangements to make. If they had nothing else, they would have their seven days.

Yes, and more. For they had compared invitations, and he would be at the Peckworth musicale tonight and the Opera tomorrow night. She would see him soon.

At last! The spies Wharton had set on Saint Charlotte (and there was a misnomer, if ever there was one) had brought him the very piece of information he needed. And his careful work to establish a set of ears and eyes in the Haverford heir's wing confirmed the news.

Charlotte Winderfield, that paragon of virtue, had spent the night with the Marquis of Aldridge, known seducer of everything in skirts. The information would add weight to the stories he intended to have whispered in the ears of every gossipmonger he knew. Charlotte Winderfield was a slut who seduced her own brother (which drove him to his death), and her continued fornication through the ranks of the *ton* were only confirmed by her current affair with the most notorious rake in the whole of England.

Wharton, or rather Stirling Whailand, was off to Tattersalls and then to Manton's to set the rumours flying.

Seeing Anthony in company proved to be more difficult thanCharlotte expected. To keep their secret, she had to behave as if nothing had changed since yesterday. She wanted to smile at him, spend the whole evening at his side, touch him, bask in the warmth of his eyes.

He seemed unaffected, nodding to her gravely from the other side of the room when she looked his way, then continuing his conversation with his mother and Jessica as if Charlotte was merely an acquaintance of no particular importance.

She sat with Sarah and Nate, and Anthony took a place a couple of rows behind her. Charlotte exercised all the willpower she had at her command and managed not to turn around, but to give at least the appearance of listening to the music. Her mind kept slipping to the events of the previous night and to wondering whether Anthony was thinking about them too.

When the musicians stopped for a rest and their hostess announced that supper was served in the next room, he made his move, bringing his ladies over to greet her party, then offering Charlotte his arm and holding her back to allow the others to lead the way.

He bent his head close to her ear and whispered, "There's a door two down from the room set aside for women to retire. Meet me inside that room? In ten minutes?"

She turned her head to meet his eyes, meaning to refuse. What came off her tongue was a breathy, "Yes."

He smiled, more with his eyes than his mouth, then left her at the door of the room, taking a couple of steps forward to say to the duchess, "I trust you will excuse me, Mama. I have seen someone I wish to speak with." He was gone before Aunt Eleanor could reply.

Was it always this easy to keep an assignation? When she excused herself a few minutes later, no one in her party made any comment. Perhaps it was her reputation. No one would think anything of Saint Charlotte heading down the passage that led to the ladies' retiring room.

Everyone else must be focused on their supper, because she had the passage to herself. She counted doors, opened the right one, and slipped into a room dimly lit with a single candle. She sensed Anthony's presence a bare second before she found herself seized and ruthlessly kissed.

Her hesitation was only momentary, any alarm immediately allayed by the dear familiar smell and taste of him. Her passion rose to meet his, and she lost track of space and time as she poured out all the frustration she'd felt at denying their changed relationship in public.

"Devil take it," Anthony said, after some time, pulling back from her lips and looking down at her. "I didn't mean to be such a beast, Cherry. Forgive me?"

"For a kiss I thoroughly enjoyed?" She lifted her eyebrows in challenge, and he grinned and kissed them.

"I intended only to tell you that I missed you. Being in the same room and unable to acknowledge what is between us—I found it hard. I wanted a few moments when I could be honest."

Charlotte chuckled. "That kiss felt honest to me."

He rested his cheek on her hair. "Honest enough that neither of us dare leave this room until we are fit to be seen, dear heart."

He was right, as she saw after more kisses, when she took the candle to the mirror over the fireplace to check that her hair was tidy. It was, but her face was flushed and her lips swollen and red.

Anthony likewise showed the effects, and not just on his lips, as his skin-tight evening breeches left him no place to hide. Charlotte asked, "Can I help you with that?"

Anthony swallowed hard. "Better not. There is no lock on the door, Cherry. I'll step outside into the cold after you are safely back with your family."

She could do with a bit of cold herself. And if her attraction to Anthony was this much out of control after a single night, how would she ever cope after a week?

She was still pondering that question in the carriage on the way home, and kept losing track of the conversation. "Charlotte, you are somewhere else this evening," Sarah said. "Are you well?"

"Perhaps a little tired," Charlotte admitted, and blushed as she remembered why. Fortunately, the darkness of the carriage hid the colour. She would have to tell Sarah if she wanted Sarah to be her alibi, but not tonight. Not in front of Nate and Drew. In the morning, then.

But the following morning, she woke with the heavy head that heralded her courses, and by the time she had breakfasted and dressed, she was sure she was about to be seriously indisposed. Perhaps the worst of it would hold off until after the Opera, and she would be able to tell Aldridge in person that they must postpone their week away.

No, that wasn't fair when he was moving the entire business of the duchy to one side to make space. She should write him a note.

She had not quite decided what to say when a footman knocked on the door. "The Duchess of Haverford is calling, my lady. Are you receiving guests?"

Aunt Eleanor? This early? Charlotte hurried downstairs and crossed the room to give the duchess her hands. "Aunt Eleanor." They touched cheeks.

"Charlotte, darling." Aunt Eleanor sat back and examined Charlotte's face, her eyes worried.

"Is there something wrong?" Charlotte asked.

"You tell me, my dear. Is there? You and Aldridge. What has happened between you?"

Charlotte blushed, and tried to withdraw her hands and turn away, but Aunt Eleanor gripped them. "Please believe me, dearest girl. There is no one I would rather have as a daughter-in-law. If only it were possible. If only that wicked boy had not ruined everything. If my son was a different kind of man, and not next in line to hold one of the highest titles in the land."

Charlotte flinched at the accusing tone, but found the strength to argue. "Is it so impossible, Aunt Eleanor? All the gossip over Ruth, and over Sarah; you helped Mama and Aunt Georgie make it go away. And no one in wider Society knows…"

The duchess nodded. "No one *knows*, my dear. Any more that they knew the truth about Ruth and Sarah. People speculate; it is what they do." She frowned "We could counter the rumours with the truth. And promise social ruin to any who continued to spread the lies. People will go on believing whatever they wish, but we can ignore anything but a direct snub. Besides, when your cousin and your sister married the men with whom they were accused of disporting, that pulled the worst fangs of the rumours."

Charlotte sighed. "Such a course is not open to me, of course. I was ruined before I even made my come out. That would be enough to damn me, without the rest."

Aunt Eleanor shrugged. "Mere ruin, and that nearly eight years ago? Only I and your closest family have anything beyond hearsay and speculation. In such a case, we ignore the truth and rumours alike. With the power your family and mine wield, we simply face the scandalmongers down until no one dares to mention the distant past. But Charlotte, darling, the man who ruined you was your own brother. The gossip will be fierce, and might well reflect on the rest of your family. Surely there is another man you can set your heart on? One whose every breath is not under such close examination as my poor son?"

Charlotte shook her head. When she pictured herself as a wife, the only man she could imagine by her side was Anthony. Not the Marquis of Aldridge. She was trained as a Society wife, and did not doubt she could manage the social and political demands of the role of duchess, but it was Anthony she wanted; the gentle man who had been kind to a lonely child, the only man ever to make her believe that marital relations might be something more than tolerable. But Aunt Eleanor was right. Being his wife would make her a target for envy and spite. Could her secret long stay hidden?

Aunt Eleanor continued. "I am concerned about more than that old scandal. We can deny it. Perhaps the Queen might be persuaded to support you. And Aldridge still has influence with the Prince Regent, and will have more when he inherits. With their backing, no one would dare to ostracise the niece of the Duke of Winshire and the wife of the Duke of Haverford."

"Well, then," Charlotte said. She knew perfectly well what the real problem was, but she wanted to hear her godmother state it.

Aunt Eleanor dropped her voice to a whisper. "Have the doctors changed their mind, my dear girl? Have your women's courses returned to normal? If not, then Aldridge cannot think of taking you to wife."

Charlotte told her what Ruth had said when Charlotte had explained the problem. "Any woman might prove to be infertile, Aunt Eleanor. Or might have only daughters, come to that." But Ruth had also said that she had known other women with infrequent and painful courses, and that they had trouble conceiving or, if they found themselves with child, difficulty in carrying to term.

"That is true, dearest. But it does not change the facts," Aunt Eleanor retorted. "A duchess has one primary role: to bear the heir. All else can be left undone or accomplished by someone else. But a barren duchess fails her husband and all of his ancestors.

"And any duke in need of an heir might come to resent and neglect a wife who fails him in such a way. The love that you have for my son will not survive years of infertility. Believe me. I have seen it over and over. And I know the Haverford men. None better. Aldridge might say it doesn't matter; he might even believe it. But it will matter, Charlotte. And it will eat away at him until he blames you and seeks consolation elsewhere."

Charlotte shook her aching head. "I think you give him insufficient credit, Your Grace."

"I know you, too. You will not tolerate his straying. He is infatuated with you, and has been for years, but do you think he has been celibate all that time? Do you think he will remain faithful if you cannot give him a son? I don't say these things to be cruel, but because I care about you both, and there is nothing worse than to be stuck in a marriage when you hate the person to whom you are yoked."

Charlotte shook her head again. Surely, she would never hate Aldridge? And he would never hate her? He was one of her oldest friends. "I have told him I will never marry," she assured the duchess who put her arms around her and offered her a handkerchief.

"I am so sorry, my dear child. I wish it could be different."

When she went back up to her room, Charlotte wrote to Aldridge. It took her more than an hour. "Yesterday evening made me realise that I am not cut out for an affair," she wrote. "I found it very difficult to keep hidden the awareness of you engendered by our night together." Not just difficult, but impossible. Aunt Eleanor had noticed, and how many others?

"I cannot in all conscience keep to our arrangement. Please forgive me." She had behaved like a wanton. She had justified everything her grandfather and father had ever said about her. She began to cry again, and struggled to subdue the tears so she could add one last thing.

"Thank you for complying with my request. I will always be grateful for your help in overcoming my fears, and will treasure my memories of our night together."

By the time she had finished, the cramps had started. She gave the letter to a footman and sent her maid for a hot brick and a tea made of the herbs Ruth had prepared for her.

She hoped Aldridge would not be too upset.

Aldridge leaned on the balustrade of Westminster Bridge and stared down into the river. Even now, several hours after midnight, the Thames was busy. Watermen rowed party-goers home in skiffs and entire parties continued in brightly lit barges as they travelled down the river. Or up, for it was that magical hour when the tide was turning and only the river current fought or assisted passages. Lighters, too, were already on the water, collecting or delivering goods to ships at anchor or from bank to bank.

He had been there for three hours, choosing a spot equidistant between two of the gas lamps that had been so revolutionary a couple of years before. The carriages that intermittently crossed the bridge ignored him, as did most of the pedestrians. Gentlemen heading to further entertainment gave way to those heading home. The night watch averted their eyes from those scurrying with nefarious intent either from trouble or to it.

Early in his vigil, he'd been accosted several times by enterprising women seeking to provide a little short-term pleasure in return for lightening his wallet, but his polite refusals must have merited a place on the gossip circuit, for he'd been left alone this last hour.

Or perhaps the news that passed around was his response to an attempted assault and robbery. The explosion of violence had been a temporary respite from his own thoughts. The brief joy of sending three armed men fleeing in disarray had swiftly dissipated, however, as had the hope that others of their ilk might dare his mood.

The risk kept him alert whenever anyone passed, which amused him, since he'd come here to toy with the idea that his life was not worth living. Clearly his body disagreed. His mind, too, which had rapidly concluded that he had a certain value to his mother and sisters. Yes, and to his brother, who would be seriously disgruntled if Aldridge died before one of Jonathan's younger sons was old enough to take charge of the duchy.

His heart was outvoted, then.

A man passed him, then stopped a few yards along and leaned against the stone to look down into the river. "Busy night," the man observed. He was clothed as a gentleman, at least regarding the shoes, overcoat, and hat, which was all Aldridge could see. The cultured voice, too, marked his status. There was something familiar about it. Aldridge searched his memory for a match.

"Been here long?" the man asked.

A name clicked into place. "Basingstoke," Aldridge said.

The vicar of one of the inner-city parishes turned to face Aldridge, and enough light reached his face to confirm Aldridge's identification. "Aldridge," he replied, moving closer. He and his wife had founded the Theodora Foundation, which offered a refuge and a training school to women who chose to leave the sex trade. Unlike many of their ilk, they treated those they rescued and those still in the game like human beings of worth. There was the word again. Worth. Perhaps if a whore could find enough worth in herself to start again a tired rake ought to make the effort.

Aldridge turned back to face the water, noting that the tide must be on the move, since the bargemen in the boat currently approaching were making heavy weather of it. "I suppose one of your soiled doves told you Westminster Bridge had attracted another jumper. If you're here to talk me out of it, you may save your breath. I do not intend to kill myself."

"I'm pleased to hear it. And yes, I was told about a fine gentleman in a melancholy mood who appeared unduly interested in the water."

"It is an interesting river," Aldridge commented. "I have never before noticed how much traffic flows by night."

Basingstoke propped himself on his own elbows and watched in silence for a while. Aldridge made a small bet with himself that it would not last above five minutes. He started counting, and had reached two hundred and seventeen when Basingstoke said, "If you need someone to help—even just a listening ear? I know we are barely acquaintances, but that can be helpful sometimes, and anything you might say to me would go no further. A matter of professional ethics, if you will."

Aldridge lifted an eyebrow. "The seal of the confessional?"

"If you wish to look at it like that."

"I do not, but I appreciate the offer." He was surprised at the strength of the temptation. He had always envied those with intimate friends, closer than brothers; people who knew one's character, all one's weaknesses, and liked one anyway. Those closest to Aldridge were dependants or servants. He had outgrown most of his associates in his wild youth, and they had never been confidants, in any case.

Perhaps that was one of the reasons that Cherry's rejection hurt so much. He had thought they were friends; had longed for a wife who looked at him and saw Anthony, and not his title, his social position, his wealth, his family connections, his political power, or any of his other surface attractions.

He must not even think of her. As well decide not to think of the Thames as it flowed beneath him, or of the bleeding hole she had made of his heart. At the very least, he must not speak of her. Shakespeare, as in so many things, had the words, and he murmured them aloud.

· · ·

"…and in my tongue
      Thy sweet beloved name no more shall dwell,
      Lest I, too much profane, should do it wrong
      And haply of our old acquaintance tell."

Hah! And there he was, speaking of her. "The sky is beginning to lighten. Dawn is more than an hour away, but the promise of it is here already." And if that wasn't a metaphor, he'd never heard one. But not one he believed. There'd be no dawn for him and Cherry. She was like everyone else. She only wanted him for what he could do for her. And now that she'd had him, she didn't want him anymore.

"Would you care for breakfast?" Basingstoke asked. "Cook always prepares more than we could possibly eat." He hesitated. "Do not feel obliged. I imagine you have many calls on your time."

Aldridge exhaled on a short laugh. "As it happens, I have no plans." Not for the next seven days. Even the couple who looked after the cottage to which he'd planned to take Cherry had been told to leave all prepared and not come back for a week. "Do you have work I could do? I am looking for something to do for the next week, and I am not used to being idle. I can drive carriages, carry water, chop wood. I can groom horses and muck out their stalls. I daresay I could learn other tasks."

Basingstoke raised his brows, but made no comment beyond, "All help is welcome. Would you be open to travelling to Hounswood? The handyman-gardener at the training school there has just broken his leg falling off a ladder, so they are short-staffed. I would normally go myself, but I promised my wife I'd attend her sister's wedding with her."

That could be made to work. He could send a note to his secretary with his change of address. Otherwise, the instructions he'd already left would cover it. He'd given Edmund the address of the cottage and his date of return. Then he'd said: *"Tell no one where I am gone. Not my mother. Not the Prime Minister. No one. Do not contact me unless something comes up that urgently requires my personal attention: my father dies, someone assassinates the Prince Regent, Napoleon invades Britain."*

He nodded his agreement. "I'm willing, but I don't know much about gardening."

Basingstoke grinned. "We need a strong back and someone who is willing to follow orders."

He lifted his brows again, this time in challenge, his lip quirking with amusement.

Aldridge shrugged. It would be something to do, and if he made a mull of it, as he'd done with Charlotte, at least his heart would not be in it, and other people wouldn't be hurt.

Basingstoke turned to walk back to his home, and Aldridge fell in beside him. "I'd rather not be known as the Marquis of Aldridge, if that is acceptable."

Basingstoke took that in his stride, too. "Grenford, then."

"Ford, perhaps. Yes, Anthony Ford."

Anthony Ford, a commoner of gentle birth who had his own reasons for helping out at the Theodora Foundation's training school for a week. Tony Ford, who had never even met a duke's granddaughter, and certainly had no reason to mourn one. Tony Ford, who undoubtedly had problems of his own in this world of sorrows, but who had a life that belonged to him, and not to a deranged despot, a title, and hundreds of dependents. Ford was a lucky chap. It would only be a week, but it would have to do.

Wharton had written to Whailand's London agent with a list of his expectations, and the man had found Wharton a small jewel of a townhouse, fully furnished, and complete with a husband-and-wife team to serve him.

It had belonged to a deceased estate, and had been sitting empty, apart from Simpson and his wife, for over a year. The agent took a six-month lease, and instructed the couple to employ the staff they needed to make Mr Whailand comfortable.

Mrs Simpson was a cook and housekeeper. Simpson agreed to

take on the roles of both butler and valet. A footman and two maids were hired, and all was prepared when Wharton arrived.

It would do. Wharton exerted his charm, assuring his new servants that he was delighted. The location was perfect. In Westminster, on a square of more modest houses surrounded by the homes of the wealthy.

From the first dinner she served him, Mrs Simpson showed that she was an artist in the kitchen, so that was some consolation for not being able to keep his usual pets close by, as he was accustomed to doing.

And Simpson had a deft hand with Wharton's boots and cravats. As for the other servants, Wharton asked only that they did their work and stayed out of his way.

Not that he would spend much time in the house. As soon as he slept off the effects of the long ride in a hideous post chaise—the person who had named them 'bounders' was saying no more than the truth—he needed to visit the little haven that had been set up for him in at a private club with an excellent reputation for meeting every need of its clients.

They would have received and would fulfil his requirements for privacy, exclusivity, cleanliness, some measure of physical beauty, extreme youth. Refreshed after all these months of abstinence, he would then be ready to put his mind to the first step in revenge. He had clubs to join and people to meet.

Reputable places and respectable people. In the Whailand persona, Wharton would stay away from gambling hells and brothels. Whailand was a gentleman of adequate, but not extravagant means, seeking a gently born bride of a similar level in Society.

Manton's was a must. Perhaps Jacksons, though he preferred to watch rather than put himself in the way of being punched. His Eton accent might get him into White's or Brooks, but that might not serve him. He would spend some time at Tattersalls.

What he needed was a garrulous fool. Someone amiable who would happily take a man from the country under his wing. Someone who was invited to entertainments that might attract the kind of maiden Whailand would be interested in courting, and that would certainly provide a fertile soil for the scandal Wharton planned to sow.

People like the Winshires and Haverfords circulated at the highest levels of Society. Wharton would not risk encountering his enemies by accepting such invitations, even if he received them. But his rumours would go in his place.

He regretted that he would not have a front-row seat in their pain. His place was behind the curtain, pulling the strings.

But I will be there for the final act, he promised himself.

22

Charlotte didn't want to leave her room. The indisposition had been a mild one, but she continued to linger long after the cramps had subsided to a dull ache. When Sarah came looking for her, several days later, Charlotte was up and dressed, though she had not made it farther than a chair by the fire.

"Darling," Sarah greeted her. "How are you?"

"Better, thank you. A little sore still, but nothing unusual." She tried for a cheerful smile. "I am just being lazy, Sarah. How are you?"

Sarah frowned. "You will have to do better than that before I believe you."

Charlotte hid the face that had betrayed her by turning to the fire. "What do you mean? My indisposition is past its worst."

"Is it to do with you and Aldridge? I have seen it coming for some time, and have been happy for you. And then at the musicale…" Sarah's arm slipped around Charlotte's shoulders. "Darling, can I help? Do you want to talk about it?"

Charlotte caught back a sob. "There is no me and Aldridge. There cannot be." She turned into her sister's embrace, wailing, "It hurts, Sarah. It hurts so much!"

The whole story washed out of Charlotte on floods of tears. Sarah limited her contribution to consoling pats and murmurs, and the occasional clarifying question. Eventually, when Charlotte had finished, Sarah sent for a washbasin of warm water, plus tea and cake, "Cake will not fix your ills, dearest, but it is hard to be completely miserable when eating cake."

Charlotte gave a watery chuckle, as her sister intended. "Thank you for listening," she said.

Sarah patted her hand. "I am your sister."

The tears welled again, and Charlotte fought them back. "Friends forever," she said, their old nursery promise.

A knock on the door announced Charlotte's maid with a tray of tea makings. She put them on a table near Sarah, and fetched a jug of water from the door. "My lady, would you like me to wash your face and tidy your hair?" the maid asked Charlotte's turned back. Charlotte shook her head, and her voice was calm when she replied, "My sister will help me, thank you, Clarke."

Sarah made the tea and put several of Fournier's delightful little confections of sponge and sugar paste onto a plate while Charlotte washed her face and pinned a couple of loose strands back into her coiffure. "Clarke would do a better job," she observed as she took her seat next to Sarah again, and accepted the cup of tea.

Sarah gave the remark an abstracted smile. She was thinking about what she wanted to say. Charlotte waited for it. On the long list of people she did not want to disappoint, her sister was highest.

But she did not expect what Sarah said. "I am so angry with Aunt Eleanor. She had no right to interfere, and she could not be more wrong. And she has upset you, which is what I cannot forgive."

"She is just trying to protect her son," Charlotte protested.

"Really? As if he was a boy in the nursery with no idea what is good for him? He is thirty-four, Charlotte, and if anyone in all of England—no, the whole United Kingdom—knows his own mind when it comes to women, it is the Marquis of Aldridge."

The martial light in her eyes softened and she nudged Charlotte with her shoulder. "Darling, Aldridge loves you and you love him. It is plain to anyone who knows you both. I do not know why the Duchess of Haverford is so determined to prevent this marriage, but it is Not. Her. Business."

"She is his mother," Charlotte pointed out. "And I am barren. The Duchess of Haverford must have sons."

"Nonsense," Sarah argued. "The Duke of Haverford must have an heir. And that is well covered. Even if you are barren, and Ruth said these things are not certain, Aldridge has a brother, nephews, a whole tribe of cousins."

"Distant cousins," Charlotte corrected. She put the tea cup down and examined the cakes as an alternative to letting Sarah see the indecision in her eyes.

"Irrelevant. The brother and nephews are enough."

Charlotte opened her mouth to point out that Jonathan was wed to foreign royalty and therefore had other responsibilities, but Sarah put a finger over her lips.

"Which is beside the point, Charlotte. You owe it to Aldridge to tell him your true objections. Then the pair of you can decide what to do. You told me, when I was reluctant to confront Nate about abandoning me, that I had to listen to him. And you were right." She gave a sharp nod and softened her dogmatic tone by taking her sister's hand and holding it gently. "Now I'm giving you the same advice. You need to tell Aldridge the truth."

"That sounds more like an order than advice," Charlotte grumbled.

"It was advice before you convinced him to take you to bed," Sarah retorted. "Now you have done so, do you not think you owe him the courtesy of explaining why he is good enough for bed sport but not for marriage?"

Shocked, Charlotte pulled her hand from her sister's grasp. "He does not believe that!"

"I think he does, and so does Nate. Charlotte, some of the women I work with saw him on Westminster Bridge several nights ago, staring into the water. They thought he was going to jump." She touched Charlotte's arm as Charlotte was about to jump to her feet, explaining, "He did not. They sent Alex Basingstoke to

Aldridge, and Alex took him home with him to his parsonage. You need to talk to him, Charlotte."

"I did not mean to hurt him, Sarah." She was crying again, but a sense of hope and wonder fuelled her next comment. "I did not know I could."

Gardening did not exercise the same muscles as riding, boxing, or fencing. Aldridge exulted in the hot bath in the scullery in the gardener's cottage, where he had a small room in the attic. One that would fit into his dressing room at any of the Haverford estates with room left over.

The bath, too was only half the size of the smallest he'd ever bathed in, and he'd had to bucket in every drop of water from the well to the kettle, and then from the kettle to the scullery. It was hot, though, and soothed the aches.

Harris, the gardener, treated his temporary apprentice with a mix of the deference due to a gentleman and the scorn of a master for the incompetent who didn't even understand the words used to describe a craft's tasks, let alone carry them out.

Mrs Harris called Aldridge 'dearie', fussed over him like an indulgent mother with one precious chick, and seemed determined to fatten him like a Michaelmas goose.

He was having dinner tonight with the vicar of St Chad's, who was also head of the Theodora Foundation training school. He had met Arthur Beauclair several times in the four days of his stay.

Beauclair appeared mild, unworldly, and a little ineffectual. But that image didn't match with the respect paid to him by residents of the training school, servants and trainees alike. Aldridge would be able to fund the canal extension he was planning without touching the duchy's investments if he had a pound for every time he heard someone say, *Mr Beauclair would not like it,* or *I need to ask Mr Beauclair,* or *Mr Beauclair will be so pleased when I tell him.*

Basingstoke, too, had said that Beauclair was both the head and the heart of the Theodora Foundation, though Basingstoke was the face, because he and his wife were comfortable with the social settings that Beauclair avoided.

What that meant for dinner, Aldridge had no idea. Dinner was at the vicarage, which was the other side of the grounds of the training school. Aldridge carried an unlit lantern, which he'd need on his way back to the gardener's cottage.

Three more days and he'd need to return to London. He didn't want to think about it. Instead, he occupied his mind wondering who else would be at dinner. A wasted exercise, as it turned out, since he was the only guest.

Aldridge was shown straight into the dining room, where the table had been set with two settings at one end, for ease of conversation. Beauclair did not bother with small talk. "Your days with us are more than half gone, Mr Ford. Have you found what you were looking for?"

What had he been looking for? A temporary escape, he supposed. "Yes, sir," he replied, and found himself explaining, though he had not intended to. "I wanted a holiday, I suppose. Time away from decisions I have to make and situations I cannot change."

"And you have found that in trimming our hedges, digging our vegetable beds, and mending our window shutters." Beauclair's eyes twinkled. "Not everyone's idea of a holiday, Mr Ford, but I am glad it has suited you. Ah. Here is the soup."

Beauclair then asked, "What are your thoughts on the situation with Napoleon," and they discussed the worrying news from Europe through a table setting mainly comprising a tasteless soup. "The cook here produces excellent meals in the English country tradition," Beauclair explained, "but will insist on attempting French cuisine. Leave the soup, and enjoy the roast to come."

The roast was superlative, and was a worthy accompaniment to a robust discussion of Napoleon's likely reactions to Murat's defeat at the hands of the Austrians, and the capacity of the British and Prussian alliance to defeat the Corsican should it come to a pitched battle.

After that setting was removed and the next laid, Beauclair told the maid, "Leave us now, Milly. You can clear the table when we remove to the parlour. I wish to speak to Mr Ford in private."

Aldridge's hands froze over the apple he was peeling. Here it came. Beauclair had recognised him, and was about to touch him up for money or political support or a job for a relative or protégé. He set the apple moving again, holding the knife so it slid under the skin. *I'm inclined to agree to his requests. He is a good man.*

"Yes," Beauclair said. "I do know who you are. We did not meet last year when I was in London with my cousin Lechton, but you attended Alex Blasingstoke's wedding. And even if I had not recognised you, enough people in the training school have seen you before that your identity is an open secret."

Aldridge raised one eyebrow as he inspected the apple to ensure he had not missed a speck of skin. "No one has said a thing."

Beauclair shrugged. "Here, we are used to people who want to leave their past behind. No one has or will say anything, and if you wish to be Ford while you are here, Ford you will be. Harris has been amused to have a marquis, heir to a duke, at his command."

Aldridge thought about some of Harris's rants about lazy gentlemen's sons who had never done a lick of a work in their lives and couldn't resist a wry smile.

"But it is about your past and your future that I wish to speak, Ford," Beauclair continued. "I had intended to say nothing, but... I was uncomfortable." He picked up another of the apples, and began to turn it in his hands. "I have been praying since you arrived, and it is clear to me that I am meant to tell you about the storm breaking over your family and your lady's."

My lady's? Aldridge had the apple an inch from his mouth. He lowered it again. "A storm? What do you mean?"

Beauclair put the apple back into the basket on the table. "I cannot be certain. Someone who hates you. A weapon they have used before. Anger, spite, envy—"

He shook his head, frowning. "I should perhaps explain... I see...connections. See is not quite the right word, but it is closer than smell or taste or hear. The clear connection between Nate and Sarah is one of the reasons I supported them when they wanted to marry. I knew what the world would say—what my bishop did say. They were minors, and I had no right to encourage them to disobey their elders."

Aldridge had his own opinion. *Better than marrying the poor girl off to Richport or Rutledge or Selby, as her grandfather threatened. Richport would have been bad enough, but Rutledge was a dissolute wife beater, and Selby was an ally of Wharton's and as mad as a meat-axe.*

Beauclair was claiming a more mystical explanation for his actions. "But I could see that they belonged together, that their connection was meant. I am not explaining myself. Perhaps there are no words for such things, at least outside of theology."

He sighed. "You are not a religious man, I think? It would be simpler to say 'God willed it', but that is not language you will accept."

"I believe in the existence of some sort of divinity," Aldridge admitted. "I am not convinced he, she, or it is interested in me. Or if he is, I do not think he likes me much."

Beauclair gifted him with a gentle smile, conveying amusement with a touch of exasperation and a large helping of affection. "You have been told He loves all his creatures, and you do not believe it because you do not love yourself."

Ouch. That struck a little close to home. Aldridge tried to fix Beauclair with the ducal glare he had perfected in front of a mirror when he was still in his teens. Beauclair didn't seem to notice.

He continued, "You must have seen the sort of connection that Alex has with his wife, and Nate with Sarah? If it makes it easier for you, just assume that I have a natural ability to notice such attachments when they are still tentative. You have such a connection with Lady Charlotte. It is strong and true."

I know. Aldridge wasn't going to tell Beauclair how many women he had known, many of them skilled beyond belief, a few (a very few) dear to his heart. He had embarked on the night with Charlotte expecting to teach her how pleasant love-making could be, and assuming he would find pleasure in the experience. What happened had blown his preconceptions out of the water. His world was still rocking nearly a week later.

But Beauclair was still wrong. "She won't have me."

Beauclair's answer was stern. "You need to find out why. The two of you are meant." He had cut his apple into several small pieces and he stopped to eat one of them while Aldridge thought about that. Aldridge couldn't think of anything to say. He tried to suppress the hope that welled regardless. Beauclair was obviously a little touched. It would be foolish in the extreme to trust his words.

Beauclair broke the silence. "However, at this time all you need to understand is that the connection with you has made Lady Charlotte a target. The storm I speak of? Its hatred is focused on you, and it strikes at Lady Charlotte to wound you. I thought you could have this week as respite before the storm broke. But I was wrong. The enemy has acted faster than I expected."

"I am sure you mean well, Beauclair, but..."

Another gentle smile, this time even more amused. "You think I am delusional, Anthony. May I call you Anthony?"

Aldridge nodded, both to the request and to the statement.

"And I am Arthur. Anthony, you can believe me or not. It does not matter. But I beg you, on the off chance that I might be right, return to London in the morning. Your family and the woman that you love are in danger, and they need you."

23

Whenever the Duke of Winshire was in London, he had a standing weekly booking for a private meeting room upstairs at Miss Clemons Book Emporium and Tea Shop. Miss Clemons was the only person who knew who had hired the room, and even she—as far as the duke knew—did not know who he met there.

No doubt she speculated—after all, he had ordered that the room be prepared with refreshments for two. But he trusted her to keep her speculations to herself.

As did Yousef, who was his usual guard on his visits. His old friend did ask, though only once, "Yakob, do you know what you are doing?"

No. I really do not. She is married, and even when she is a widow—which will be soon, by all accounts—will she want to marry again? Will I?

He had no answers. Unless it was already an answer that he could not resist these weekly meetings, and neither could she.

He stood when the Duchess of Haverford entered the room, shutting the door behind herself. "Eleanor. You made it."

She threw back her heavy veils to disclose her smiling face. "James."

"How was the baptism?" *I missed you last week.* He wouldn't say that. Anything about their feelings was forbidden territory for as long as she was tied to another man.

Eleanor sat herself in front of the tea makings and he took the chair on the other side of the table, where he could watch the deft movements of her competent hands. "Such a sweet baby, James, and the couple, very happy. So lovely to see." Her smile was wistful. "I wish Aldridge would settle down."

"He and Charlotte seem to be moving in that direction," James observed and was surprised when her lips stiffened and her eyes narrowed.

She shook her head. "Aldridge will not marry Charlotte, James. I am sorry, but it isn't possible."

Before he could ask why, the door crashed open. His niece Sarah stood in the doorway, her eyes flashing and her chest heaving. "Your Grace, how could you?"

James rose, protesting, "Sarah!"

She ignored him, slamming the door shut behind her and storming across the room to lean on the table so that her face was only a foot from Eleanor's alarmed one. "We trusted you. Charlotte trusted you, and all the time you were working against her."

"Sarah?" *What on earth was she talking about. And how did she know to come here?*

Sarah didn't seem to hear him, her focus all on Eleanor, who was protesting, "No! I love Charlotte. It was to save her as much as Aldridge…"

Sarah shook her head, a vigorous repudiation. "Don't you think they are old enough to decide their own fates, without your interference? You have broken my sister's heart, and Aldridge's too."

"Better broken now, while there is still time for them to find another," Eleanor insisted.

Sarah's lip curled. "Is that what Aldridge was thinking when he stood on Westminster Bridge for several hours the night after you had told Charlotte to reject him?"

Eleanor had been pale, but at this she turned white as a sheet. "Aldridge? No! What are you saying?"

Sarah shook her head, impatiently. "He did not jump. At least as far as I know. He went off with an acquaintance. But he might have, Your Grace. If he is as heartbroken as Charlotte, he still might."

"He has not been home since that night," Eleanor whispered. "His staff will not tell me where he is. Oh, Sarah, he would not. What will I do?" She cast around her wildly for her shawl, her bonnet, her umbrella.

Sarah straightened, and seemed to see James for the first time. "I beg your pardon, Uncle James. I went to Haverford House and then I remembered it was Thursday, which is the day you meet the duchess for afternoon tea, and so I came here."

With some part of his mind, James noted that Sarah—and so, probably, his other relatives—knew about his regular meetings with Eleanor, but that was a discussion for another time. "Sit down, Eleanor. You will gain nothing by rushing out of here in such distress. Sarah, you had better explain what has happened. What is all this about Eleanor interfering between Aldridge and Charlotte?"

In a few words, Sarah outlined what Eleanor had said to Charlotte, and how Charlotte had reacted. "But Eleanor," he said, when he had heard Sarah out, "you have another son and grandsons by him, and Aldridge has a whole battalion of cousins, besides."

"Distant cousins," Eleanor dismissed them with a wave of her hand. Her colour had returned, but only in two hectic spots, one high on each cheekbone. "The Haverfords have always succeeded father to son, since the first foundation of the line. And I have worked my whole adult life to keep the duchy strong for Aldridge and his sons."

She was up and pacing, all her attention inward, though she still addressed James. "You don't know how many times I have had to manoeuvre to replace an incompetent steward that Haverford has installed with one who knew what he was doing, or how often I have smoothed over an alliance between houses that Haverford had come close to destroying. And all for Aldridge."

James shook his head, trying to comprehend. "That is admirable, Eleanor, but what has that to do with his marriage? If he loves my niece…"

Eleanor's eyes flicked from James to Sarah and back. "But that is precisely it, James." She held out a hand, begging his understanding. "Grenford men fall in love, it is true. Aldridge is no different to his father in that way. He has been in love a number of times, and with the most unsuitable of women."

She blinked at his growl. "I do not mean Charlotte. But the women before her. He has always got over them, James, even the mistress he wanted to marry. Better for Charlotte to suffer a little now than to live through his loss of interest."

"Eleanor, you cannot seriously compare Aldridge and Haverford." By the time Haverford was Aldridge's age, he had been a byword for corruption and dissipation.

Eleanor glared down her nose at him, her chin jutting pugnaciously. "You have no idea. You have not suffered as I did. You don't know how Haverford berated me—what he called me every time my courses came. Even worse when a pregnancy failed. I dread that for Charlotte."

"Aldridge is not Haverford," James repeated, pity for Eleanor's sufferings softening his anger at her meddling.

"Not in many ways, James, but in this, yes. Would you expect me to discount a thousand years of tradition and throw away all my work for the sake of something as ephemeral as a Grenford in love?"

"I would expect you to allow two adults to make their own decisions, Eleanor." James picked up his own coat and his hat, and offered Sarah his arm before turning back to the duchess. "It seems I have greater faith in your son than you do. He is a fine man, grown far beyond the reputation that still clings to him."

"But James…"

James ruthlessly overrode her. "I would happily give my niece into his keeping, with every confidence. Their love is demonstrably of the kind that endures. As I understand it, the connection has survived nearly eight years, and the direst of experiences."

He stopped once more before walking out the door, and refused to soften as Eleanor sank back into her chair, tears running down her cheeks. "I believe," he told her solemnly, "that love of the kind that builds a family of the future is more important than slavish adherence to the customs of the past. I am deeply disappointed that you cannot feel the same way."

24

Charlotte needed to speak to Anthony face to face, to tell him about her inability to give him an heir and see whether he still wanted a future with her. For she was not sure how she would live without him. She sent a message, asking if she might visit, and received a polite reply signed by a secretary. "I regret to inform your ladyship that Lord Aldridge is away from town. I will ensure he receives your message when he returns."

After some thought, she made enquiry at Blasingstoke's parsonage, but the vicar and his wife were also away from home, and the servants denied all knowledge of Lord Aldridge.

"I cannot talk to him if I do not know where he is," she grumbled to Sarah.

"You can sit around and mope until he returns, or you can come out with me and Nate this evening," Sarah suggested.

What if he does not return? Charlotte was not going to say the words out loud, fearing to make them more concrete. The mental image of Anthony staring into the Thames from Westminster Bridge kept reverberating in her mind. She had always known he was haunted by a deep strand of melancholy, but he would not go that far. *Would he?*

She was in no mood for a rout or a ball, but she had accepted the same invitations as Sarah a fortnight ago, and it was too late to send her regrets. She put herself in the hands of her maid, and was ready by the time Sarah and Nate arrived in their carriage.

Her first hint that something was wrong was in the reception line. She smiled a greeting at an acquaintance, who suddenly found it necessary to turn away to speak to someone else. It kept happening, and a space opened up around the three of them—a space surrounded by backs, frowns, and the hum of whispers.

When they reached the reception line, the hostess flushed a deep red. "Lady Charlotte... I did not expect... that is..." She turned to her husband, who spoke to Nate. "Under the circumstances, Lord Bentham, perhaps it would be best if you took—er—the sisters home."

Nate's face had turned to granite and his voice was icy. "What circumstances would those be, Lord Fenton?"

The man cast a desperate look around him and stammered, "No smoke without fire, what? Best just to go home." His wife slipped her hand into his and he pressed her hand to his heart, before pleading, "Look, Bentham, my wife has planned this for weeks. Don't make a scene."

Nate stood his ground. "What. Circumstances."

"Not the place to talk about it," Fenton insisted. "Ask me tomorrow. Ask anyone. It's all over town."

They've found out about me and Aldridge. Charlotte touched her brother-in-law's arm. "Let us leave, Nate. We are not welcome here."

"I will remember this, Fenton," Nate commented, his statement all the scarier for its conversational tone.

They left, Charlotte on one of Nate's arms and Sarah on the other, the crowd separating before them as if afraid of contamination.

Uncle James had not gone out that evening, having shelved his plans to attend the Opera after the altercation with the Duchess of Haverford. He was in his study with Yousef, but called through the open door when they arrived.

Drew was there before them. "Bad evening?" he asked.

"That prat Fenton threw us out," Nate told him. "Something about 'circumstances'."

"Circumstances, eh?" Drew commented. "The manager of my club told me, very politely, that my membership had been temporarily suspended pending investigation of 'circumstances'."

"Did the club or Fenton give you any information about these 'circumstances'?" Uncle James asked. He had poured each of them a brandy, even the twins, and was handing them out.

Another arrival in the hall proved to be Jamie and Sophia.

"Surely you haven't been shunned, too?" Charlotte asked, as Uncle James poured a brandy for his eldest son and a port for Sophia.

"Oh dear," Sophia replied. "Has it come to that?"

Uncle James summarised the situation. "Charlotte, Sarah, and Nate were turned away from the Fentons, and Drew's membership of his club has been suspended. Do you know what this is about?"

Sophia accepted her port. "We came to tell you that the whole town is buzzing with stories, many of them about the Winshires, others about the Haverfords. People have been dredging up history going back to Aldridge's childhood, and every scandal he has ever been connected with, plus a few I've never before heard. Jessica has gone home in tears."

"And the same with our family," Jamie added. "Every incident that can be misinterpreted or cast in a bad light, right back to your duel with Haverford when you were a young man, Kaka."

Yousef swirled his coffee thoughtfully. "It sounds like Wharton, Yakob," he suggested. "Were not he and his witch of a sister masters of the nasty rumour?"

"You're right, Yousef," Jamie agreed. "Let us track the stories to their source and stamp on the snake's head."

"Which will not stop people repeating them," Sarah pointed out, "and how are we to prove they are not true?"

"We cannot," Charlotte said, slowly, remembering her conversation with the Duchess of Haverford. "We should not. We simply face the scandalmongers down and refuse to bow our heads. We speak not to petty people with evil minds but to those with real power. The Queen will receive Mama, I am sure, and you could talk to the princesses, Sophia. Kaka, you have influence with the Prince Regent. If they will show their support in public, that will help."

Sophia nodded approvingly. "Yes, Charlotte is quite right. For every rumour we disprove, another will pop up, even worse. Why, they are saying that you seduced your own brother, Charlotte, and that he killed himself as a result. Yes, and that the reason Sarah ran away with Nate was that you and she were disporting with the rakes at one of Richport's orgies, and Grandfather was threatening to make you each marry one. Also that Charlotte has been Aldridge's mistress ever since. How can people swallow such rubbish?"

The room swirled around Charlotte. Someone took her hand in a firm grip and advised her to breathe. Sarah. She took a sip from the brandy glass held to her lips and the burn of the alcohol brought her back.

"A kernel of truth," she croaked, then took the glass from Sarah and sipped again. Her voice steadier, she said again, "A kernel of truth. Richport had an estate next to Applemorn Hall, where Sarah and I were living when Sarah fell in love with Nate. I met Aldridge that summer." She smiled as her uncle and cousins, without moving, shifted into warrior mode, alert as hawks sighting the rabbit. "He was a perfect gentleman, and kind to a little girl," she assured them.

She looked around the room. She knew her family loved her, and Yousef was fiercely loyal. But surely, they would look at her differently if she told them the other morsels of truth in that litany of lies. Her brother Elfingham had raped her. She had spent a night with Aldridge.

Sarah squeezed her hand. "I imagine we shall find other morsels of truth buried in some of the other rumours. Although some seem to be made out of whole cloth. I imagine it unlikely in the extreme that Aldridge killed a circus performer who happened to look like the Rose of Frampton in order to allow his mistress to adopt a new identity and marry his friend Lord Overton."

Drew, Sophia and Jamie each had a rumour to quote, all of them ridiculous.

The attacks on Uncle James and the rest of the family three years ago had been staged to win public sympathy and disguise the fact that Uncle James was an imposter—an Easterner who had known the real son of the deceased duke when he was in prison in Persia. The attacks were real enough, as Charlotte knew. The rest was nonsense.

Aldridge had sold his brother Jonathan to slavers, along with his brother's wife, Prudence Wakefield, who was a former lover of his. They would be slaves to the Saracens yet, but Prue whored herself to buy her escape. Or Jonathan did. Charlotte had heard Prue speak of how she and Jonathan had been kidnapped from the London docks, and of how they'd escaped into France. So another farrago of lies.

Uncle James and Aunt Eleanor had been lovers in their youth, and had resumed their affair when Uncle James returned to England.

Charlotte spoke again when the chuckles died down. "We need Aunt Eleanor." She or Mama, but Mama had gone to Leicester to be with Ruth in her confinement.

Sarah started to protest and Uncle James frowned, but Charlotte held up a hand. "No one is better at the politics of Polite Society. And these rumours concern her and her family, so she will be working to combat them. It is better strategy to work together."

"Charlotte is right," Sophia said, oblivious to the undercurrents. "A pity that Aunt Grace and Aunt Georgie are both from town. Still, Aunt Eleanor will be able to marshal Society's dragons on the side of right."

"Yes, and the Wakefields will know how to track the rumours back to Wharton, wherever he lairs," Uncle James agreed. "We have a plan, my children. I suggest we sleep on it, and send for the duchess and the Wakefields tomorrow."

Wharton was pleased. He could not risk entering the finest of drawing rooms, but at the lower-level entertainments he attended, the campaign of rumours was going well. Aldridge would end up with nothing. Perhaps the authorities would investigate the man's imprisonment of his father, but even if the old duke really was mad, Wharton had allowed for that. The rumour that the madness was hereditary would do nicely.

The doctor's story, that he'd been fired because he refused to poison the old man, might even point to Aldridge already beginning to lose his mind.

But that was only a small part of the price Aldridge would pay. The fact that Richport had been driven from England proved that even a duke was not immune to social censure. Once the rumours did their job, Society would cast out Aldridge, his mother, and his sisters—yes, and his lover, too. Her first. It had taken Elspeth a long time to discover the identity of the whore that Elfingham was so upset about, but she'd figured it out, and Wharton had found the doctor who treated the girl for the clap.

Wharton giggled. Saint Charlotte! What a laugh. She'd never be able to hold her head up again. Perhaps she would kill herself? That would be one in the eye for Aldridge.

The man was disgustingly rich, and refused to gamble like any normal man, but he speculated. A few nasty accidents in his canal works. A run on one of his banks. His investors would leave him in droves.

Not that Wharton had time for all of that, as the griping in his belly told him. Never mind. He would live long enough.

Let the rumours run for a week or two, and let the two ducal families feel the full weight of their disgrace. Then would come the grand finale. The infernal device was being constructed. Mullins, the footman he had in his thrall, had made a copy of the key to Aldridge's front door. Wharton would go out in a blaze of glory, and he would take his enemy with him.

Aldridge arrived home by nine of the clock, having left Hounslow on a borrowed horse as soon as the sun was high enough to give light to ride by. Despite all his rational rejection of Beauclair's folderol, the man's conviction left him with bad dreams, none of which he remembered. But he woke early, with a paradoxical combination of dread and hope. Dread of whatever this storm denoted; hope that Charlotte was not, after all, lost to him.

Beauclair had come down to the stable to see him off, and had given him an odd parting message. "Remember Samuel and John the Baptist," he said, and gave another of his charming smiles. "I don't know what that means, Anthony, but I woke up with the remark in my mind and the thought I should tell you."

Very Delphic. Aldridge wasted little time thinking about, instead wavering from joy to despair as he imagined what awaited him in London.

Richards met him at the door to the heir's wing. "Welcome home, my lord. Mr Markinson was here a few minutes ago to say he is sending an urgent dispatch to you this morning, my lord. Lady Charlotte called and asked to speak with you. And Her Grace has asked to be notified as soon as you arrive."

Aldridge regarded his butler, his brows raised. "Trouble, Richards?"

Richards sniffed. "Foolish gossip, my lord. I have said it will not be tolerated, but I fear that my influence is limited to this household."

Aldridge handed over his gloves, hat, and coat. "I will go and find Markinson. Send to my mother and tell her I will do myself the honour of waiting on her in an hour. Have a bath prepared in my room, and tell my valet to lay out appropriate wear for a call on the Duke of Winshire." Or, at least, on his niece, which Richards could probably work out for himself.

Charlotte had called. But there was trouble, so probably she needed his help. Still, it was a good sign that she turned to him, was it not?

All three secretaries got to their feet when he entered the room, and Edmund said, "Thank God. I was about to send you a message, my lord."

"So Richards tells me. Gossip, he says. About me, I assume. How bad?"

"About…" Edmund took a deep breath and let it out again. "Read my report, my lord. All three of us collaborated on it. When we heard about the first rumours, we thought it best to find out exactly what was being said. So, we went out into the coffee shops and clubs, where people like us gathered, and"—he waved a thick package that he lifted from his desk—"this is the result."

Aldridge's brows shot up again. Bad indeed, if it affected his personal life, his estates, and his business interests. He took the package Edmund passed him and quickly scanned it, breathing more rapidly as he turned the pages. The temper he had spent a lifetime learning to control was on a very short leash indeed by the time he reached the end.

With difficulty, he kept his voice calm. "Thank you, gentlemen. These allegations are scurrilous, and will be addressed. However, I am conscious that the reputation of the master reflects on that of his secretaries. If any of you wish to tender your resignation…?"

"No, sir!" The denial exploded from Edmund. "Whoever is behind this—my lord, I want a hand in bringing him down."

The other two agreed, just as fervently. "Excellent. And you have made a good start with this report. I agree it is an attack, and much like those the man Wharton has waged against the Duke of Winshire and his family before. I see more coffee in your future, Rook. Hawk, perhaps you might do me the favour of looking over some horses at Tattersalls? No need to say who you are representing. Edmund, I feel sure the arrangements for the duchess's ball require a visit to a number of merchants?"

The secretaries nodded, but as he turned away, Aldridge had another thought. "Her Grace has asked to see me. I think we might assume that this nonsense has reached Society's drawing rooms. It is foolish, I am sure you will agree, to think to use social approval and disapproval to fight the Duchess of Haverford on her own ground."

They returned his smile. Rook even laughed. But as Aldridge returned to his own wing and his bath, he was not amused. How dare that scum malign Charlotte! And what of the accusation that she was Aldridge's mistress? Was it a shot in the dark? Or did he know about that night?

Mama was waiting for him, pacing back and forth, every fractious movement conveying anxiety, though as he entered, she was telling Jessica and Frances that they had nothing to worry about; that she and Aldridge were going to fix it.

"Of course, we are," Aldridge agreed. Whereupon his mother destroyed the effect of her calming remarks by casting herself into his arms and bursting into tears. Alarmed, he patted her back while sending a questioning glance at his sisters.

After a moment, she pulled away and dabbed at her eyes with a small lace-trimmed square of embroidered linen.

"I apologise, Aldridge. So embarrassing for you, and your cravat —such a nice knot, dear, and now all wet. I was so worried about you, dear. You left no word, and Mr Markinson would not say where you were, and I heard you had been seen on Westminster Bridge at night, and I was so frightened, because I knew you were unhappy, and it is all my fault, and now these horrid stories, and I am so glad you are home!"

"I am sorry you were concerned, Mama. I was perfectly safe." His conscience gave him a kick. "I should have let you know where I was going, but it was a spur of the moment impulse."

She was shaking her head. "You are an adult, Aldridge. You have every right to make your own decisions." And she burst into tears again.

Aldridge hovered, helplessly, while Jessica helped her to a chair, and Frances poured her a cup of tea. "I am glad you are here," Jessica told him. "Some awful stories are going around. Aunt Eleanor has been really upset. Frances and I don't know what to do."

Mama had composed herself again. "I am perfectly well, dearest Jessica. You need not be concerned for me."

"I know about the stories," Aldridge said. "Markinson has given me a report. Lady Charlotte called for me yesterday, presumably about the gossip. I've sent a message to say Mama and I will visit this morning. You and Frances had better come too. I've ordered the carriage, so go and fetch your bonnets."

Mama put her cup down and half rose from her chair. "You will have to go without me, Aldridge. I will not be welcome there." The tears rose again and she blinked them back. "You both look well enough for visiting, girls. Run and get your coats and bonnets. Do not forget gloves, Frances."

That was a rather transparent move to get his sisters out of the way. What could be wrong? It could not be that silly feud. Mama had been meeting the Duke of Winshire since just after he arrived back in England. In secret, she fondly thought. "Have you had a disagreement with the Duke of Winshire, Mama?" Aldridge asked.

She swallowed hard, and stood erect, her chin raised and her lip trembling. "He is angry with me, and you will be, too. I told Charlotte that she must not marry you."

Aldridge couldn't believe his ears. "You what?"

"I had reasons, but..." She took a deep breath that shuddered on a sob. "I was wrong, Aldridge. I still think my reasons are good, but the decision was not mine to make, and so I will tell Charlotte. I am very sorry, Aldridge."

Aldridge paced across the room, gritting his teeth and clenching his fists, afraid to speak lest his anger exploded. *Mama told Charlotte not to marry me.* The betrayal cut deep. He wondered at her reasons, but he could not ask if he was to retain any equanimity at all.

Before he had wrestled his feelings under control, the butler appeared with a message that he handed to the duchess, and Frances and Jessica came back into the room followed by a maid carrying their coats and bonnets.

Aldridge forced a smile and a nod for his sisters, then turned when his mother said his name. "Aldridge, I will get my bonnet and come with you, if you will permit. The Duke of Winshire has sent to ask if I will help to manage these rumours. He suggests we also include Matilda and Charles."

Aldridge inclined his head. "I will send them a message. Your earl, too, Jessica? Or have you not accepted him yet?"

Jessica's eyes glittered and she hoisted her chin. "Yes, send for Colyton. I might as well find out where I stand."

Brave girl. He managed a smile for her. "We will go via the office and write a note," he said. He offered an arm each to his sisters and nodded coldly to his mother. "We will meet you at the carriage, Your Grace," he said, and then felt guilty when she paled still more at the formal address. He would consider forgiving her when he knew how badly she had hurt Charlotte.

25

Once again, the Winderfield family—those currently in London, at least—gathered to combat misinformation.

The note from Aldridge came while Charlotte was still dressing for the day after a restless night. She went down to breakfast to find Rosemary and her shield sister, Mariamne, Drew, Uncle James, Yousef, and the warrior Yahzak already there, and Sophia and Jamie arrived soon after. Nate and Sarah came next, and Prue and David Wakefield joined them.

Prue and David brought Tony, who had been staying with them. They were also accompanied by their eldest daughter, Antonia, whom Charlotte examined surreptitiously. The girl had been the subject of one of the rumours—it claimed that she was Aldridge's daughter, conceived when he had stolen a march on David who was courting Prue. The gossip said Aldridge had abducted her, making her his mistress, and then abandoned her when she became pregnant.

All untrue, Charlotte was sure, and if Antonia did have Aldridge's eyes, why, she also shared them with David, Jonathan, and Jessica. And Tony, come to that. The two of them could easily be brother and sister. Even the age gap, only two years, supported that impression.

Then Aldridge arrived with the duchess and two of his sisters. Something inside Charlotte settled to see him, and the small smile that curved his lips as soon as he caught her eye.

Uncle James, after greeting Aldridge, raised his voice over the hubbub of conversation to say, "The Hamners are still on their way, but let us begin."

"Will you begin without me?" Aldridge asked. "I would like, if Lady Charlotte permits, to have a private word with her ladyship."

He met her eyes. His face was set in a bland mask, but his eyes yearned. Charlotte did not wait for Uncle James to respond, but crossed the room and beckoned. She led him out into the passage and along to a little parlour that—because of its size and barely operable fireplace—was seldom used, except when interviewing an upper servant or someone seeking support for an ill-favoured political or philanthropic idea.

It wasn't the right place for the coming discussion, but it was closest, and Charlotte couldn't bear any further delay. In moments, she would tell Aldridge that she was barren, and his response would decide the rest of her life. But how would she tell him?

He spoke first, falling to his knees in front of the chair she'd taken, and enclosing her hands in his. "Cherry, my mother says she told you not to marry me, and I have been desperate to know whether you would have said yes without her interference."

The social mask had gone. His eyes burned into hers from a strained white face. She blurted, "I am barren, Anthony. That is why your mother is against our marriage. I cannot give you an heir."

Aldridge gripped her hands more tightly. "Is that all? My brother has two sons and his wife is with child again. I have at least six distant cousins in line to step into my shoes after Gren and his sons. I have heirs aplenty, my heart's dearest love. I want you. I need you, Cherry, as my wife, my duchess, my partner in all things. Will you marry me?"

"You are sure? You will not come to… resent me?"

"Cherry." The gentle protest, the hurt in his eyes, melted her last resistance.

"You won't, will you?" Her question was a soft crow. She leaned forward to fall to her own knees and into his welcoming arms. "You love me. You have given your word, and you never break your word."

He accepted her kiss, but pulled back before she could deepen it. "You have not given yours," he pointed out.

Charlotte's chuckle was born in joy. "Yes, Anthony. Yes, I will marry you." She lifted her mouth again, and this time he took it, and nothing was said by either of them for a timeless stretch that ended only because of a knock on the door.

"Charlotte and Aldridge?" It was Sarah's voice. "Colyton and the Hamners are here. Uncle James sent me to fetch you."

"Come in, Lady Sarah," Aldridge called, as they got up from the floor and began putting one another to rights. "Cherry, my love, will you marry me immediately? Quite apart from my need for you—though I hope you won't discount that—nearly all the rumours that are not ancient history will be defanged if you are my marchioness, and not merely the audacious wench that sought me out in my own bed." He waggled his eyebrows and Cherry administered an admonitory tap on the forearm.

"He's right," Sarah said. "A wedding will be just the thing." She was conducting them back to the main drawing room as she spoke. She flung open the door, "I give you, the Marquis and future Marchioness of Aldridge!"

In the flurry of congratulations that followed, Aunt Eleanor stayed in the background. But she approached Charlotte as the others in the room settled back to weaving the new betrothal into the plan they were making. "Charlotte, my dear. I do not expect you to forgive me, but I am very happy you have accepted Aldridge." Her eyes tracked her son, who was laughing as he evaded ever more extravagant propositions from his sisters for celebrating his hasty wedding. "He is so happy, Charlotte. It gives me hope, and makes me even more aware I was selfish to intervene."

Charlotte kissed her cheek, and was rewarded by her lover's

approving smile. "All I ask is that you are happy for us, Aunt Eleanor."

Aunt Eleanor brushed at her cheek. "So silly. I have wept more in the past twenty-four hours than I have in many, many years. I am happy for you, dearest. Very happy."

Aldridge finally fulfilled his errand at Doctor's Commons late in the afternoon, and stopped in at the Winshire mansion on his way home to report his success.

Many of the others were already there, returned from afternoon calls on those they could count as allies. The agreed strategy had been to refuse to comment on any of the scandalous lies and half-truths, but to simply to ignore them, and to carry on as if Society had no option but to do likewise.

It was, as Aldridge had pointed out, mostly ancient history, anyway, and no one would care about it in a day or two, when new scandals came along to amuse the *ton*. The accusations that he was killing his father would annoy the committee from the House of Lords, who had sat as judges at the duke's competency hearing a year ago. They would not like their probity to be called into question, and would back Aldridge as a result. As for the claims that Cherry was his mistress, making her his wife would sink those without a trace.

Still, it was good to hear that he was right. He was greeted with the news that the tide of opinion had already shifted. No surprises there. Given the number of titles and the level of influence they could summon to their side, the result had been a foregone conclusion.

Not one to leave things to chance, Aldridge's mother had sent to Windsor, seeking an audience with Queen Charlotte, and the Duke of Winshire and Mama had called on Carlton House this afternoon. "His Royal Highness says he will be pleased to attend your wedding here at eleven tomorrow morning, and hopes to kiss the bride," the duke reported.

Aldridge frowned. "Tomorrow? But I thought this evening…" He had beguiled the long wait watching the slow turning of the wheels of ecclesiastical law by imagining in detail what he and Charlotte could explore together tonight, and he was in no mind to give up the reality for the Fat Adonis.

"A great honour, do you not think?" his mother said. "I have sent an invitation to Her Majesty and to the Princess Royal, too. I do not expect the queen to join us, but I have hopes for the Princess Royal. With such signs of favour, none will dare to snub us."

He wanted to respond to the note of anxiety in her voice, to her lowered eyes that would not meet his, but he was still angry with her, and his voice was cold when he replied, "Should any dare to serve the future Duchess of Haverford with a cold shoulder, I shall know how to respond."

"Of course." Charlotte's beloved voice, accompanied by the touch of her hand as she slid it inside his upper arm, soothed his irritation. "But it would be foolish to refuse royal favour for the sake of a few hours, would it not, Anthony?"

He looked down into her lovely eyes, and his lips curled at the corners without his volition. "If it pleases you, my love, I am content." He could not resist adding, "Even if it does mean I must wait until tomorrow to have you to myself."

She blushed, and the Duke of Winshire turned away, covering his mouth and coughing, but not before Aldridge had seen the twinkle in his eye.

"I will need to let Alex Basingstoke know the change of time," Aldridge added. *Oops. A decision made without consulting her, and just hours after asking her to be his partner in all things.* "Unless you have someone else that you would prefer to perform the ceremony?"

"Alex would be perfect, and please tell him that his wife and their children will be welcome, Anthony."

He loved the way she called him by his own personal name. His heart overflowing, he kissed her on the nose, right there in the crowded drawing room, then blushed when he looked around at the smiling audience. *I'm in serious danger of losing my reputation for being incapable of love.*

"Join us for dinner, Aldridge," the duke suggested.

"I had better go home and get changed, then. Will you see me out, Cherry?"

After a very pleasant, if incomplete, interlude in the small parlour on the way to the door, Aldridge went out to his curricle, which was being walked around the mews courtyard by a pair of boys dressed as gentlemen, with the groom who had been asked to walk them watching on.

The heavy eyebrows, dark hair, and hawk profiles hinted at their origin. "You are the Duke of Winshire's youngest sons," Aldridge guessed.

The taller of the two bowed, while the other held the pair of horses, murmuring to them as one of them attempted to lip his ear.

"I am Thomas Winderfield," said the tall one, "and this is my friend Jamir ibn Yousef. You are the Marquis of Aldridge, and you are going to marry my cousin Charlotte."

"I am," Aldridge agreed. "So, we shall be cousins, Lord Thomas. Thank you for walking my horses."

"They are superb, Lord Aldridge," Jamir enthused. "A different breed to our Turkmen horses, but you can see that they have noble ancestors."

Thomas grinned at his friend and told Aldridge, "Jamir hopes you have time to show us their paces, but is too polite to ask." Jamir nudged Thomas in the ribs, none too gently, then had to soothe one of the horses, who took offence at losing his attention.

Aldridge was amused. "And do you wish to see their paces too, Lord Thomas?"

"It is a wonder beyond imagination, Lord Aldridge, but Thomas prefers machines," Jamir reported.

"I like horses, too," young Thomas protested.

Aldridge could do with some company, to take his mind from the unexpected delay in his nuptials. "I am going home to change and then will return here for dinner. If the two of you have the permission of your fathers, you can come with me," he offered.

The two boys shot each other delighted looks. "Thank you, sir. We'd love to," Thomas said, with another elegant bow, as Jamir passed the lead rein to the groom. With Jamir at his heels, Thomas took the steps back into the house three at a time, and disappeared through the door.

They were back in less than five minutes, with the duke's lieutenant Yousef, Jamir's father, to give the required permission.

London streets were no place to give a pair of high-bloods their heads, but Aldridge let them stretch their paces as the busy traffic gave way to the quieter roads leading towards Richmond. Both boys were ecstatic, and Jamir expressed the earnest desire to one day have a pair just like them, and just such a curricle. Thomas—when asked—admitted that the height of his ambition was to drive a railway engine. "But your curricle is very nice, Lord Aldridge."

"You might drop the 'Lord' since we are practically cousins," Aldridge suggested. "And you, too, Jamir, if you wish."

"Not in front of waladi—my father," Jamir commented, and grinned. "Thank you, Aldridge."

26

At Haverford House, Aldridge requested a fresh team in three quarters of an hour, and sent for his valet. He left the boys in the billiard room. "I'll have someone bring you refreshments," he promised.

He was tying his cravat while his valet stood by with an assortment of cravat pins when Jamir burst into the room, Richards on his heels. "Aldridge, come quickly," Jamir demanded.

"I am sorry, my lord," said Richards, grabbing Jamir by the arm. "The boy got past me."

Aldridge held up a hand. "Wait, Richards. Jamir, what is it?" The boy's eyes were wide and strained.

"There is a man…" Jamir stopped and visibly composed himself, closing his eyes, folding his hands across his breast and taking a deep breath. Then, standing straight and tall, he reported, "The refreshments did not come, sir, so Thomas said we should remind the footman. We saw him farther down the hall, but he was with a man, dressed as a gentleman, not a servant. The man carried a large bag. It was dark where we were, and they did not see us. The man said to the footman, 'Show me to Aldridge's bedroom. I will place the device there, and you will wait thirty minutes and then fetch Aldridge'."

His brows drew together and he wrinkled his nose. "We followed, sir, and they came into your apartments, but stopped at another room. The Sultan's room." He waved back in the direction of the playroom. "Thomas stayed to watch them, sir, and I came to get you."

Aldridge took off at a run, plucking a battle axe from a display in the passage as he passed. *Thank goodness I hadn't put my boots on.* Jamir, too, ran on stockinged feet. He and Thomas, lurking by the playroom door with a knife in each hand, must have taken off their boots to move more quietly.

The door to the playroom was partly ajar, and Aldridge could hear conversation. No, a monologue. "Such a surprise for dear Aldridge. Mullins, are you still here? Go and fetch your master. Tell him…" He snickered, and Aldridge recognised Wharton's throaty giggle. "Tell him Charlotte is here, and wants to make passionate lo-o-ove all night long." Another snicker.

"What about my sister? You promised…" That was the footman, Mullins.

"I will not trouble your sister after tonight, Mullins. Run your message, boy. But be quick! The device goes off in twenty minutes, and counting. The sooner you get back with Aldridge, the sooner I will tell you how to find your sister. Now where shall I place myself? Ah, yes! Perfect. Right under the portrait of Baroness Overton." He giggled again, the pitch rising, but Aldridge had ceased to pay attention as the footman emerged from the room.

He stopped in his tracks as he saw Aldridge, axe at the ready, and squeaked his fright when Thomas stepped up beside him and put a knife to his throat.

Aldridge beckoned Mullins away from the door, and Thomas marched along with him, keeping the knife in place. Once they rounded the corner of the passage, Aldridge said in a low voice, "Keep your voice down, Mullins, or I shall give Lord Thomas the nod to slit your throat. Now. What device is Wharton talking about?"

Mullins looked confused. "Don't know no Wharton, my lord. That there's the Beast. He has taken my sister, my lord. He says he'll put her to work in the brothels if I don't do what he says."

"The Beast can't be trusted, Mullins, you know that. But you also know that I always keep my word. I will help you find your sister, but you must help me bring down the Beast." Aldridge nodded to Thomas, who removed the knife and stepped back. "Now, tell me about the device. Black powder?"

"I think so, my lord. He says it will blow half the house sky high when the timer reaches its end."

Thomas said something in another language, an interjection that, from the tone, could probably be translated by an expletive. He changed to English to say, "I knew I'd seen the man before. Aldridge, I talked to him two weeks ago at an exhibition of clock-work mechanisms."

"By his count, we still have fifteen minutes," Aldridge said. In moments, the plans were made. Richards and a group of armed footmen went round to the playroom's other door. More armed footmen followed Mullins and Aldridge. "Stay out of sight until I have him subdued," Aldridge instructed. "Boys, stay here. I don't want the job of explaining to your fathers how you came to be shot or blown up."

Aldridge entered the room a pace behind Mullins, his duelling pistol hidden behind the footman. Richards had the matching gun. Wharton was lounging on the massive bed, preening for his reflection in the mirrored ceiling, but with one eye steadily on the door and the barrel of his own pistol hard against the head of a trembling hall boy.

"Surprise!" he said, then put on a falsetto voice. "Oh, Aldridge. I am ready for you, Aldridge. We shall light up the night together, Aldridge."

Aldridge showed his own weapon. "Give it up, Wharton. My men are blocking all the exits and will attack on my command."

"But Aldridge, I don't plan to leave. I am going to die tonight and take you with me. And this sweet little boy. A pity, but there it is. The duke is dead, long live the duke." He kicked a package of papers towards Aldridge. The seal was broken, but most of it still adhered to the document—Aldridge could recognise it from across the room as the steward's seal from Haverford Castle. "Mullins didn't tell you about the letter from Haverford Castle. Naughty Mullins."

He turned a snarl on the footman. "Naughty, naughty Mullins. You told Aldridge. No pretty little sister for you!"

Haverford was gone—to whatever hell awaited him. Aldridge shelved the notion to deal with later.

Wharton was still talking, crooning almost. "I win at last, Aldridge. Haverford, I should say. But only for the next few minutes. Then it will be Gren's turn. Pretty Gren. You should have let me have him, Aldridge. Haverford. I told you years ago I would get back at you, and I have." He giggled again. "Do you like all my pretty stories?"

A shadow moved near the other door. Slowly, with extreme stealth, Thomas wriggled along the edge of the room, until he disappeared into the deeper shadows at the head of the bed.

Whatever he was up to, Aldridge needed to keep Wharton talking. "Is that it, Wharton? All these years and you have been sulking because Gren wanted you to leave him alone?"

Wharton pushed himself upwards, and screamed, "Liar! He loved me. And I loved him."

"He came and begged me to protect him. You were a man grown, and he was a little boy in your power."

"Liar," Wharton screamed again. "You took him away from me and you will have to pay!" But his gun did not waver from the hall boy's head. Matthew. The boy's name was Matthew, and he was Richards' grandson.

"Your plot has failed, Wharton," Aldridge told the villain. "Even as we speak, the Prince Regent and Queen Charlotte have intervened to kill the lies you spread."

"But they are not all lies, are they? And people will always wonder, especially about your saintly whore. Did she pant for you Aldridge? Or did she say her prayers while you rode her? Everyone knows she is your lover, Aldridge. She is ruined."

"Have a care, Wharton. You speak of the Duchess of Haverford."

"No!" It was another screech. "You lie! She refused you, and how I laughed when I heard it."

"But today, she accepted me, and agreed to allow me to use the special licence I fetched from Doctor's Commons this very day." Aldridge bowed slightly. If Wharton shifted just a little more, Aldridge could target his heart while avoiding the boy. "I have you to thank for her willingness to wed straight away, Wharton."

But Wharton pulled the boy tighter across his chest, growling deep in his throat. "I hate you. I hate you."

"Got it." The voice came from the shadows and Thomas stood, a box-like object in his hand. "I have disarmed the timing mechanism, Aldridge, and removed the firing device from the fuse and the fuse from the container of powder."

"No-o-o!" Wharton heaved the boy from him and fired wildly in Aldridge's direction as he rolled from the bed and hurled himself through the window, bursting the mullions.

Aldridge went straight over the bed and Richards around, but by the time they reached the window, Wharton was disappearing behind the hedge at the bottom of the stairs into the garden. Aldridge fired anyway, but the chancy shot missed.

"Quick," he said to Richards. "Get out searchers. Be careful. He's armed and dangerous."

He led the way down the stairs and out of the library into the garden, then followed in the direction Wharton had been running—towards the river.

The garden was designed to trick the eye with a series of vistas, and even in the fickle twilight, they would not have been able to see far ahead, but they could hear Wharton giggling as he ran. "Have a care," Aldridge called back to those who followed.

But there was no ambush, no explosion. Instead, as they reached the water gate that opened to the Thames, Wharton pushed a boat from the wharf and rowed out into the river, there to back his oars to keep from running with the current.

"Catch me if you can!" he shouted, and then stroked into the water and shot off down river towards London.

"It's a trap, my lord. Your Grace," Richards suggested.

Almost certainly. "We can't let him get away again," Aldridge replied.

"I know where he lives," said Mullins. "I can show you, my lord."

Aldridge made up his mind, pointing to several of the footmen and to the remaining pleasure boats tied up to the wharf. "You, you, and you. Follow Wharton. Stay out of pistol range, but see where he goes." He turned to the grooms. "You and you, saddle a horse and chase the boats downriver. Try to keep them in sight, if you can. Take extra horses for the footmen. The rest of you"—he nodded to the other grooms—"saddle horses as fast as you can. I want to leave here within minutes. I'll take you and you as backup, so go with Richards and he'll make sure you're armed. Thomas and Jamir, take a horse each and return home. Tell the Duke of Winshire I need help. What is the address, Mullins?"

They were nearly as fast as he hoped. He was on the road less than ten minutes after Wharton was swept away, and the man's address was some distance from the river, so if he was heading to his own place, he would need to cross almost a mile of streets.

It was a good time of day to gallop hell for leather through Chelsea, Knightsbridge, and Mayfair. Tradespeople had ceased their deliveries and most of the *ton* were not yet on their way to their evening entertainments. Still, people turned to stare as Aldridge, with the two boys close and the grooms trailing, raced along the streets, at one point leaping over a cart that was turned across the way.

They had left the grooms far behind when Aldridge drew his horse up at the turn where the boys needed to peel off for the Winshire mansion. He pointed, and they grimaced, but obeyed.

Alone, now, he set his horse back to the gallop, murmuring into its mane, "Not far now. Good boy. Good boy."

It was a narrow townhouse in a row. The door was wide open. Aldridge hitched the horse to the area railing, and drew the pistol, which he had reloaded while waiting for the horses. He should wait for the others, but if Wharton was in there and had another device, there wasn't time.

He ignored the open door, instead creeping down the area steps and trying the door into the kitchen. It was unlocked, and the kitchen showed signs of having been hastily abandoned. As he crept up the stairs, he could hear Wharton singing, in a rich mellow tenor which somehow added to the discordance of the particularly filthy lyrics.

The man was sitting on a chair facing the door, a gun in his hand and another of those devices at his feet. Aldridge had a clear shot, but hesitated. The man was an evil fiend, had earned death for any of dozens of illegal acts, and had, in fact, been condemned to hang. *I can't shoot him in the back.*

But if he spoke, he might miss his shot. And then it was too late. Mullins burst in the front door, screaming, "Where is my sister? Where is my sister?"

Wharton calmly shot him in the shoulder, which punched him backwards. No help there. The gun was a repeater. Aldridge took aim, but before he could resolve the dilemma of whether or not to shoot without announcing himself, Wharton decided to taunt Mullins.

"Your sister is dead these four weeks, you fool, and serve you right. You betrayed me."

"I did everything you said. You said she was safe. You said you wouldn't hurt her."

"Safe at the bottom of the Thames. Beyond hurt, Mullins. But she hurt plenty before she died." And he threw back his head and laughed.

Mullins hurled himself on his tormentor, ignoring another bullet as it slammed into him. He knocked Wharton from the chair, and they rolled around in the hall, onto and over the device.

Aldridge moved around them, trying to get a clear shot, and then Thomas shot into the hall, followed by Jamir. Thomas dived for the device and dragged it out of the reach of the combatants. Jamir met Aldridge's raised eyebrows with a sheepish smile. "We gave the doorman a message for my father and the kagan," he explained. "Thomas thought he might be needed."

Thomas was on his feet again, the device abandoned. "Get out!" he shouted. "The mechanism is jammed. I can't open it to get to the fuse and I think the flint has sparked."

Aldridge didn't hesitate. He grabbed a boy by each arm and pushed them ahead of him through the door. Out on the street, his footmen were arriving, and beyond them came a phalanx of Winshire's riders, with Winshire himself in the lead, a son on either side.

"Get back!" Aldridge yelled. "It's about to blow up!"

The sound of the explosion covered his last words. He shoved the two boys to the ground and hurled himself on top of them. Then something hit his head from behind, and darkness fell.

Anthony had only been knocked out for a matter of seconds, Nate said, but Charlotte had seen the bruises and cuts peppering his back. He'd saved Thomas and Jamir from more than a bruise or two, covering them with his own body as masonry and glass rained down on them. And, so Nate said, his riding coat had mostly saved him.

He'd been carried back to Uncle James's house, complaining bitterly about not being allowed to walk and demanding to be taken home, but subsided when Charlotte had scolded him. "You will stay here for the night, and you will let me look after you, Anthony. You have a wedding to attend in the morning, remember."

Uncle James made not a murmur about her spending the night in Anthony's bedroom, but he sent her maid to sit with them. Clarke slept in the corner, a curb on amorous congress that Anthony declared entirely unnecessary, since he was too sore to do all the wicked things he had been planning ever since Charlotte accepted his proposal.

He then proceeded to detail them in a low voice, punctuated with several drugging kisses and caresses that set her wishing even more fervently for his return to full health. He had the power, even

wounded as he was, to make her almost forget they had an audience. Except that Clarke had begun a set of transparently false
snores and was keeping her eyes studiously shut.

"Clarke is awake," she whispered to Anthony.

The scoundrel replied, soft voiced, "Does that mean you do not
want me to do this? Or this?"

Can one squeal in a whisper? Apparently so. She slapped the offending
hand. "Behave!" she hissed.

"Do I have to?" he whined, like a small child, then spoiled the
effect with a yawn. "I'm not tired," he grumbled, which was a
patent untruth, and so she told him.

He pulled her head down until her ear was close to his lips. Even
so, his words were so quiet she had to strain to hear them. "I am
afraid I will wake up alone, Cherry, and it will all have been a
dream. You won't make me be a duke all by myself, will you?"

Anthony's hidden vulnerability had always melted her heart, but
never so much as now, when he let slip the mask he wore to tell her
how much he needed her. "Go to sleep, Anthony my love. I will be
here when you wake up, and it will be our wedding day."

As it was, he slept for no more than an hour, and then they
talked again, softly so as not to disturb Clarke. He explained the tiny
nuggets of truth in Wharton's lies about him.

Prue had once borne his daughter, but Anthony had not known
of Antonia's existence until shortly before he and Cherry met, and
by that time, she and David had met and fallen in love.

Jonathan and Prue had been kidnapped by Wharton, but
Anthony was to blame only for buying Jonathan a ticket on a ship
bound for the Mediterranean; one that happened to be owned by
Wharton and the other criminals in a ring that stole and traded
people.

And there had indeed been a circus performer, still was—as far
as Anthony knew. She had put on a convincing performance in
which the Rose of Frampton died in a riding accident in full view of
half the ton, while watched by Baron Overton and his new bride,
the real Rose.

In return, Cherry told him of her dreams before the incident, and admitted he was about to fulfil them. But she did not plan to give up the new dreams she had embraced since the incident. "Can I set up schools on our estates, Anthony?"

"I have already done so, Cherry darling, but you shall be in charge of them all and will change anything you don't like."

He slept again. Charlotte lay down beside him and slept too, and woke somewhat refreshed and incredibly aroused to find him caressing her breasts.

Clarke slept through it all. *Clarke deserves a raise.*

They breakfasted together, then Anthony's valet arrived, with everything he needed to dress for his wedding, and with a package that Anthony said he had sent for. "Wharton had Mullins intercept it," he explained to Charlotte. "If it is what Wharton claimed it to be, I had better read it this morning."

"I shall leave you to it, then," Charlotte suggested. "Clarke will be waiting for me."

Anthony did not look up from his letter, but held out his hand and pulled her to his side. "Read with me?" he asked, and tilted the paper so she could do so.

The gist was immediately clear. The Duke of Haverford had died peacefully in his sleep in the early hours of yesterday morning. Charlotte's immediate thought was that Anthony was in mourning, and they would have to put off the wedding.

Anthony did not agree. "I will have to tell Mama and your uncle, my darling," Anthony said, as he folded the pages again. "I would like to ask them to keep it a secret until after we are married. Do you agree? It is nobody else's business, after all."

Charlotte thought there might be some disagreement on that. "You had better let the Prince Regent know when he arrives," she warned him.

"Yes. Wales will kick up stiff if we spring it on him when Basingstoke introduces us to the witnesses as the Duke and Duchess of Haverford." He grinned at the thought, and added, "He won't mind as long as he knows. He didn't like my father either."

Two hours later, they were dressed in their finery. Either Clarke and Anthony's valet had coordinated their efforts, or some good spirit had decided to bless the union, for both bride and groom were dressed in shades of green and gold.

Charlotte wore a new gown she had ordered in March and never worn. It was of the palest mint with great flounces of cream lace embroidered with golden and silver flowers backed by a tracery of rifle green leaves. The fabric of Anthony's coat matched the tracery, and the thick embroidery that trimmed the edges was gold and silver. He wore the coat over a gold waistcoat and cream breeches, and his cravat was pinned with a cut emerald that matched the one in the centre of the necklace Aunt Eleanor had brought to Charlotte while she was getting dressed.

A necklace, earrings and tiara—gold set with pearls and diamonds, accented with those brilliant emeralds. "Aldridge—Haverford, I mean; it shall be so hard to get used to saying that—Haverford wanted you to wear these today, Charlotte. They are not Haverford stones, but came to him from my mother." Her eyes filled with tears. "You will look lovely in them, dearest."

Charlotte accepted her hug and kissed her on the cheek. Anthony was still angry with his mother, she knew, but Aunt Eleanor had meant well, after all. She gave the jewellery case to Clarke and sat to have the tiara carefully inserted into her coiffure and the earrings and necklace put on.

Then it was time to go down, to a chapel filled with flowers and guests. Nearly all of them were family, on one side or the other, and in some way, including the Overtons.

Anthony was pale, except where one of his bruises stood vivid purple over one of his cheeks. Still, he refused to sit in a chair, but stood tall beside Charlotte, saying his vows in a clear voice that sounded through the chapel.

Then came the moment that they turned to the witnesses and Basingstoke's voice rang out. "Your Highnesses, Your Graces, ladies and gentlemen, I give you the Duke and Duchess of Haverford."

Her hand through his arm, Charlotte felt Anthony stiffen at the title. She had just enough time to whisper, "I love you, Anthony," before the Prince Regent reached them, to shake the new duke's hand and salute the new duchess with a kiss.

EPILOGUE

MAY 1816, LONDON

Today's boisterous family gathering at Fournier's pastry shop was a final get-together before the Duke and Duchess of Haverford sailed for the continent. They were taking the wedding journey they'd had no time for last year. Their wedding had been followed by the funeral of the former duke, and then His Grace had taken his seat in the House of Lords in the anxious weeks that remained before Napoleon was finally defeated at what was now being called the Battle of Waterloo.

Marrying the day after his father's death was a minor scandal, but the erstwhile Marquis of Aldridge said he could not cope without his beloved, and his mother and her uncle supported him. All the other scandals that Wharton had tried to stir died with the villain, for Haverford and Winshire allies, from the Prince Regent down, spread the story of the jealous schoolboy turned slum king who had used lies and violence to pursue revenge for imagined slights even against two of the highest families in the land.

Now, with Europe at peace again and the ducal estates all in order, Cherry and Anthony were off to visit Anthony's brother Jonathan in the small grand duchy of Elchenburg, somewhere to the east of the German Confederation.

Tony was going with them to meet Jonathan, who had cheerfully confirmed by letter that Tony's mother had been one of his first *affaires de coeur*. He proclaimed himself keen to meet his son. Tony was less certain about meeting Jonathan, declaring that David Wakefield was his father now. Cherry and Anthony would have kept him. Jonathan, with the consent of the Grand Duchess, had offered him a permanent home in Elchenburg.

Given a choice between three households, he had joined the growing Wakefield clan, the second oldest after Antonia. The Wakefields also had seven other children, four more of whom had been brought into their family as strays.

The entire crowd of Wakefields, down to the baby, had come to see the Haverfords and Tony off. So had Mama with Aldridge's youngest sister, Frances, Uncle James, Aunt Georgie and Aunt Letty, and Cherry's mother. Plus, all the other brothers, sisters, and cousins of the duke and duchess. Which meant a crowd of Hamners, Lechtons, Suttons, Chirburys, Ashburys, Redepennings, and Winderfields. The Overtons were there, too. Cherry had insisted on the invitation, telling everyone that he and Lord Overton were close enough to be brothers and she and Lady Overton had a lot in common.

Leaving aside the nursemaids, footmen and guards—which they never did, ensuring that they had their own refreshments while the family enjoyed theirs—they were fast growing sizeable enough for a battalion.

Jessica was absent. She and the Earl of Colyton had been wed last week, and were travelling to his country estate on their own marriage journey. Anthony knew that Cherry was uneasy about the match, but Jessica was determined and the Dowager Duchess was satisfied, so Anthony had given the bride away with a plea to a higher power to look after her. Jessica did make a lovely bride.

Mama and Uncle James were sitting together, smiling at their gathered families. They had begun their weekly meetings again once Mama was out of her blacks. Would anything more come of it? Anthony hoped so.

He turned his attention from them to watch Cherry as she

moved among the crowd, stopped often by a little girl or boy and bending to hear whatever secret they wanted to whisper to their Auntie Cherry. She was a favourite with the children, who had adopted Anthony's name for her, though they still addressed him as Uncle Haverford.

He saw her brace herself as she greeted each infant, though he was certain no one else noticed. The family had produced several babies in the year since their wedding, and each was a stab to his Cherry's heart. He loved her all the more for the gallant way she pasted on a smile, embroidered tiny caps and gowns as gifts, accepted the responsibility of being a godmother, and doted on each tiny being with all the appearance of delight.

He could give her every material possession she might wish. He could, and did, give her himself. He would give her this, if he could. They had spoken of taking wards, as his mother had. But Charlotte wanted to wait. She had conceived once, almost six months ago, and carried the baby for three months before losing it.

"Perhaps," she said, "we might be granted our Samuel." He had told her Arthur Beauclair's remark about Samuel and John the Baptist, and she had immediately connected it with two barren women, Hannah and Elizabeth, who were at last given sons.

And perhaps, while they were with Jonathan, he could convince his brother and his brother's wife to let him foster one of their sons in a decade or so, once he was old enough to go away to school, and educate him to be duke after him.

All Anthony really needed was his Cherry.

SECOND EPILOGUE
HAVERFORD CASTLE, JUNE 1830

Lady Sarah Grenford was not at all impressed with the scrap of humanity ensconced in the Haverford cradle. "He is very little, Papa," she complained. "He cannot walk. He cannot talk. All he does is cry and sleep. I wanted someone to play with."

"He will grow, Princess Sally," Haverford assured her, his own eyes devouring the heir his duchess had delivered, much to the surprise of them both, after fifteen years of marriage.

Sally expressed her opinion in a noise that was rude even for a lady of only seven. "Humph!" Haverford should probably reprimand her, but her nurses did enough of that, and if he did spoil her, just a little, Cherry would make sure she kept her feet on the ground. He kissed her cheek, instead.

Sally had not finished. "I do not know why you and Mama needed another baby. You have me."

"We have so much love to give, Sally darling," Cherry said from the bed, "that you were all filled up with it, so we needed another baby to have the love left over." Haverford lifted his daughter in his arms and carried her with him while he crossed to the bed to kiss his wife's cheek.

"I hope we did not wake you, Cherry mine."

Her hand came up to caress his face and she smiled. "His little lordship will be awake shortly and demanding his lunch. Perhaps you might call for tea, Anthony? I would like a cup while he is still asleep."

"I will do it, Mama!" Sally offered, wriggling to get down.

Cherry and Haverford, hands clasped, watched her strut importantly to the door and open it to give her message to a hall boy. "I am the most blessed of men," Haverford murmured to his wife. "You filled my cup to overflowing just by becoming mine, then you gave me our Sally, and now…" He chuckled even as his eyes watered. "My cup of happiness is much bigger than I ever dreamed possible."

Cherry squeezed his hand. "Mine, too, Anthony."

Sally came skipping back to the bed. "When is Lord Aldridge going to wake up, Papa?" she asked.

Haverford raised an eyebrow. "Who told you to call him Lord Aldridge, darling?"

"Nurse. She said he is the Marquis of Aldridge, and I must treat him the respect that is due to the heir of the House of Haverford." The mutinous curl to her lip showed what the little girl thought of that instruction.

Haverford picked her up and put her on the bed beside her mother, who wrapped an arm around her and tucked her into her side. "Nurse is usually right, my precious, but in this instance, she is wrong. Your little brother is the Marquis of Aldridge and he is heir to the House of Haverford. But he is also your baby brother, and a dear little boy. Do you remember his name?"

She wrinkled her nose in concentration. "Jonathan Anthony Charles George Grenford," she pronounced, correctly, and beamed at her own cleverness.

"Precisely," Haverford agreed. "Call your baby brother Jonny, Princess. Mama and I plan to do so. I will have a word with Nurse. In our family, he will always be a person first and a title second."

He put an arm around both his ladies and kissed the cheek of the woman to whom he had always been Anthony. Then, when the hope of the Haverfords set up the mew that signalled a coming demand for Food Now, the Duke of Haverford returned to the cradle to bring Jonny into the circle of arms.

THE END

See overleaf for more places you can find Aldridge.

THE ALDRIDGE STORY

The Marquis of Aldridge first stepped onto the pages of my stories in 1807 (his time) and 2015 (mine). *A Baron for Becky* was—at least in part—about a rake with a big heart who loves his mistress enough to help her to a happy ending with his best friend. It is in three parts, set in 1807, 1810, and 1813.

Aldridge has been a secondary character of mine ever since. Here are some of his appearances.

In 1805, he was in *Unkept Promises* (the heroine, fleeing from smugglers, interrupts Aldridge's idiosyncratic take on a garden party. He popped up again later in the book, most of which is set in 1812.

In 1807, he became involved in an investigation into blackmail and murder in *Revealed in Mist*. Awkward, since he was connected to the two investigators: David Wakefield was his half-brother, and Prue Virtue, a long-lost girlfriend.

His reaction to the events in *Revealed in Mist* send him into a three-month drunk during which he meets Charlotte (mentioned in *To Tame the Wild Rake*). Being abducted and dumped in Becky's garden brings him to his senses (*A Baron for Becky*).

Later the same year, the hero and heroine of *A Raging Madness* meet him out Christmas shopping with his mistress.

In 1812, he appears several times in *To Wed a Proper Lady*. For example, he is second in a duel during which a sniper is found in the bushes ready to kill his principal's combatant and his second. He seconded Wesley Winderfield, a protégé of his father, and the opponent was Lord Andrew Winderfield, seconded by his older brother Jamie.

He is also present in *A Suitable Husband*, as the head of the Grenford family, supporting the poor relative, Cecilia Grenford, the heroine of the novella. In 1812, Cecilia is rescued from penury by the Duchess of Haverford and finds herself organising a house party, which runs over into 1813.

He appears in other authors' stories from the same box set, *A Kiss for Charity*, by Sherry Ewing, and *An Open Heart*, by Caroline Warfield.

As the half-brother of the heroine, he appeared frequently, of course, in *Melting Matilda*, set in 1813 and early 1814.

And *To Claim the Long-Lost Lover*, in which the heroine is Sarah, Charlotte's sister, has him too many times to mention here.

You will also find him and Cherry with their children in the Wattpad novel *Never Kiss a Toad*. I wrote this with Mariana Gabrielle. It explores what happens when her rake's son seduces my rake's daughter. It's way too long, needs extensive cutting and quite a bit of rethinking to bring the themes out and reduce the stray plot lines. But we posted it as we wrote, and will one day edit it down to something reasonable.

You'll find him playing a rescuer role when I need a passing (somewhat tarnished) knight for a fair maiden. Two of the newsletter subscriber short stories he appears in are *Miss Winston's Honour* and *The Mouse Fights Back*. He has frequently wandered onto my blog and the pages of *The Teatime Tattler*. And from time to time, he has helped out at Facebook parties.

He has been a great bit part actor, and I'm thrilled to have finally given him his own starring role.

ENJOY THESE BOOKS BY JUDE KNIGHT

Regency books

The Return of the Mountain King series

James Winderfield, exiled third son of the Duke of Winshire, is back to inherit the ducal title.

In 1812, high Society is rocked by the return of the Earl of Sutton, heir to the dying Duke of Winshire. James Winderfield, Earl of Sutton, Winshire's third and only surviving son, has long been thought dead, but his reappearance is not nearly such a shock as those he brings with him, the children of his deceased Persian-born wife and fierce armed retainers, both men and women.

The Duke of Haverford, his one-time rival in love, sets out to destroy him, and his children with him, but Sutton is no longer the friendless, open-hearted youth who was exiled for his temerity. Even inheriting his father's title won't stop his enemies from trying to kill him. But no one, his people whisper, ever wins against the King of the Mountains.

As the new Duke of Winshire's two older children and his twin nieces navigate society to find acceptance and a love of their own, Winshire rekindles his acquaintance with the influential and beloved matriarch, Eleanor, Duchess of Haverford. Their time is long past; their friendship, though, is golden.

Paradise Regained (prequel novella)

James yearns to end a long journey in the arms of his loving family. But his father's agents offer the exiled prodigal forgiveness and a place in Society — if he abandons his foreign-born wife and children to return to England.

With her husband away, Mahzad faces revolt, invasion and betrayal in the mountain kingdom they built together. A queen without her king, she will not allow their dream and their family to be destroyed.

To Wed a Proper Lady — The Barbarian and the Bluestocking (novel 1 in the series)

Everyone knows James needs a bride with impeccable blood lines. He needs Sophia's love more.

James, eldest son of the Earl of Sutton, must marry to please his grandfather, the Duke of Winshire, and to win social acceptance for himself and his father's other foreign-born children. But only Lady Sophia Belvoir makes his heart sing, and to win her, he must invite himself to spend Christmas at the home of his father's greatest enemy: the man who is fighting in Parliament to have his father's marriage declared invalid and the Winderfield children made bastards.

Sophia keeps secret her *tendre* for James, Lord Elfingham. After all, the whole of Society knows he is pursuing the younger Belvoir sister, not the older one left on the shelf after two failed betrothals. Even when he asks for her hand in marriage, she still can't quite believe that he loves her.

(This book was first published as a novella, and has been extensively rewritten to make it a novel. The novella was in the Bluestocking Belles' collection *Holly and Hopeful Hearts*.)

A Suitable Husband

A chef from the slums, however talented, is no fit mate for the cousin of a duke, however distant. But Cedrica Grenford can dream. (novella)

To Mend the Broken-Hearted — The Healer and the Hermit (Novel 2)

Trained as a healer, Ruth Winderfield is happiest in a sickroom. When she's caught up in a smallpox epidemic and finds herself quarantined at the remote manor of a reclusive lord, the last thing she expects is to find her heart's desire. A pity he does not feel the same. She must return to London's ballrooms, where the wealth of her family and the question over her birth make her a target for the unscrupulous and a pariah to the high-sticklers.

Valentine, Earl of Ashbury, is horrified when an impertinent bossy female turns up with several sick children, including the two girls he is responsible for. He hasn't seen his niece and his daughter—if she is his daughter—since his faithless wife and treacherous brother died three years ago. He reluctantly gives them shelter. Even more reluctantly, he helps with the nursing.

When Ruth goes, she takes his heart with him. When jealous relatives lie about their time together, Val must face his past and win her back, not just for himself, but for the children he has come to love.

Melting Matilda (A novella in the Bluestocking Belle's collection, Fire & Frost, published as stand-alone in May 2021)

Sparks flew a year ago when the Granite Earl kissed the Ice Princess under the mistletoe. Matilda Grenford is a lady and the ward of a duchess, but the daughter of a famous courtesan. Charles, Earl of Hamner, seeks a countess of impeccable bloodlines, not one whose scandalous birth would offend every noble ancestor back to the Norman Conquest. But neither of them can forget that kiss.

To Claim the Long-Lost Lover — The Diamond and the Doctor

Sarah Winderfield has refused dozens of marriage offers since Nathaniel Beauclair convinced her to run away with him eight years ago, and then disappeared without a word or a trace. But now she needs a husband. She has a child to love and to protect, and the child needs a father.

She does not expect to meet Nate when she ventures back into the marriage mart. Should she let him explain why he deserted her? Can she believe him?

Dragged back to England to feed his father's pride in family, Nate refuses to give into the man's demands that he take a wife. But his father mentions Sarah Winderfield, he rushes to London. Those who beat and abducted him insisted that she was to be married within the month, but she is still single. Surely they can find again the promise they believed in when they were young?

Through a labyrinth of old rumours and new enemies, two long-lost lovers must decide whether or not to claim one another, and win the bright future they both desire.

To Tame the Wild Rake — The Sinner and the Saint (this book)

The whole world knows Aldridge is a wicked sinner. They used to be right.

The ton has labelled Charlotte a saint for her virtue and good works. They don't know the ruinous secret she hides.

Then an implacable enemy reveals all. The past that haunts them wounds their nearest relatives and turns any hope of a future to ashes.

Must they choose between family and one another?

The Golden Redepennings series

True love is rare and elusive, but they won't settle for less.

Candle's Christmas Chair (A novella in *The Golden Redepennings* series)

They are separated by social standing and malicious lies. He has until Christmas to convince her to give their love another chance.

Gingerbread Bride (A novella in *The Golden Redepennings* series)

Mary runs from an unwanted marriage and finds adventure, danger and her girlhood hero, coming once more to her rescue.

Farewell to Kindness (Book 1 in *The Golden Redepennings* series)

Love is not always convenient. Anne and Rede have different goals, but when their enemies join forces, so must they.

A Raging Madness (Book 2 in *The Golden Redepennings* series)

Their marriage is a fiction. Their enemies are all too real. Uncovering the truth will need all the trust Ella and Alex can find.

The Realm of Silence (Book 3 in *The Golden Redepennings* series)

Rescue her daughter, destroy her dragons, defeat his demons, return to his lonely life. How hard can it be?

Unkept Promises (Book 4 in *The Golden Redepennings* series)

Mia hopes to negotiate a comfortable marriage. Jules wants his wife to return to England, where she belongs. Love confounds them both.

Other Regency books

A Baron for Becky

She was a fallen woman. How could the men who loved her help set her back on her feet?

House of Thorns

His rose thief bride comes with a scandal that threatens to tear them apart.

Lord Calne's Christmas Ruby

One wealthy merchant's heiress with an aversion to fortune hunters. One an impoverished earl with a twisted hand. Combine and stir with one villainous rector. (novella)

Revealed in Mist

As spy and enquiry agent, Prue and David worked to uncover secrets, while hiding a few of their own.

The Beast Next Door (A novella in the Bluestocking Belles collection *Valentines from Bath)*

In all the assemblies and parties, no-one Charis met could ever match the beast next door.

Lunch-length reads: story collections

Hand-Turned Tales and Lost in the Tale

A double handful of short stories and novellas. *Hand-Turned Tales* is free from most eretailers. Try the range of Jude's imagination one bite at a time, in a lunch-length read.

If Mistletoe Could Tell Tales

A repackaging of six published Christmas stories: four novellas and two novelettes. Because nothing enhances the magic of Christmas like the magic of love.

Hearts in the Land of Ferns

Five stories all set in New Zealand: two historical and three contemporary suspense. All That Glisters has been published in Hand-Turned Tales. The other four have all been published in multi-author collections, but never before in a collection of Jude Knight stories.

ABOUT JUDE KNIGHT

I've always wanted to be a novelist. I was a good enough reader to see that the first two attempts (one when I was fourteen and one in my early twenties) weren't good enough to publish. Then along came life. A seriously ill child who required years of therapy; a rising mortgage that led to a full-time job; my own chronic illness… the writing took a back seat.

As the years passed, the fear grew. I'd waited so long. If I never finished any of the dozens of novels I started, no one would ever judge them.

My mother believed in me, and on the way home from that great lady's funeral, I realised I'd left it too late for Mum to ever hold a print copy of one of my fiction books. So I replaced the fear of finishing with the fear of not finishing, by telling everyone I knew that I was writing a novel.

In the years since I published my first fiction book just before Christmas in 2014, I've published eleven novels, as many novellas, a heap of shorter stories, and more novellas in group anthologies. I plan to keep going till I run out of years.

I write historical fiction with a large helping of romance, a splash of Regency, and a twist of suspense.

I then try to figure out how to slot it into a genre category.

I'm mad keen on history, enjoy what happens to people in the crucible of a passionate relationship, and love to use a good mystery and some real danger as mechanisms to torture my characters.

In my other identity as Judy Knighton, I've been a plain language consultant specialising in contracts, insurance policies, and financial disclosure statements. Fiction is more fun.

www.ingramcontent.com/pod-product-compliance
Lightning Source LLC
Chambersburg PA
CBHW030930210726
48290CB00007B/2139